BODY OF WORK

Very Personal Training – Book 1

KARLA DOYLE

Body of Work
VERY PERSONAL TRAINING–BOOK 1

Cassie has fantasized about the ginger-haired personal trainer for months. Brian is friendly, but never more—until he appears on her doorstep and shows her how much her flirting has affected him. The more she's with him, the more Cassie wants the fairytale, not just hot sex with the 6'2" hunk. She can give Brian full access to her body, but after her ex's reaction to her explicit photography business, sharing her secrets, and her heart, isn't an option.

Brian knows better than to break the rules. Don't date gym members. Keep his inner beast on a leash during sex. Cassie tested his resolve on number one her first day in the gym. Shattered the second rule when he touched her. The petite pixie shares his preferences in the bedroom. She makes him laugh and love—but past mistakes haunt him, emotionally and tangibly. Cassie's worth the price he'll pay for breaking the rules. Now he must convince her to give him her heart.

Books in the Very Personal Training series are individual love stories with happily ever afters and no cliffhangers. There are character crossovers between books, but each can be read as a standalone story.

BODY OF WORK—Book 1
(Brian & Cassie)

WORTH THE WAIT—Book 2
(Sam & Leigh)

For my love...whom I met at the gym.
And for Amanda—I'd be lost without you. Truly. (Now stop worrying
about the tire!)

Big hugs to Andie, Lisa C., Tristina & Grace. Your endless support &
insightfulness mean the world to me.

Chapter 1

CASSIE

"YOU'VE BEEN GETTING LATER and later." Brian's face appeared from behind the bench to smile down at her. "This is the third night this week you're closing the place."

"Is it?" As if she didn't know. Hitting the gym at 11:00 p.m. was playing havoc with Cassie's sleep. Between the adrenaline rush from weight training and the pheromone rush from tracking Brian as he worked, she tossed and turned for at least an hour after she got home. No amount of toy time took the edge off.

She pressed the bar up and would have set it on the rack, but Brian shook his head and held up two fingers.

"Two more."

"Slave driver."

"Nah, just keeping you from slacking. Come on, show me what you've got."

If only he were referring to her naked body writhing on top of him instead of her quaking muscles as she committed every ounce of energy into pushing the barbell up from her chest.

"Done. I can't do another one."

Brian's hands covered hers on the bar, blocking her from quitting. Also, setting off a riot of naughty thoughts about what they could do on this weight bench. Thank god her face was already beet-red from the workout.

"You can do it, I'll spot you."

"Check my membership—I'm not paying for personal training."

"No charge for my services tonight."

In that case, she had a list of services she'd like to add to her tab. Sweaty, naked services that did not involve this barbell. "Fine." She inhaled while lowering the bar for what felt like the fifty-fifth repetition, rather than the twelfth. Half-way, that's all she had left. She quit mid-descent and started the upward pressing motion.

Brian shook his head again. "No stopping. I want you to go all the way down."

A giant snort burst out. "How am I supposed to focus on my form when you're talking dirty to me?"

The barbell dropped to her chest, whooshing all the precious oxygen from her lungs. Any chance she had of completing the last rep was officially dead.

"Help?" She batted her eyelashes exaggeratedly, making him laugh. It wasn't the smoldering expression of passion she fantasized about, but he had a great laugh and an amazing smile, both of which were currently directed at her, so she'd take it.

His hands gripped the bar on either side of her breasts, his fingers grazing her spandex-covered torso. Covered with sweat, yet she shivered. Good lord, could she get any more desperate for him?

His fingers twitched and something flickered in his blue eyes. "I'm tempted to keep you pinned there awhile."

He what? She stared up at him, but whatever she'd seen in his eyes disappeared quickly enough to make her question whether she'd seen it at all.

"But since it's closing time, I'll let you go." He plucked up the barbell she'd practically killed herself to press and returned it to the stand.

What she wouldn't give to see Brian bare-chested, to watch all those muscles flexing and rippling without a t-shirt hindering her view. If he was fully naked and poised over top of her, ready to fuck her with all that power, so much the better.

"Catch your breath yet?"

She blinked. Blinked again. Yup, he was still there, big hands curled over the bar, grinning down at her. Oh god, her fingers were this-freaking-close to her nipples. Another thirty seconds and she probably would've been stroking them.

"I'm good, thanks." She scrambled from the bench, tripping over her feet as she walked to the nearest station for a bottle of spray cleaner and a rag.

A little friendly attention and she'd become a bumbling, hot-and-bothered mess. She needed to give up the futile flirtation attempts she'd repeatedly thrown his way for the past several months. Find an attainable guy, hustle him into her empty bed and ride him until she didn't get mental images of Brian Black every time she closed her eyes. Call that tomorrow's plan. That, and hitting the gym when Brian *wasn't* here, instead of essentially stalking him at his workplace five times a week.

She grabbed the sanitizer and turned, shrieking when she face-planted into a wide expanse of chest. "Geez, you need bells on your shoes or something." She looked up, then up some more until she got to his face.

A tidy, super-short ginger beard and mustache framed sensual pink lips. Did the man ever *not* look delicious? Much more of this innocent contact and she might not make it out of the building before giving in to her body's aching demands. A quickie in the ladies' locker room—solo edition.

"I spoke to you twice. I guess you didn't hear me."

Hence his smirk. They were alone in the gym and he'd been a dozen feet away, max. Once again, he'd caught her daydreaming—this time at midnight.

"Just calculating how quickly I can de-sweatify that bench and get out of your way. I'm sure you're sick of being polite when I keep holding you up at closing time. Especially on a Friday."

"I'm not being polite. And I don't mind staying late if you're the reason." He relieved her of the cleaning products, but didn't release her hands in the process. Not only were they hostage beneath his strong, rough palms, his thumb was brushing back and forth over her skin.

That couldn't be accidental, right?

Holy crap, holy crap, holy freaking crap. All the times she'd joked around with him, tossed out the innuendos, outright told him how hot he was…he'd always seemed amused, heck, he came back for more, day after day, but not once had he returned the sentiment. But this, now? If only he'd *say* something…

"I have to wipe everything down anyway, so don't worry about the bench."

Okay, not quite the something she'd hoped for. Because she'd foolishly let her imagination get the jump on reality. The touch wasn't a caress, duh. He was being his super-friendly self and offering to clean her equipment, nothing more. Probably so he could get out of here faster. Go hook up with a date or something. Ugh.

"I'll hit the change room and leave you to it, then."

He let her fingers slide free. "Sure."

The perma-smile she couldn't get enough of—gone. Not that she blamed him. The gym had officially closed five minutes ago. By rights, he should've kicked her out the door already. Instead, he'd allowed her to finish her routine. Her way of thanking him for that—drooling all over herself while staring at him with what had to be moony eyes. Time she took a hint and stopped pinging the poor guy with lame come-on attempts.

"I'll be quick. Just because gym time is the highlight of my day doesn't give me an excuse to hold you up more than I have. I'm sure you have something much more exciting to do when you leave here."

"Take your time."

"Thanks, but I'll hurry." No reason to prolong the agony.

Inside the locker room, she groaned and pressed her back against the lockers. Her reflection stared back at her from across the room. She wasn't the hottest female at the gym, but she wasn't too shabby. She'd had a decent—yet respectable—amount of boyfriends and lovers, several of whom had told her she was beautiful. Beautiful might be a stretch since she didn't have the long hair, long legs or big boobs most men preferred, but if she appraised herself honestly, she was pretty enough. Good skin and an athletically trim figure. She'd give herself a solid seven-point-five out of ten. Maybe not in Brian's league, but taking a stab at him—or more accurately, several dozen stabs—had been worth the attempt. Sometimes über-hot guys went for the more ordinary girls. It happened all the time in the movies and romance novels—there had to be real-life examples.

Just not where Brian was concerned. She dropped onto the bench with a sigh. His recent arm candy included a stunning blonde with massive boobs who *did* qualify as beautiful. One of his ex-girlfriends was a hard-bodied fitness pageant competitor whose legs probably went higher than Cassie's nipples. The list didn't get any less extraordinary. Yes, she'd used a variety of investigative techniques to acquire this information. And yes, she'd been a moron to think she could be next in line. Attempt made, defeat acknowledged.

She stripped off her tank and bike shorts. A shower would be great, but she certainly wasn't taking the time for one now. Blotting the perspiration from her skin didn't make it less sticky or easier to wrestle the baby-doll tee and short denim skirt into place. Crap, she'd been in here almost ten minutes already.

Beyond the locker room door, the loud whir of heavy-duty machinery kicked on. She stuffed her workout gear into her backpack, scooped up her purse and cracked the door a couple of inches. Perfect timing. Brian was across the gym, pushing a huge-ass industrial vacuum around the weight room. Plenty of distance and noise to prevent more awkward conversation. She threw up one arm in a goodbye wave, tucked her chin to her chest and hightailed it the heck out of there.

BRIAN

Brian rolled to a stop on Sloane Street. He killed the engine and stared through the rain-covered window of his Jeep at the white bungalow. If he did this, if he knocked on Cassie's door at a quarter to one in the morning, there'd be no going back.

A man could only take so much. The petite brunette had caught his eye from day one. She'd been torturing him for months—chatting, teasing him with comments that made *her* blush, openly flirting with him while she exercised. He'd have made his move immediately if not for his stupid contract.

Which led him back to the decision at hand—to knock on her door or drive away?

He scooped the cell phone from the passenger seat. Weighed it in his palm and took another glance at her house. Light escaped around the edges of her closed curtains. If he didn't grab this opportunity, the odds of him getting another like it were slim. Fuck it, he was going for it.

Still raining and no sign it planned to let up. The drops cooled his skin, not the fire churning in his gut. He made short work of the distance to her door, each long step knotting his insides a little more. Yeah, he was nuts to do this. Nuts and committed to seeing it through. Worst-case scenario, she'd tell his boss and he'd get fired. Yeah, that'd suck—on multiple levels.

He stopped a couple inches shy of the doorbell. Looked at the pink-covered phone in his hand and considered its owner. Her eyes, her smile, her body. The way everything inside him came alive when she laughed with him at the stupidest thing. Totally worth the risk.

He swallowed hard at the muted sound of the chime. Resisted the urge to press his face to the glass and look through the small window in her front door. Twenty seconds later, he rang again. Maybe she hadn't heard it. Or maybe she was hiding in a corner, waiting for him to leave. Another minute and he'd assume the second and haul his ass back to the car.

The outside lamp came on. Cassie's eyes popped into view in the lower portion of the window. They locked with his, instantly changing from a cautious squint to wide with surprise. The tip of her nose appeared, then her top lip. She had to be standing on her toes now. The rest of her mouth followed, curled in a smile. That's all it took—he was a goner for the thousandth time.

The thunk and scrape of metal as she unlocked the door ramped up the tension in his gut. When that door opened, things were going to change, one way or another.

Her soft voice and pretty eyes greeted him through a narrow crack. "Brian? What are you doing *here?*"

"You dropped your—" The door inched open. Wide open. Holy hell, there went his jaw, all the way to the ground. He'd seen Cassie in gym clothes and street clothes. Hot, sexy, adorable—those descriptions all fit, depending on the moment. Cassie in a silky, Oriental-patterned robe that barely reached the tops of her thighs and didn't close all that well in the front, wet hair framing her face…a word didn't exist to describe the sight. "You're dripping." Oh yeah, smooth opening statement right there.

"So are you." She giggled as a fat drop of water fell from his nose.

"It's really coming down."

"Thanks for the late-night weather update. Is that part of a membership upgrade?"

Messing with him now, was she? Exactly how he liked it. "Only for my favorite member." He pulled her cell from his pocket and offered it up. "You dropped this."

"Oh my god, where? I didn't even notice it was missing."

Restraint, he needed a bundle of it. In reaching for her phone, Cassie's robe gaped enough to give him one hell of a view. Add that to the charge that ran up his arm when their hands brushed and he nearly forgot the question. "Ladies' change room, near the lockers."

"How'd you know it was mine?"

He forced his eyes upward and—bam. Caught in the act of ogling her body. *Classy, man.* The door ought to be slamming in his face any second.

Instead, she waved the phone side-to-side. "Hmm?"

"I tapped the email icon. Didn't read anything, but I figured cassiebunny69 had to be you." The blush she got was unmistakable. "You might want to consider a passcode for your phone."

"Guess I got lucky that you found it, not somebody else."

Got lucky—his cock liked those words. At this point, his cock was a hell of a lot more optimistic than the rest of his soaked-to-the-skin self. "You going to the gym tomorrow?" A reasonable question to ask at one in the morning while standing in the pouring rain. Yeah, not too obvious.

"I'm not sure…" She turned the phone over and over in her hand. "Will you be there?"

"I will."

"What time?"

Time to play this out, see where it led. "Whenever you need a spotter."

"You're not working?" She stared up at him, pretty eyes getting bigger when he shook his head. "You want to…work out with me?"

"Actually, I want to do a hell of a lot more than work out with you, Cassie." Lightning cracked behind him and the street lost power. Fantastic timing, nature. He could barely make out Cassie's silhouette, let alone read her expression. For all he knew she was frozen in front of him, too scared to respond or make a move. "Go inside and lock the door. I'll see you at the gym sometime."

"Brian, wait…" Her small, soft hand latched on to his arm. She pulled him closer, over the threshold, close enough to smell the shampoo she'd used and feel the waves of heat rippling from her freshly showered body. Close enough for him to make what could end up being a huge mistake.

Thunder boomed and electricity streaked the sky again. Three seconds' worth of light was enough. His hands found her waist—so tiny beneath his grip. She submitted to his tug, gasping when she connected with his drenched t-shirt.

"I'm getting you wet."

A sexy giggle floated up. "It's not the first time." Her palms flattened against his chest, the tips of her fingers curling into his pecs. "It happens every time I see you…and sometimes when I'm just thinking about you."

The girl could flirt and she had a subtly dirty sense of humor, but this, telling him she got wet because of him—fuck. He had to know for sure.

"You should shut your door before your house is wet too." He slid his hands over the silky robe, up her back, into the damp hair at her nape. "What side of the door do you want me on?"

"The inside. I want you inside."

All he needed to hear. He walked her backward, pushed the door closed. Fumbled around for the deadbolt with one hand. Without the moonlight and flashes of lightning, he was as good as blind in a house he didn't know. Hopefully he wouldn't break anything—or worse, launch them down a staircase or something—because now that he had her in his arms, he had no intention of letting go for a single second. To hell with finding his way to a room. He put an arm out, located a flat surface and turned them toward it.

Cassie's back hit the wall with more of a thud than he'd planned.

"Shit, sorry."

"Don't be." Her hands snaked up his chest, her nails

making him shudder as they scraped the back of his neck then pushed through his hair. "I always wondered about this, how it would feel."

Felt like fucking heaven to him. "And?"

"Very soft." She arched her body tight against his. "Unlike the rest of you."

If only she knew the truth of that statement. Most days he had to stand behind the counter or some piece of equipment at least once while the hardness she'd inspired eased. No amount of standing around would relieve his hard-on now, only coming. He'd agree to almost anything at this point to have it be with Cassie, instead of his fist and a bottle of lotion.

"I can't count how many times I've thought about touching you."

Her fingers trailed over his beard. "Maybe you should forget about math and just—touch me."

He smoothed his palms down, over her hips, then back up, past the dip of her waist to the curves of her breasts. Through the satiny material didn't cut it. He needed skin. Her skin.

"Back up."

"Okay." She resumed her position on the wall, giving him better access. Her breath quickened as he followed the front edge of her robe to its belt.

He worked the knot free. Paused when she sucked in a breath and held it. "Too fast?"

"No, don't stop."

One light tug and the belt fell to her sides. The robe had to be hanging open now. Fucking blackout. All that beautiful skin waiting for him and he couldn't see a damn thing. His hands would have to do what his eyes couldn't, starting at the top.

He followed her shoulders to the slender column of her

neck. Cupped her face between his palms. "I've wanted to kiss you since the first day you smiled at me."

"That was months ago."

"Tell me something I don't know." He laughed with her, then caught a lock of cool, damp hair and tucked it behind her ear, letting his hand linger on her jawline. "I've never looked forward to going to work as much as I have since you started talking to me. Best hour of my day."

"I had no idea you were..." Her head shook against his palm.

"Such a huge coward?"

Another head shake.

Once again, he wished he could see her, though for different reasons. No more joking. "All the time I spent hanging around your machines, talking to you, you couldn't tell I was interested?"

"I thought you were just being friendly. Why didn't you say something, or I don't know...pin me up against a locker?"

The woman must be a mind reader. In his imagination, he'd done all kinds of illicit things to her at the gym. Bent her over a weight bench and fucked her doggy style, tied her wrists to the barbell and eaten her pussy until her screams of pleasure echoed off the walls. So many things.

He gathered her wrists in one hand and gently held them above her head. "Is this what I should've done?"

"For starters."

The quiver in her voice made him smile. He swept the pad of his thumb along her lips, biting back a groan when she teased his finger with the tip of her tongue. He'd spent a lot of time thinking about her mouth and the things he wanted it to do to him. One tiny lick on an innocent spot had him aching for more.

"Then this?" He brushed her ear with his mouth. Kissed

her neck, her jaw, the dip below her mouth. Then, those full lips. The bottom one first, lightly, before pulling back.

"Yes, please."

For months he'd gotten hard from the sound of her laugh. Her whispered begging—goddamn. His cock might bust right through his pants if she kept it up.

He cupped her neck with his free hand. Leaned in and found her lips, both of them this time, soft, warm and eager. So fucking eager. She opened for him immediately, moaning into his mouth. She arched toward his body, his cool, wet clothes not deterring her for a second.

He pushed the robe off her shoulders as far as her position allowed. She shivered, then froze as his hand moved lower. He pulled back from their kiss. Waited. She didn't tell him to stop, but she didn't relax, either. She tilted her head at his nudging, offering her neck. He buried his face against her silky skin and inhaled. The hint of fruit with something even sweeter, something unnamable. She sighed, her body relaxing as he kissed and licked his way down her neck, along her shoulder.

"I need both hands, one isn't enough to touch you the way I want." He released her arms and they fell to his shoulders. "You're so soft." He smoothed his fingers along her collarbone. Lower, over the slopes that led to two hard tips. "Except here." He cupped her breasts, strumming the nipples with his thumbs. "These are…" How corny would it be to say amazing or incredible?

"Tiny, I know. That's the trouble with wearing push-up bras—the unassisted boobs are a disappointment."

"I'm only disappointed that I can't see them."

"Brian."

More blood surged to his groin. The stern tone really worked for her. "They feel perfect to me."

She tried to wiggle free of his hold. Not happening. Not like this.

"I'm barely a 32B and you prefer big boobs."

"Do I? Thanks for the update." He grinned at her huff. Her head might be annoyed at his teasing, but the rock-hard nubs between his fingers told him her body didn't mind. "What else do I prefer, since you've got me figured out?"

"Tall women. Long hair."

"So, the opposite of you."

"Yes."

"Wrong." He snagged her hand, cupping it over his engorged cock. "Still think you're not exactly the woman I want right now?"

"That *is* pretty convincing," she said, making him laugh again.

Laughing while groping each other for the first time. With any other woman it'd be awkward and weird—hell, with anybody else it wouldn't happen—but with Cassie, it fit. Like everything else was going to fit—perfectly.

He skimmed over her flat stomach. Another couple of seconds and there'd truly be no going back. Lower. Goddamn, nothing but more smooth skin. "So fucking soft and warm." He slid two fingers between her legs. "And wet."

"Tell me something I don't know," she said, mimicking him.

"I will if you will."

"You first."

"Deal." Back and forth he stroked, sinking deeper into her folds, giving her clit extra attention at the end of each pass. "You make me crazy hard. Like I am now." He dipped inside her, finger-fucking her knuckle-deep while she moaned near his ear. "I've gotten off thinking about you every day since we met."

14

"Where do you, oh god, do it?"

He brought his second hand in on the act, flattening his palm above her pubic bone and rocking his thumb across her clit. Another moan filled his ear, this one choppier, more desperate.

"Most of the time, lying on my bed. Sometimes in the shower. A couple of times in the employee washroom at the gym."

"While I was there?"

"Yeah. Had to. That or stand behind the counter until you left. Disgusted with me?"

"The opposite. If I'd known, I would've snuck in there with you."

Fuck, another of his fantasies. "Are you noisy when you come? Would we have gotten caught?" He rubbed harder, faster. Fucked his fingers deeper into her pussy.

"I don't—I—" Fingernails bit through his t-shirt, curling into his shoulder. Something thunked against the wall—her head, probably—and her grip on his fly tightened like a vise. Thank god for that spur of pain, it kept him from shooting in his pants like a tenth-grader watching porn.

More than ever, he wanted the damn power to come on. But he didn't have to see her to know she was more beautiful than ever—it was all around him. The sounds and scent of her arousal, the heat of her body. "You're so fucking sexy." He nipped her neck, her earlobe. "Don't hold back, come for me."

Her hips rocked forward, grinding onto his touch. She panted and moaned, the low, erotic sound vibrating through his body while hers jerked hard against his hands. For him, all for him.

Chapter 2

CASSIE

"OH GOD. THAT WAS..." No, she would not be a loser and say it was the best orgasm she'd ever had. But holy crap, it might've been.

"Just the beginning," he said, lifting her and guiding her legs around his waist. "Direct me to your bed. Now."

For the first time since Cassie bought it, she was thankful for a small house. She took a second to get her bearings in the darkness. With the curtains drawn and the power out, the only hint of light came from the jasmine-scented candle she'd lit when she got home. Since she couldn't see it anymore, she must have her back to the hallway.

"The hall runs front to back. There's a candle burning in my bedroom, halfway up on the right."

"Convenient," he said while moving.

"Yes, it's all part of my big plan. First, I planted the phone where you'd find it. A little long-distance mind control and you were at my door. Then, I willed the power to go off so you'd come inside and, you know, take care of me."

He laughed as the amber glow from the candle came into view.

"And voilà," she waved toward the open doorway, "candlelight."

"Sneaky and you have superpowers, I had no idea."

"There you go, something you didn't know about me."

"That's cheating." He strode to the bed, holding her close even after she uncurled her legs from his waist to kneel on the mattress.

After the near pitch blackness of the front hall, the candlelit room seemed bright. Bright enough to see every detail of Brian's face, mere inches away. The twinkling blue eyes, the ginger-blond eyebrows that were a few shades lighter than his close-cut hair and beard, lips that belonged on a sculpture of a Greek god—all right here for her to admire while he stared right back. Brian was in *her* bedroom, holding her in his arms. He'd already given her an orgasm that'd turned her legs to jelly and unless the roof caved in, he was about to fuck her. This couldn't be real.

"Your turn to fess up, cutie." He'd called her that at the gym. Those times, the pet name had sounded friendly and casual. Hearing him use it when he wanted her to spill some naughty secret, cutie sounded anything but innocent.

"I took—" Holy crap, was she really going to tell him this? His eyes tracked her tongue as she licked her lips. Yep, she really was. "I took your picture at the gym. With my phone. More than one picture, actually."

A massive grin spread across his face. "You really are sneaky. What did you do with the pictures?"

Oh, the usual, propped the phone against her pillow and looked at them while masturbating. "Nothing." She sounded like a woman who'd crossed the desert without a drop to drink.

"I'd like to see that."

Oh god.

"But not now. Watching you do *nothing* would mean taking my hands off you, and I don't think I can do that tonight. Not for longer than it takes to do this." He let her go to peel off his t-shirt, push down his uniform khakis and kick them aside. The boxer briefs followed suit.

Oh. God. As she'd imagined from the snug fit of his t-shirts, he had shoulders like five-pin bowling balls. Ridges of muscle carved his abs into two strips of rectangles. A light dusting of blondish-ginger hair on his broad chest tapered to a southbound trail. His cock jutted upward, long, thick and extremely hard.

"Wow. I'm totally going to be picturing you *this way* every time I see you at the gym."

"I want a picture too."

"No problem, I'll grab my camera."

All that hard manliness blocked her escape. "A picture of *you*. To call up every time you walk through the door…other times too." He pushed the robe from her shoulders, shaking his head when she tried to catch it in the crooks of her elbows. "All the way off."

The silky fabric slid the remaining distance, leaving her fully exposed in front of the sexiest man she'd laid eyes on— and in her secret line of work shooting erotic photos, she'd seen a few.

Brian's gaze traveled over her body, from her damp hair to her quaking knees. "This is a pretty picture."

"If I'd thought for one second you would ever be looking at my naked body, I would've spent my savings on a boob job instead of new camera equipment."

"Would've been a waste of your money." His palms slid under her breasts, cupping them as he had in the darkened hall.

She groaned, one part pleasure, two parts dread. Good god, her itty-bitty boobs practically disappeared in his hands.

"Some guys love big breasts, the bigger the better."

"Not exactly breaking news to the small-chested girl you're fondling."

His lips grazed the top of her breast, the warmth from his chuckle raising goose bumps all over her body. "I don't care how big they are—"

"Or aren't?"

"Or aren't." Another chuckle. "I'm more of a nipple guy than a breast man. I like," his tongue swirled around one of her tips, "gorgeous, responsive," his lips latched on and suckled hard before letting it slide free, "nipples." His eyes flicked to her face. "Even better if they're bite-sized."

That was the warning he gave before nipping her distended bud. Balance failed her and she toppled backward. Not a bad thing, since she took him down with her. Her legs parted for him, or maybe he nudged them apart. Didn't matter who or how, or even why. He was between her legs, covering her with his massive body, scraping and tugging at her nipples with the exquisite pleasure that rode the edge of pain.

"Harder—bite me, make me scream." Not something she'd ever demanded of a new lover, but with Brian...

Growling vibrated against her breast. He clamped down harder. His teeth...god, his teeth. Heat flared beneath his mouth, spread through her body. He increased the pressure. Found her other nipple with his fingers and squeezed.

Forget restraint, she just—wanted. She clawed his back, got her hands lower, on his butt, pulling him tighter on top of her. She curled her legs around him. His cock pressed against her clit, rubbing, sliding back and forth. Pushing her closer, closer. He released her nipples and she groaned in protest.

"Scream for me." He bit down again, rocketing sparks to every cell in her body. He ground his hardness onto her clit, pressing her flat to the mattress while she flew out of her skin, out of her mind.

And screamed his name.

BRIAN

Cassie screaming his name while bucking beneath him like a barely restrained animal stole the last of his control. Hands and mouths were everywhere. His and hers, clawing, grabbing, kissing, licking, biting.

"Fuck me."

As commanded, his cock angled lower. It bumped her entrance, so fucking wet and hot he could barely keep from sliding inside. The slightest move and he'd be buried. Deep. Fucking this tiny goddess in ways she'd never forget. Ways he'd never fucked any woman, always holding back for fear of terrifying them, or worse, hurting them. Cassie's demands had unlocked his beast. He sure as hell hoped it wasn't an act, because that key was fucking gone.

She managed to wiggle despite his mass pinning her. Soft heat hugged the head of his cock. "Fuck me..." The sexiest rasp he'd ever heard said the words he wanted to hear. "Fuck me hard."

Call it a fucking miracle that reason pushed harder than his cock. "Condom." One word was about all he could manage at this point.

"Crap. Right," she said, followed by an irritated tsk.

That was the Cassie he knew—cute, too sweet to use bad

words. He needed that reminder before he fucked everything up, permanently and irreparably. She didn't know what she'd asked, or how much—and how hard—he wanted to give in to her request.

"Bedside table, top drawer, unless you brought your own?"

Hell yeah, he'd come prepared. But waste time rifling around for his wallet? No chance.

She gave a frustrated sigh, her full, expressive lips set in an adorable pout when he lifted his weight. Two very different women lived in her hot little body, and he wanted them both. He went in for another kiss before pulling away completely. Sweetness and passion mingled, tempting him to take a stupid chance and slide between her legs again.

"Mmm...hurry. I need you."

Damn. In more ways than one. "Don't go anywhere."

"Would you try to catch me if I did?"

"Try?" Back turned, he smiled while scooping a condom packet from her drawer. "You're as good as caught if you think you're getting away from me now."

Fabric rustled behind him. A puff of Cassie's breath plunged the room into darkness. "Guess that means you're it." The hardwood squeaked under her scurrying footsteps and the door closed with a halfhearted slam.

The little brat. She had a head start and a lay of the land. But he had the candle—lit again, thanks to the matches he'd spotted in the drawer and some minor fumbling around—and he had motivation. He also had a huge grin on his face. He'd always pegged Cassie for a fun-loving girl, but naked hide-and-seek during a power outage, hiding from the "it" she'd just begged to fuck her hard—that took playful to a whole other level.

He tucked the condom between his palm and the candle. Managed to open the bedroom door without too much noise.

Sneaking up on her still bordered on impossible. The flickering would give him away, but he was sure to kill himself and possibly trash her house without it. Besides, let her see him approach. Let her get an eyeful of what was to come—literally—once he found her cute little hiding ass.

Combing the main floor of her bungalow didn't take long. No sign of her in the spare bedroom, bathroom or front hall. Ditto for the kitchen. He did a quick sweep of the living room. Comfy-looking couch, hardback chair that nobody in their right mind would choose to sit in, oversized coffee table—but no Cassie.

"Come out now and I'll go easy on you for running out and leaving me hanging—or, not hanging, actually." He expected a giggle or a snort. Nothing. At the lack of response, he padded out of the room. One more place to check—downstairs. He turned the knob on the last unopened door. Pushed it open and stepped into a spacious back entryway. He aimed the sputtering candle around what had to be the classiest mudroom in town.

"Nice back door," he called, loud enough for her to hear him in the basement, wherever she might be hiding. "And *yours* is going to me mine when I find you." He'd come here hoping she wouldn't slam the door in his face, now he was promising her perfect little behind a spanking, if not more. He was fucking nuts, saying shit like this. "Ready or not, I'm coming down."

Something metal scraped in the living room. He froze mid-step, waited. A quiet giggle. A soft thud and more giggling, this time less subtle. Thought she'd fooled him, did she? He set the candle on the floor and crept through the mudroom, down the short stretch of hall to where he planned to end this game—and end it well.

One peek around the archway showed him the source of

the noises. Moonlight streamed through the now-open curtains, showcasing one incredible ass and pair of legs, her bare feet bouncing lightly off the arm of the couch. So petite, she didn't fill the space between the two ends.

A big brute like him had no business getting personal with a tiny thing like her. She'd already proven she had the power to strip him of good sense. If he went too far, hurt her...he'd be lucky if it only cost him his job. But goddamn it, he wanted her. With his head, dick and yeah, more. Somehow he'd have to keep a rein on the beast she'd released minutes ago. He had to.

He rounded the corner and leaned on the doorframe. "Told you I'd catch you."

"I let you. You'd have been searching 'til dawn if I hadn't given myself up." A mischievous smile came his way. "You suck at hide-and-seek."

"Maybe. I'm better at seek-and-hide." He stepped into the room, his hand wrapped around the item seeking to hide deep inside her body.

CASSIE

"I like the sound of that game."

His grin calmed the wild thumping in her chest—then stirred it again for much better reasons.

That'd been way too close. She'd wanted Brian to catch her, preferably after a rowdy chase around the couch or kitchen table, anything that would've ended with his blood pumping and his hands on her body in a strong, purposeful grip. But rather than search in the most obvious hiding place —standing behind the floor-length drapes—he'd done a quick *man-look* around the room, then disappeared down the hall. Into what any ordinary homeowner would use as a mudroom, but in her house served as a small lobby for her business. That part—no big deal. Then he'd called out that he was heading downstairs. He'd been way too close to seeing her studio, currently set up for tomorrow's photo shoot with the Mancusos. Thank god she'd lured him back up the stairs in time.

She shifted to a seated position so she could assess—okay, ogle—him from a better angle. Though the power hadn't returned, the worst of the storm seemed to have passed, and enough light filtered through the picture window to give her an incredible view of naked, mouthwatering man. The silver tone of the moonlight gave his skin a glowing quality. Every ginger hair from his head to his thick, muscular legs seemed to carry a spark. The man was beautiful in the most raw, masculine way she'd ever seen.

"I'd love to shoot you."

"Kind of an extreme reaction to losing hide-and-seek."

"With my *camera*." God, his smile. That alone was a photographer's dream. As for the rest of him…that was any woman's dream. He'd certainly figured in all of hers the past couple months. A couple more steps and he stood across from her, only the table separating her from over six feet of powerful, aroused man.

"Glad to hear it."

"No guns or dangerous stuff for this girl."

"Good to know." His jaw ticked, his amazing smile dropping from twenty out of ten to seven or eight. Still solidly charming, but definitely missing something.

She crooked a finger at him. "Come closer."

"Table's in the way," he tipped his head at her bruiser of a coffee table, "if I come over there, I'll practically be on top of you."

"Like I said, come closer."

He chuckled. Bent and picked up the clunky, heavy metal

piece with ease. It'd taken two people to carry that thing into the house. Brian lifted it and set it aside as if it were made of matchsticks.

"Wow." Seemed to be her word for the night. Wow to his strength. Wow to the fluidity of his movement. Wow to the long, thick cock pointing at her mouth so temptingly. "I'm calling you next time I move."

"I hope you call before then."

Only the most perfect thing he could have said. She looked up and good god, those eyes staring down at her. Dizziness washed over her—okay, call it what it was, a swooning spell—and she grabbed his thighs for bracing.

"God, you're solid." A deep laugh filled the room. Made her nipples go diamond hard. Oh crap. "I meant your quads, not your," she dropped her gaze to his cock, "okay, that's pretty solid too."

"Because of you."

The hair on his legs rasped her palms as she dragged them higher. Tentatively, she circled his cock at the base. Well, almost. Quite a circumference he had. She met his eyes again, sliding her hand up and down his length as she did. He smiled. A nice, controlled smile. That wouldn't do. She wanted the Brian from the bedroom, the one who bit and pinched and rutted on her like a wild animal in a mating frenzy.

"You liked biting me." Muscles stiffened beneath her touch, but he didn't answer. She took a breath and went for it. "I like to use my teeth too." At this, his eyes widened. So did his smile. In the semicircle of her fingers, his cock twitched and strained forward. Thank god. Some men were so stupidly protective of their dicks, the slightest scrape of teeth and they looked at her as if she intended to bite it off.

"Show me."

She didn't go right for the bull's eye. Instead, she tipped her head and started with the tops of his thighs. Not too hard, but enough that he'd feel the twinge of heat that followed any decent nip. She cupped his sac, drew it out from between his legs. She administered a long lick from the underside to the base of his cock, smiling at the shudder that went through him. She took one of his balls into her mouth. Sucked it, scraping her teeth over the tight, ridged surface as she released it.

"Fuck."

"You like my teeth on you."

"Oh yeah."

"I like it too." She gave his other testicle received the same treatment. Changed the angle of her head and relaxed her jaw, opening wide enough to take both at once. She worked her tongue along the middle. Sucked hard. Added the pressure of her teeth.

A string of curses filled the room. Then a demand. "Mouth on my cock."

Heat flared between her legs. She squeezed her thighs together for friction. Released his cock to rub her clit for a quick second of relief she shouldn't need after the orgasms he'd given her. She eyed his cock, standing at attention. Hand still moving between her legs, she said, "Feed it to me."

"Cassie…" His voice was husky, strangled. "Careful."

Exactly what she didn't want to be. Was so tired of being. She arched her back, leaned in and put her mouth very close to his shaft. "You want my mouth on your cock, my teeth on your skin."

"Yes, but—"

"Then feed it to me."

One hand cupped her cheek. A soft touch that increased

in pressure as his hand reached her chin. He hooked his thumb firmly over her bottom lip. "Open."

Yes, god yes. She let him semi-force her lips apart, biting the tip of his finger as she feigned resistance. Even in the low-lit room, the flare of his nostrils was obvious. He liked it this way—raw, a little bit rough. Perfect. The hum between her legs increased. She opened her mouth but kept tension in her jaw, making him work to gain entry.

He grabbed control, pushed inside, over her waiting teeth. He groaned as she took him, inch by slow inch. And he was a lot to take. His cock hit the back of her throat, triggering her gag reflex. She pinched her eyes shut. Tried to breathe through her nose as another inch filled her mouth. Too much, he was too much. She reached for the base of his cock to control his entry, but he brushed her hands away. Fed her more of his length.

She stared up at him, begging with her eyes that he relent. Brian shook his head. He didn't hold her, didn't physically force her to take more of him, yet she didn't pull away. She couldn't. This is what he wanted and god help her, she wanted to give it to him. She squirmed in place. Focused on breathing only to choke again.

"Easy, relax." The words drifted down, a deep, rich sound that wrapped around her like a caress. The sweetest touch without a single finger on her body.

The panic eased and she let her jaw go slack. She flattened her tongue, welcomed him, a red carpet for the cock she wanted to please more than any before it.

"That's my girl. Just like that." His fingertips brushed her forehead, the gentleness a contradiction to the dominant slide of his cock in and out of her mouth.

The possession in his words, his tone, everything about

him, sparked her deep-seated need. Bite and be bitten. Claim and be claimed.

She wrapped her arms around his hips and dug her fingernails into his firm, meaty butt. The move earned her a quick thrust into her mouth. She sucked him hard, hollowing her cheeks in attempt to hold him in place. God, the purely male smell of his skin. The salty taste of his desire on her tongue. The way his girth and length filled her mouth, making thoughts of anything but him impossible. If only she could keep him here, deep in her mouth, savor him all night and never let him go.

She could. With her teeth, as she'd promised.

"Fucking hell." He ground the words out as her mouth closed around his cock, his body going completely still as she dragged her teeth up his shaft. "More of that."

She brought a hand around to steady his cock, casting her eyes up his tower of a body as she did so. No denial this time. Instead, his fingers threaded into her hair, pushing it off her face, presumably to better his view of her work.

And work him she did. Up and down she bobbed, licking and scraping his hot skin as she took him deep into her mouth, over and over.

"On the head, just the head, nice and hard."

Sweet Christmas in July. She released all but the tip of his cock—her favorite part if ever she had to choose. She sucked it. Dragged her teeth over it in every direction. Laved it with the flat of her tongue, then pressed her teeth into it…a little, a little more, a little more.

"Fuck, fuck yeah. Fuck, stop before I come."

She stared up and shook her head. Let him come. Let him lose control in her mouth.

He jerked back, growling when her teeth didn't automatically grant his request. In the moonlight, his eyes looked almost silver, and they shone with pure, animalistic need. He tore into the condom packet. Rolled it on without taking his eyes off her.

"Turn around. Knees on the couch."

Her pussy ached for her to obey. And she did, though not fast enough for Brian's liking. He cupped her waist, grunting at her wriggling as he bent her over the back of the couch. One of his massive hands spanned her lower back, pinning her in place. His knee knocked her legs apart and his free hand slid along her wet slit.

"So fucking hot." The couch dipped under his weight. The hair on his legs brushed her hamstrings. He slid his hand higher, one finger teasing up and down the valley of her ass, making her moan. "The way you respond, the shape of your body. The things I want to do to you...things I shouldn't do, but fuck, you make it so hard to resist."

"Do them. Do anything to me."

His cock nudged her pussy. "Hands over the back of the couch. Stop moving."

Again she obeyed. Anything to get him inside her.

He gave her the tip, nothing more, then stopped. "If I go too far—"

"You won't."

"I don't want to hurt you."

"You won't—at least, not more than I want you to."

"Fuck, Cassie, you don't know."

She turned her head so she could see him. A jumble of emotions seemed to grip his face at once. Lust, agony, concern. They wanted the same thing, she was positive of it, but Brian refused to give in, to trust her.

Her eyes flitted about, searching for something that'd free him. "Moon. If I say moon, you're," no, she refused to say the word hurt, "then it's too much."

"Moon." Wheels turned behind his intense eyes. "You sure?"

Everything changed when she nodded. The air practically crackled around them.

He bent over her back, caught her neck between his teeth and shook his head like a beast with prey in its mouth. Sparks shot from the contact point, raced to her nipples, lower, in a straight, frantic line to her pussy. "Harder." The skin under his mouth burned. "God yes, like that. Fuck me—fuck me now."

His growl rumbled against her neck as he filled her. Smoothly, urgently. God, the fullness, the sweet, sweet fullness. He pulled back, pushed inside her again. Then again.

Already, her body knew him. Craved his mass, buried deep. "Do those things to me. Whatever you want, do it."

"Cassie…" His rhythm faltered, briefly, then changed. He pounded into her, forcing the air from her lungs.

"Again. Harder."

He slammed inside her again. Pulled out completely, stung her ass with a well-placed smack, then plunged his cock deep into her pussy.

Every stroke, every heated slap, pushed her closer to the edge. The ridges of corduroy abraded her nipples, teasing them with the taste of friction. She caught them in her hands. Squeezed them until fire spread beneath her fingers. If only he could bite them while he fucked her. Do it all, all at once. Fuck her pussy, fill her ass, bite her nipples, make her burn. Make her come until she couldn't breathe, couldn't move. God, she was close, so close—she wanted to come so bad.

"I want that," Brian half-growled into her ear.

She'd said it aloud? Oh god.

His arm banded her hips. Two fingers slid between her legs, surrounded her clit. Rubbed her hard, pinching and pulling the nub mercilessly while he continued to fuck her with deep, rough strokes.

"O-oh god yes…" She shattered, inside and out. Her skin sizzled. Blood pounded in her head. Every muscle tensed and spasmed until she lay boneless beneath him, a limp rag doll hanging over the back of the couch.

She blinked the stars away and found him staring at her. Not quite smiling, but close. "This is the best dream I've ever had."

He chuckled, his hand stroking sweat-dampened hair from her cheek. "Me too."

"I may have to lose my phone at the gym again."

His hand curled around her hip. "Only if I'm there to find it."

Possessive about her? Wow. "I'd rather not take that chance, and I'd be lost without my phone. How about I just… invite you over?"

"When?"

Seven days a week ought to cover it. "Tomorrow night?"

"Can't. I bounce at Blur every Saturday."

"Right, of course. I was only kidding anyway." Maybe the darkness would help hide the word *liar* stamped all over her face with that one. She wiggled free of his body. Months since she'd taken a man to bed, yet two seconds without Brian inside her and she resented the void.

"Hey…" The hand that'd been on her hip trailed up her body to her chin. With a hint of that enchanting dominance, he tipped her face until she was forced to look him in the eye. "I'd call in if I could. For you, I'm tempted."

"Oh." And wow ten times over. "Well, you could, um, pretend you found my phone when you're done with work."

"It'll be late. Later than it was tonight."

"I don't care if you wake me up." A little on the desperate side, but whatever. Too late now.

"I bet you're cute when you're sleeping."

Oh, that smile. If she fell in a pool of that smile and drowned, she'd die happy. "Want to go down the hall and find out?"

"Yeah."

"Really? I mean, you don't have to stay, if that's too—you know, too much."

He caught her lips in a kiss. Soft, warm, lingering—it squashed her insecurities completely and left her breathless when he drew back to look in her eyes.

"Let's go to bed."

Chapter 3

BRIAN

FUCKING PHONE. He should've muted it before falling into a sex-induced coma in Cassie's bed. Now he had to choose between releasing her and letting the insistent caller ruin her opportunity to sleep in. And after last night, he owed her the extra rest.

He eased his leg out from under hers. She mumbled something incoherent and curled tighter to his chest. So damn cute, the way she resisted his exit from their cozy nest. The ringing ended, only to start up again immediately, for the third time. The person on the other end of that call better have a life-or-death situation.

He scooped his pants from the floor, waiting until he was clear of her bedroom to pull the cell from his pocket. The screen told him two things. One, it was way too fucking early to be out of bed, especially when the bed he'd left had warm, naked Cassie in it. And two, somebody at Iron Works had a shitty work ethic.

"Yeah," he said by way of answering.

"Still sleeping at eight thirty—must've been a late night."

Not just work calling, but the owner. The guy who kept dangling the juicy carrot of partial ownership in Brian's face. Guess he'd forgo the sarcasm and let Trevor needle him a little.

"I closed last night. Didn't get out of there until after twelve thirty." Tack a couple of hours onto that for the fucking and late-night talking in bed, and he'd had all of five-or-so hours' sleep.

Trevor's phony laugh came through the cell. "I bet there's more to it than that. What was her name—no, scratch that question. Who gives a shit what her name was, right? Better question, was she worth the sleep deprivation?"

The guy was a no-class womanizer, but Brian forced himself to laugh as if he agreed. "Yeah, definitely." And that part was one-hundred-percent true.

"Lucky bastard. I scored one at Frenzi when the power went out. Big tits and lips to match. She couldn't keep her hands off me in the bar, but when I tried to get her primed in the BMW, she froze up. Wouldn't let me touch her, looked at me like I was a pervert when I suggested she suck my dick on the way to my place. All I got out of it was missionary in the dark. Put her in a cab after instead of driving her home. Why bother, right?"

What a dick. If Trevor wasn't holding Brian's future in his hands, he'd tell the guy exactly what he thought of him. "Better luck next time."

"I'll choose better tonight. Maybe I'll take home two to make up for last night."

Brian had nothing against casual sex or kink, but Trevor's attitude toward women made his blood boil. Good thing the asshole kept his presence at the gym to a minimum. Speaking of which, hopefully the idiot wasn't saying all this shit within earshot of members. "Are you up front?"

"Sitting in my office. I need you to come in."

"Somebody call in sick?" Code for hungover on a weekend morning.

"That twit with the big fake tits, Shanna, and she's not sick. Try still drunk from last night. I'd fire her ass if I hadn't fucked it already."

Unbelievable. The dick had made Brian sign a contract prohibiting romantic involvement or sexual contact with members, yet he was fucking his employees, thus rendering them un-fireable when they pulled shit like calling in wasted.

From where Brian stood—which happened to be buck naked in a member's living room—Shanna had more brains than he'd given her credit for. She'd essentially traded her ass for job security and the ability to completely slack off. This bullshit would stop when he owned a share of Iron Works, that was for damn sure.

"When?" he asked, shrugging on his pants.

"Half an hour ago. Eight-to-three shift."

"I'll be there as soon as I grab a shower."

"No time for that, I have a nine-fifteen tee-off. Be here in ten."

Asshole. "On my way." He stuffed the cell in his pocket and took a look around the room. Pretty nice in the daylight. Walls and furniture in shades of brown. Cream-colored curtains and chunky metal accessories. Not a prissy thing in sight—a living room any guy would be comfortable in. Cassie even had a decent-sized TV. If she liked sports as much as she liked sex, he might ask her to marry him.

The random thought stopped him mid-stride. A couple months of easy conversation and one hot night didn't mean he should cash in his savings for an engagement ring. But damn, coming home to Cassie after work every night—not difficult to imagine.

He crept into the bedroom and collected his shirt and socks from the floor. He'd been right, she was cute when she slept. So damn adorable he didn't want to disturb her.

She murmured in her sleep, her eyebrows drawing together. Her hands moved to her breasts, cupping them. Cute, hell yeah. Sexy, double that. If he hadn't agreed to go to work, he'd burrow under the sheets and bury his face between her legs for a wakeup call. His cock thought that was a great idea. It wanted him to tell Trevor to cancel his fucking tee time and actually work for a change—while Brian spent the day making Cassie come as many ways as possible. And that list got longer by the second.

He bent to whisper in her ear, then thought better of it. One sleepy smile from Cassie and he'd be lost in her. Last time he checked, nobody was paying him to fuck, so he'd better haul ass to the gym.

He resisted kissing her—barely—and went to the kitchen. Another nice, tidy room. Navy and stainless steel with shots of yellow here and there. And the woman stocked quality food. He grabbed a couple pieces of fruit for breakfast on the go. Snagged a notepad from the fridge door and scribbled a short note. He closed the door behind him and jogged to his Jeep. Leaving sucked, especially this way, but he'd see her later tonight. With that to look forward to, nothing could ruin his day.

CASSIE

Wow, he'd certainly left his mark. Cassie smiled at her reflection in the full-length mirror on the back of the bathroom door. An oval bite mark on her neck and three small spots that were definitely bruises from his fingertips digging into her hip. Nothing on her nipple, surprisingly. Kind of disappointing. The tenderness when she moved spoke of how well he'd used her pussy. If he meant what he'd said, tonight he'd do it all again. A shiver rippled through her. Tonight was too far away.

She stepped to the vanity to re-read the note he'd left on her kitchen counter.

Good morning, Cutie. Got called in to cover somebody's 8-3 shift. I wouldn't have answered the damn cell, but I didn't want it to wake you. Stuff to do after work, then I'll probably grab a nap before bouncing because somebody very hot and sexy wore me out. Not complaining, though—last night was incredible. You were incredible. See you soon.

So the man wasn't a poet. The note still scored nicely on the romance scale. He'd enjoyed last night, enjoyed *her*. Then he'd spent the night wrapped around her, a gentle giant replacing the rough lover from earlier. God, she was totally hooked, so much worse than before. She wanted him. Daytime, nighttime, as much as she could get. She just had to be smart. Keep him in her bed and out of her studio.

Not that he'd have a problem with the explicit subject matter in her body of work—show her a man who didn't enjoy naked photos. The trouble with disclosing her boudoir business fell into the opposite column. The few guys she'd told had been *too* interested, expected her to show them "the dirty pictures". The one time she had shared... She shivered.

Never again. Since the breakup with Lance—after which he'd used that sharing against her—she'd vowed to keep all the skin she shot hidden. The only people who knew about her alter ego's work were her clients. And Nana, regrettably, since she'd been the one to bail Cassie out of the Lance mess. Going forward, nobody else would know. Nobody. That's how it had to be, period.

Speaking of clients, the Mancusos would be here at three. Since she'd already prepped for their session, she had time to hit the gym—for the sixth time this week. Training had been part of her regular routine since her early twenties, but this was definitely the most dedicated she'd ever been. Because of her increased motivation—Brian—she could see the beginnings of a six-pack on her midsection. She twisted to see them flex. Raised her arms to shoulder level and curled her fists upward, making her biceps pop. Not too shabby. Her triceps and shoulders could use some extra work, though. Maybe she should splurge on some personal training.

She smiled at the idea, already picturing Brian bossing her around in the gym, his hands on her body as he guided her movements. Definitely worth dipping into her savings a little.

She hustled down the hall to her bedroom. New gym clothes rarely made it to the monthly budget and the pickings in her drawer were slim. He'd already seen her in her birthday suit, so her limited wardrobe shouldn't make too much difference. She chose cut-off sweats that showed a little more butt than appropriate, and one of her former extravagances, a Nike workout tank with a built-in bra that boosted her breasts. A couple of barrettes to keep her unruly hair from poking her in the face, her cross-trainers, and ready or not, she was off.

CASSIE

Tons of cars packed the Iron Works parking lot. Cassie found a spot in an outer row and locked her faithful little Ford. Nobody would want to steal it, especially parked next to a BMW worth at least four times as much. One day she'd upgrade her vehicle. After she'd banked enough money to buy a location for her studio *separate* from her home. She patted the hood as she walked away. Even with her increasing referrals, she and the Ford had many more years together.

She spied Brian's dark-green Jeep near the door. Due to last night's storm, the top was up and the doors in place. Not the norm. The man preferred it stripped to the bare bones, a deathtrap on four thick wheels. She'd only seen him driving it one time, but the image was a keeper. Ginger-haired lumber-jack of a man with one hand on the wheel, one hand on the roll bar overhead, his left foot sticking out the doorless gap as he peeled into the lot. A man's vehicle had never done much for her until the day she saw Brian in this Jeep. Consider her among the converted. Now she couldn't help thinking about sex every time she saw a green Jeep—any green Jeep. But especially this one.

She walked along the driver's side, her fingers lightly trailing along the warm metal. Considering what it might be like to go for a ride triggered old fears. What if the thing rolled? What if they hit a bump and without doors or a roof, she was thrown clear of the vehicle? No, she wouldn't go there, to ancient history and heartache over her loss. Not with much better scenarios to focus on. Such as Brian driving them somewhere off the beaten path, tying her to one of those padded roll bars and fucking her until she screamed loud enough to be heard all the way to the city. Oh boy. Also not the thing to be thinking about right now.

She stopped a couple feet from the gym door. Yanked her shoulder bag around front and feigned rooting through it. She could pretend she'd forgotten some important item. Drive home and masturbate instead of working out. With the hum building between her legs, she'd probably be riding her vibrating dildo for a good twenty minutes. That had to count as cardio. Heck, if she knelt and kept her knees bent, it'd be a leg workout too.

"Hey, Cassie. Don't usually see you here on the weekend." Sam, another of Iron Works' personal trainers, paused beside her to hold the door open. "Coming or going?"

She couldn't help smiling, and not because Sam was incredibly hot, though in an entirely different way from Brian. If she answered "coming", she wouldn't be. Not for at least an hour. She'd never had an orgasm at the gym, though she'd certainly gotten close on the stationary bike. Dangerously close the times Brian was in her field of vision while she pedaled and ground her clit into the saddle.

"Drag her in here, Sam." Brian's voice snapped her back. She followed the toe-curling sound to where he stood behind the front counter, arms folded across his chest, a panty-melting smile on his face. "Or I'll come over there and do it myself."

Sam nodded toward the opening. "You don't want to mess with the big guy. Better do as he says, or next thing you know, he'll be hauling you out for his Sunday boot camp."

"His boot camp?" She tried to focus on Sam while they crossed the entry area to the desk. Tried. Hard to do with Brian unabashedly stalking every step she took. "Is that a new class—I haven't heard about it."

"Not new, and not here." Sam flashed a grin. He really did have an incredible smile. "Forget about the boot camp, you don't need it. You get any better-looking and we'll never get any work done while you're around."

Such a flirt, Sam. Always chatting up the female membership, spreading his charm and no doubt inciting some hot fantasies. Just not in her.

"Hey, Jacobs. I'm off in an hour. You and me and the gloves, and I'm not talking about hitting the heavy bags."

Sam let a laugh rip, then tipped an invisible hat at her. "And with that warning, I'm off to prep for a sparring match."

She watched Sam until he disappeared around a corner, then turned back to the desk to scan her membership card. "You and Sam are going to box? I might have to stick around to see that."

"If you want to see me punch the cocky smile off his face, be my guest."

From everything she'd observed and heard the past few months, Brian and Sam were buddies. Good ones. The scowl on Brian's face didn't support that theory. He hadn't tried to hide his possessive nature, nor did she want him to, but jealous about Sam being, well, Sam?

"Um, okay," she said. "Maybe I'll take a pass."

He handed her the standard-issue white towel offered to all members when they worked out, but when she accepted it, he used it to pull her closer, rather than letting go. "You'd rather not see me damage his pretty face?"

The counter separated them, but it might as well have been air. Heat rolled off him—it surrounded her, sparking a riot of conflicting sensations inside. "I'd rather not see *you* like...however this is."

He released the towel, and the lack of tension made her stumble backward. "Have a good workout."

As if that would happen now, with Brian obviously pissed at her. Did he seriously think she was interested in Sam, especially after last night?

She went through the motions, stashing her things in a

locker, working through one of her upper-body routines in a zombie-like state. Three sets of curls with the bent bar, super-setted with skull-crushers and close-grip presses for triceps. Then, seated military presses for her shoulders, alternating with decline-bench abdominal crunches. Twenty minutes gone and still no sign of Brian in the weight room. Not even for a peek.

"Where'd you leave your amazing smile?" Sam appeared at the high end of the crunch bench. Shaved head, sparkling eyes, nice teeth. His black tank stretched across a fine chest, nicely rounded muscles popped along his shoulders and down his arms. A light sheen of sweat gave his tanned skin an irresistible glow. He could've stepped out of a muscle magazine, he looked that good. And he seemed like a nice guy, beyond his flirtatious nature.

"Because if *you're* not smiling, there's no hope for the rest of us schmucks," he said as she finished her fifteenth crunch and grabbed the bar holding her feet in place.

"There's always hope. I'm just distracted today. I'll bring my smile next time, promise." She swung her legs down and stood in front of him. "Are you and Brian really going to spar?"

Sam gave one of his easygoing laughs. "Hell no, I'm not putting on gloves against him today."

"So he *was* kidding around. I couldn't tell for a few minutes there."

"Oh, he was serious." He winked. "I'm just not stupid."

Ah. Apparently Sam got his kicks from stirring the pot. Why didn't that surprise her? "Okay, well, I'm headed to the cable machine."

"Me too," Sam said, falling beside her.

Coincidence? No, she'd bet her grocery budget that Sam

was still in shit-disturber mode. Surely Brian would've clued in to that by now.

She clipped a rope to the cable for triceps press-downs. Straight ahead of her, Sam jumped, grabbed the stationary wide-grip bar and pulled himself up until his chin reached the bar. He controlled his descent and repeated the move, again and again. When he'd finished—after god knows how many reps, she'd certainly lost count—she was still standing there with the rope in her hands, not a single repetition achieved. Worse, Sam had caught her staring. Much worse, so had Brian, from where he now stood, half a dozen feet away.

She smiled at both men, her eyes lingering on Brian. "Maybe one day I'll be able to do those."

"I bet you can now." Sam crooked his finger at her. "Come here and give it a try."

"Oh, I don't think so…I doubt I could even reach the bar using the step box."

"I'll give you a boost," Brian and Sam said in perfect sync. Crinkles formed at the corners of Sam's hazel eyes. Darts shot from Brian's blue ones.

Wow. The testosterone level in the area might've blown the roof off if they weren't in an industrial building with thirty-foot ceilings.

"You're not working today. Leave helping the members to me."

This whole situation seemed to be amusing the crap out of Sam, who grinned and nodded toward the front of the gym. "Exactly what I was thinking. You have two people waiting at the counter, you'd better go make some protein shakes." After a glare from Brian that would've left most people quaking in their cross-trainers, Sam simply chuckled. "C'mere, Cassie. I'll give you that boost." As soon as Sam reached for her, connected with her elbow, Brian disappeared.

"I really don't think I can do this." And she wasn't just referring to the pull-ups. Innocent as it was, ridiculous as it was, having Sam's hands on her body felt, well…wrong.

"Sure you can. Hands up, ready and…grab it."

"Oh my god." Arms shoulder width apart, she dangled. "Now what?"

"Now pull yourself up."

"That simple, huh?" Heat spread through her shoulders, back and biceps as she attempted to defy gravity. "It's too hard."

"Bullshit. You can't weigh more than a buck-fifteen and you're in here five days a week, working the weights. Pull yourself up."

She gave it everything she had, her upper body shuddering more with each inch she gained. Her muscles screamed at her to quit. She didn't. One—she had to do at least one.

Below her, Sam clapped. "Almost there, keep going."

She gritted her teeth. Pulled. Saw the white bar before her eyes. "I did it, oh my god, I did it."

"Great, now slowly drop down three-quarters of the way, then do it again."

The only words her muscles registered were *drop down*. Not the slowly part. Definitely not the do-it-again part. She hit the rubberized floor with a thud, knocking the box over and turning on her ankle in a monumental display of graceless spaziness.

"Crap." Stronger words sprang to mind, but she bit her tongue while hopping about, trying to shake off the throbbing above her ankle bone.

Sam's hand curled around her waist. "Quite the dismount."

"You okay?" This from Brian, who suddenly loomed over

them, eyes darting back and forth over their faces, then down to where Sam's arm disappeared behind her back.

"I'm sure it'll be fine after I ice it. Think I'm done for today, though."

"I'll help you to the locker room," Sam said.

Brian's face turned ruddy, his mouth a thin, straight line. "I think you've helped her enough."

"And I think you should check who's standing by the front desk and get back to it."

There went the testosterone again. And again, Sam won by pulling the work card.

"It's okay, I can walk on it." She tried disentangling from Sam and failed. He urged her along, away from Brian, supporting her as she hobbled. He even waited while she retrieved her bag from the locker room, then insisted on accompanying her to the front, where Brian stood beside a dark-haired guy in a Hilfiger golf shirt that probably cost as much as she spent on groceries in a week.

She knew the type—the kind of man who liked impressing people. If the overpriced shirt didn't give that away, his phony smile, thick gold chain and two chunky gold-and-diamond rings sure did. She preferred Brian in his navy work t-shirt any day.

Mr. Slick extended his hand. "Trevor Ritchie, owner and general manager. Brian tells me you fell from a piece of equipment and hurt your foot."

Oh, nice. Thanks a lot, Brian, for making her sound like some twit who didn't know her way around a gym. She got it, though. He was simply protecting his employer, and possibly his job. For him, she'd go along with the ditzy-woman-at-gym thing.

"Like I told these two, I'm fine. I was in awe of Sam's pull-ups, so he helped me up and cheered me on. The fall was entirely my fault."

The owner leaned back against the counter. Stuck his hands in his pockets. She had no desire to look at this guy's crotch, but her eyes were drawn to the steady movement beside his fly. *Please god, let him be playing with his car keys in there.*

"Sounds like you might enjoy some personal training."

She caught Brian's eye and smiled. "I was actually thinking that this morning."

"Then it's settled. I'll credit your membership with five sessions, on the house."

The offer was clearly a bribe of some sort, but her budget-minded side didn't care. Five sessions, no charge—not turning that offer down. "Thank you, I can't wait to take full advantage of one of your trainers."

Behind her, Sam laughed out loud, as was his way. "Sign me up for that job."

In front of her, Brian snorted. "I think one pull-up with you was probably enough for her, Sam."

Trevor ignored their subtle battle, his attention staying on her. "We have three other personal trainers, one of whom is a woman, if that's your preference, Ms...?"

"Johnson. Cassie. Actually, I'd prefer Brian. We've gotten to know each other some. Having him train me seems like the natural next step."

Brian's mouth ticked up, just a bit. Was he thinking of last night too? Inside the spandex tank her nipples tightened, the tingling sensation spreading lower and settling insistently between her legs. Last night, they'd gotten to know each other a whole lot better. He'd trained her how he liked his cock sucked—hands-free, until every hot, thick inch of it was deep in her throat. What would he train her to do tonight?

"All the ladies want Brian." Trevor's smirk gave her the

crawlies. He raised an eyebrow at the man she'd chosen. "Do you have time in your schedule for a few sessions with Cassie?"

All business, Brian stepped behind the counter to the computer. "Let me check." A couple of clicks later, he said, "I've got some slots open that might mesh with your usual workout schedule."

She limped to the customer side of the steel-and-black counter, leaned on the high-gloss top and pulled out her phone. She swiped her finger across the screen and tapped the numeric pad that popped up, winking as he watched. "Passcode. Proud of me?"

"Always a good idea."

God, that smile. She countered with one of her own that probably paled in comparison, then brought up her calendar app. "Okay, I'm ready for you."

A low chuckle left his lips as he looked at his monitor. "Monday at three?"

"Nope. I have a portrait sitting booked in the afternoon."

He scrolled and clicked. "How about at eight?"

"Another client."

Blue eyes lifted, settling on her face. "Busy lady. Sounds like the portrait business is booming."

"It gets me by."

"I bet you're being modest."

"Not really." More like skirting the truth. Portraits and light commercial work brought in enough to pay the bills, but she'd never get ahead if that's all she did. The *other* stuff is what put money in her savings account, even if it held her back in the relationship column.

They settled on late Tuesday night for her first session. A crazy time to train by most people's standards, but it'd give her time to wind down from her evening booking before what would undoubtedly be an hour of intense physical conditioning under Brian's tutelage. Plus, the gym would be a ghost town by that time. Perfect, should her personal training take a more personal turn.

"Looking forward to it, Cassie. Anything else I can do for you today?"

He probably meant protein shakes and energy bars, but she couldn't resist the opening. "Not now, but I'm looking forward to later." Before he could answer, Trevor sidled up, brushing against her side in what felt like a deliberate act of contact.

"You roped Brian into coming back to the gym later? Workaholic, this guy. An easy job for him, though. You're already in great shape."

Goose bumps rose on every inch of skin Trevor touched—and not in a good way. If this was his normal behavior, ick. "Not compared to some of your members, but thanks."

"Don't sell yourself short, shortie." Trevor lightly tweaked her waist. "I'm sure watching you train later won't be a hardship."

Talk about unprofessional. Owner of the gym or not, this guy needed to back off. Or be pushed off. "Brian's not training me tonight, we have other plans, right?"

Brian stared. Trevor stared. From across the lobby, Sam stared. Metal clanked in the weight room, music drifted from the speakers and the phone rang on the wall. All of it faded until all Cassie heard was her own heartbeat.

Brian looked her square in the eye. "The only plans I have later are at my other job."

She didn't allow her jaw to drop. Wouldn't, especially in front of a sleazeball like Trevor Ritchie. Instead she pulled it together. Waved her hand at Brian with an accompanying pfft. "Kidding, gotcha." She dropped her phone into her bag and patted the side. "Wouldn't want to lose that. You never know what kind of jerk might find it." Brian's mouth became a taut line. Bull's eye. But she could still do better. "Sam, would you mind if I leaned on you out to the parking lot, my ankle's kind of throbbing."

Sam was at her side in two seconds. "My arm is your arm."

BRIAN

Cassie walked out the door with Sam half draped around her, and there wasn't a damn thing Brian could do about it. If Jacobs had a brain in that shiny, shaved head of his, he wouldn't come back in today.

The oversized wall clock taunted him. Another half hour before his shift ended. More, if the three-to-closing person wandered in late. With it being a gorgeous Saturday afternoon in July, and his replacement being Traci, the odds of that ran pretty high. Fuck. He had to talk to Cassie. Needed to. Soon.

"I'd say Ms. Johnson has a crush on you."

Add shit to that fuck. Now he got to deal with Trevor. "Nah, she's just the joking-around, nice-to-everybody type." No lie there.

"Know much about her?"

That she liked to be bitten, the harder the better. That she gave the most intense, enthusiastic head of his life. That her skin smelled like citrus mixed with soft female and her mouth tasted like heaven. "Not really, just casual stuff."

"Do you know if she's single?"

"No."

Trevor smirked. "No, you don't know, or no, she's not single?"

Damn it. If Brian had taken two minutes to tell Cassie

they had to play down their relationship while at Iron Works, none of this would have happened. Cassie wouldn't think he was the world's biggest jerk. His dick boss wouldn't be nosing around Cassie's profile on the computer.

"I don't know." He bristled as Trevor jotted Cassie's home address and other personal information on a notepad. Phone numbers, email, birthday. A total violation of her privacy. Fuck. "But based on things she's said, I suspect she has somebody in her life." Him, if he hadn't completely fucked everything up today. And even if he had, he'd still do whatever it took to shield her from his scumbag boss.

"Well, whoever he is," Trevor ripped the page free, "he's no competition for me."

Chapter 4

CASSIE

CALL THAT A LESSON LEARNED. Or relearned, because it wasn't the first time she'd been burned. Cassie fastened her seat belt and willed Brian to feel the heat of her long-distance glare as she exited the parking lot. The mess from minutes ago didn't fall entirely on his extra-wide shoulders though. She knew better than to take sex talk as gospel. Lance had promised all kinds of things while hopped up on sex endorphins—to set a wedding date, to stop pressuring her to do a threesome, to keep her secrets. All lies. She should've known better, then and now.

Things with Brian had just seemed so…natural. Far more than the rollercoaster year she'd spent with Lance. Stupid, maybe, but she and Brian had clicked since day one, and last night had taken that connection to an amazing place. More than a night of incredible sex, or so she'd thought. Because she wanted it to be more with Brian.

Truthfully, he'd done her a favor, squashing her in front of his grossly inappropriate boss. He'd reminded her that people —men, in particular—were unpredictable and not always trustworthy. Better that she remember that now, before she accidentally let him further into her life than the bedroom. Sharing all her secrets with Lance had cost her dearly. She literally couldn't afford to make that mistake a second time.

The other thing she wasn't going to do again was turn tail and run. Certainly not because of one flub where she'd assumed more than she should have. Awkward as Tuesday might be, she'd walk in there with her head high—as high as her five-foot-two frame allowed—and be all about the exercise. Brian wouldn't get the satisfaction of knowing that he'd gotten under her skin when he'd marked it.

By the time she pulled into her driveway, the anger had dissipated. A good thing, since she had important clients arriving soon. She hurried through the house to her bedroom, stripping off her gym clothes as she went. She tossed the lot on the bed, swapping the spandex and booty-revealing shorts for some of the semi-professional, nice-girl-next-door items that put most clients at ease. Cream-colored top, tan Capri pants and last, but most important—soft-soled flat sandals. Casual, quiet camouflage, she considered it.

A bit of soft makeup, a couple adjustments to her barrettes and she was ready. She scooped the gym clothes from her bed, her hand lingering on the rumpled sheets. Even after the mixed-up mess with Brian at the gym, she couldn't help thinking about what they'd done in that bed—and smiling at the recollection. She'd come five times last night. Five. The last time, with his mouth, had gone on and on for what seemed like forever, completely frying her circuits. She'd barely registered his good-night kiss as he spooned in behind her, his hard-on wedged between their bodies.

What kind of man goes down on a woman, gets her off in

spades, but doesn't demand or expect gratification for himself? Not the kind she expected to drop her the next day. The more she reflected on last night, the more his behavior at the gym hurt her head. She had no issue with two bodies bumping and grinding to temporarily meet mutual needs, then moving on. But nothing about last night felt like a one-night stand. His unexpected appearance on her doorstep, his hesitancy to make the first move. The sex itself...she'd never had anything like that in any of her casual encounters, if ever. Then there was the cuddling. She'd woken a few times throughout the night to find his arms still closed tightly around her—protective, possessive.

Something had changed *after* he'd left her bed this morning. He'd taken a call on his cell, written a note in her kitchen and left. Only...the front door had been locked when she left for the gym. Oh god, he'd gone out the back door. In the light of day.

She limp-jogged to the rear of the house, heart pounding against her ribs as she searched for anything that might've given her away. The Cassie Johnson Photography sign hung on the wall behind a chair and telephone table. The only business cards in the holder matched the sign. Nothing alarming about those items—no trace of her alter ego anywhere in this room. But what if he'd gone downstairs? He didn't have reason to, but what if he had, out of simple curiosity?

She clutched the railing and took the basement stairs as quickly as possible. From halfway down, the seating area came into view. Three white, butter-soft leather chairs and a matching full-length couch formed something of a circle around a low, round, glass-top coffee table, much like a sophisticated rec room. Farther to the right lay the studio area where she did her commercial work and traditional portrait sittings. The left side of the basement housed her L-shaped desk and its two black leather office chairs. A few feet along, filing cabinets and shelves of camera equipment. Still nothing that would send him packing.

But if he'd made it all the way to the bottom for a better look, as in, around the partition wall… The bed, she could justify. Had used many times for G-rated photo shoots, like the time she photographed the Grady family, all four wearing red pajamas, tucked under an heirloom quilt. Such a great picture. If he'd seen the bed today, though, adorned with the Mancusos' toys for the shoot—oh god.

A double knock rattled the back door. "Come in," she called up while taking the basement stairs faster than her ankle cared for. She smiled while pulling the door open. A genuine one, because not only were Paolo and Beth Mancuso her most lucrative clients, they were truly wonderful people and shooting them was a treat for her eyes and her heart. They'd become friends.

"Hey, guys." Cassie waved them inside. "How many times have I told you to knock and walk in?"

"I told Paolo to open the door, but he wouldn't." Beth pulled her gorgeous husband in behind her. "He worries that we might catch *you* doing something naughty, since this studio is in your house, not in a separate building, like your old place."

Exactly why Cassie was eating truckloads of no-name pasta in an attempt to bank cash faster. Damn Lance for being the world's biggest douchebag. She'd had such a great setup—two-story century home on a picturesque street with a coach house tucked privately in the back. *That* had been a wicked studio. No amount of renovations to her basement would bring it to that level of awesome. At least she hadn't lost her business when she'd been forced to sign over her property. But it'd come pretty darn close and the Mancusos knew that, though few others did. If not for them sticking by her and Nana writing a check, she'd be taking passport photos at the Walmart portrait studio. She had a lot to be thankful for.

She gave Beth an affectionate squeeze, then released her. "Listen, as long as you come in my back door, I guarantee you won't catch anything."

Paolo and Beth blinked at her and broke into simultaneous laughter.

"All right, all right. Enough laughing at the foot in my mouth, let's move this downstairs."

As usual, Paolo insisted the ladies descend before him. Such a gentleman—with his clothes on, anyway. Cassie led the way, not wanting to get between husband and wife. She poured three glasses of Chianti and took a seat across from the couch where her clients had settled.

This warm-up time made the experience more comfortable for most people, which resulted in more intimate, natural photos. Better photos meant return business and word-of-mouth referrals. Anybody with a steady hand, good lighting and a decent camera could take pictures. Capturing raw, real emotion was an altogether different story, especially when the subjects tended to be naked and...busy. Call her cocky, but she had a knack for it, and credited the prep time she invested in *people* as part of that knack.

Sometimes clients sat and chatted for an hour, or knocked back a couple of drinks before they relaxed enough to do whatever it was they had in mind. Repeat clients like Paolo and Beth had started out that way. Now they rarely needed much of a primer.

Camera tucked in her lap, Cassie sipped her wine and opened the conversation. "How's business at the restaurant?"

"Excellent." Paolo gave Cassie his eyes, but his hand stayed on Beth's bare knee, just below the hem of her skirt.

"The new features are all hits and the pictures you took for the menu are beautiful, simply beautiful. You need to come by, sit at the chef's table, enjoy some of them."

"One of these days." When she had a wad of cash and nothing practical to save it for—yeah right.

"Our treat," Paolo said, as if reading her mind. "And bring somebody special. Tell us you've found a man who makes you happy."

"Um, sort of..." How romantic would that be, eating at the nicest Italian restaurant in the city with Brian's hand moving up her leg—much like Paolo's was on Beth's—under a linen-covered table? Only Brian had taken himself out of that equation and left her solo in more than this fantasy. "One day soon, maybe I will," she lied. "Thank you."

"Our pleasure." Paolo's words were meant for Cassie, but his attention had moved entirely to Beth.

Such a gorgeous couple. Paolo's Mediterranean complexion, his dark eyes and hair, contrasted with Beth's fair skin and sleek, light-blonde mane. Watching them together was exquisite. And yes, a turn-on. Anywhere from simmering to explosive, depending on the shoot. Judging from the accessories Paolo had dropped off earlier in the week and the speed at which the couple across from her were warming up, Cassie would probably be in a hot-and-bothered sweat at the end of their appointment.

Paolo took the glass from Beth's hand and set it on the table. He cupped her face between his hands and spoke softly to her, something in Italian. Cassie didn't understand the meaning of his words, but the emotion and intent couldn't be missed. *Everybody should have a love like this in their lives.* Somebody to share absolutely everything with, fearlessly. Somebody who demanded your body, heart and soul so they could cherish those things with every cell of their being, forevermore.

Cassie lifted her camera, subtly began to shoot. Six feet away, Paolo's palm skimmed up Beth's thigh, pushing the flimsy skirt to her hips. Beth's legs parted, offering access to her husband's strong hands. He stroked the narrow swath of black fabric between Beth's legs, whispering in Italian while kissing her neck. Beth leaned back on the arm of the couch, unbuttoning her silky camisole top to expose unrestrained breasts.

Even as a card-carrying member of the *I Love Cock* society, Cassie couldn't help staring at Beth's perfect rack, especially when Paolo's mouth closed over the top of one pink peak. Inside her bra, Cassie's nipples responded to the visual stimuli. Once the camera was engaged, she usually thought strictly about shadows and angles, whether or not to zoom. Not with the Mancusos. They'd gotten to her from the first session—which consisted of clothed yet suggestive poses and kisses—and they continued to affect her, regardless of the dozens of times and ways she'd photographed them. It wasn't just the things they did in front of her lens, it was the connection between them while they did it— whatever the *it* might be. Thank god her inner professional knew to continue capturing images, rather than sit and gawk.

Paolo's dark head moved down Beth's body, his tongue swirling inside Beth's bellybutton—an act that made Beth giggle and thrash. His next stop elicited a different response. Cassie slid from the chair to get a better angle of Paolo's mouth teasing his wife's pussy through her panties. They'd love these shots. Paolo's near-red tongue pressed against the black lace. The beautiful line of Beth's arched back, the black skirt banding her hips. The perfect O her red-painted lips formed as she climaxed.

Beth's arms closed around her husband's neck as he lifted her. Silently, all three moved to the other side of the partition wall. A white zone like the other areas, this one contained a large white-blanketed bed. Cassie had three headboards to suit a variety of shoots—black wrought iron, Mission-style cherry wood and a pretty white-upholstered one. For today's shoot, Paolo had chosen to go without. Kind of surprising, given the props he'd dropped off. A glass dildo chilled in a black ice bucket, a silver bullet vibrator in front of it. Then came the restraints. Black suede cuffs and red silk scarves indicated Beth would be tied up for the pictures, but without a headboard, apparently she wouldn't be tied down. Whatever Paolo had planned, Cassie had no doubt Beth would leave here a satisfied, happy woman.

Cassie switched to her new Canon Mark III, adjusted the Nifty Fifty lens she'd selected for this shoot. She moved around the room, capturing Paolo's and Beth's bodies from different heights and angles as they tangled together in a frenzy of kissing, tugging and grinding. Beth's clothes fell to the white-carpeted floor, along with Paolo's black dress shirt. Cassie took a couple shots of the strewn items. A picture of dirty laundry to some, perhaps, but she knew today's clients would appreciate the erotic quality of the simple shots.

As soon as Paolo reached for the scarf, the dynamic between the couple changed. Beth's body went pliant, allowing her husband to blind her with the carefully folded red silk. He spoke to her while tying the blindfold and cuffing her wrists. Although Paolo kept the volume of his voice low enough that Cassie only made out single words here and there, the tone was unmistakably firm. Not harsh or cruel, like the Doms in those staged porn videos. Regardless of Paolo's commands, or the actions he took, his voice always held a reverence for Beth that stirred Cassie's heart, as well as the longing low in her belly.

Paolo was a demanding partner, sexually. Unyielding and rough at times. Through it all, his complete adoration of Beth was more obvious than the sun on the most brilliant summer day. And it went both ways. Cassie had shot her share of engagement and wedding photos, pictures of couples allegedly at the pinnacle of true love. None of those brides or brides-to-be compared to the depth of emotion Cassie saw in Beth's eyes. Every time Paolo reddened Beth's porcelain skin with his palm, paddle or teeth, Cassie saw Beth's love for him ratchet higher. She gave what he wanted. He took what she needed him to take.

Paolo stretched Beth's arms above her head. He had only to touch her knee and she parted her legs, enough to give him —and their photographer—a peek of the pink between her legs. Paolo stood back from the bed, wordlessly cuing Cassie to move in and shoot solo pictures of Beth. An easy assignment, this. Beth was breathtakingly erotic, especially as Paolo had arranged her.

"I'll be right back." Paolo's whisper tickled Cassie's ear, though she doubted he noticed her shudder. He was entirely focused on his wife, as always. "I picked up a surprise for her, but it's out in my car."

Cassie nodded, her mind racing as Paolo snuck, half dressed, from the basement. The surprise might as well be for her, the anticipation of it made her that giddy. She circled the bed, capturing a dozen frames of Beth before Paolo reappeared. Cassie always took an abundance of pictures, and more so with the Mancusos. Graphic, explicit shots, of course. But not all fell into the X-rated category. The majority of pictures, including those she took while Paolo and Beth were fucking right in front of her, were better described as erotic or highly sensual. Cassie knew without looking at the screen on her camera that today's images would be some of her best work. Their sessions always produced incredible images, for reasons other than Cassie's keen eye and steady hand.

After returning, Paolo trailed his fingers up the inside of Beth's leg, past her pussy to her breasts. "I bought something for you, *mia amata*. Not something you've asked for, not one time, but something I want to use on your beautiful body. May I?"

"Yes."

The trust, so automatic and freely given, tugged at Cassie's heart. Turned it a shameful green.

The small box in his hands couldn't be more than four inches square by an inch high. Not much would fit in there, toy-wise. Definitely not a new paddle or flogger, nor a dildo or plug. A small vibrator, possibly. None of those items matched his description, anyway. After all Cassie had seen them do together, what could he have bought for his wife that she'd never once requested?

Paolo stood beside the bed. No physical contact, yet the electricity of their connection crackled. Cassie kept her eye to the camera. She caught the moment he lifted the box's lid. Focused on its contents—*her* curiosity had nothing to do with it, nothing at all—and forced her lips to stay shut when she saw the gift.

Building the anticipation, Paolo jingled the small metal dangles near Beth's ear.

"Jewelry?"

"Of a sort." He pooled a silver chain between her breasts, keeping its ends in one palm.

"A necklace?"

"No." With his free hand, he dragged his nails over her curves, bringing her nipples to full rigidity. He plucked one between his fingers, then the other, back and forth, until Beth rocked beneath his increasingly firm touches. "Careful, *cara*, don't let my gift slide away."

Beth stilled instantly. "I won't."

Cassie held her breath, and not only to steady the camera in her hands. She stepped to one side, changed angles. Anything to distract herself from becoming fully immersed in *their* moment. On edge, finger poised over the button, she waited to freeze time.

Paolo held Beth's breast firmly in his palm. He brought his mouth down on Beth's for a sensual kiss that would make a gorgeous picture. Cassie continued to shoot as he pulled back from the kiss. Full yet utterly masculine lips curled into a wicked, lusty smile. Dark eyes with a truly unfair amount of long lashes focused on Beth's face. Paolo would shake his head at these images, but Beth would cherish them.

The small movement of Paolo's hand caught Cassie's eye. Thank god, or she would have missed what would surely be the most important shot of this session. With no hint or warning to Beth, Paolo closed the first alligator clamp on her waiting nipple.

BRIAN

Brian's fingers twitched. Get the hell off Cassie's street before she noticed him sitting out here, or go make a giant ass of himself? No brainer. He yanked the keys from the ignition. Hopped out of the Jeep and stalked across the street toward her bungalow. To think, he'd come here to apologize at minimum, beg if necessary. Then some Italian stallion had jogged down the driveway—shirtless and grinning ear to ear

—and grabbed a small black box from his Cadillac. Boxes like that usually held jewelry the likes of which Brian couldn't afford, might not be able to afford for the next decade.

He ignored the front door, opting to follow the guy's route to the back. The inside door was open, as were the screens on the outer aluminum door. Convenient for him. A good sign too—if they weren't worried about privacy, the guy might be here to stand in front of Cassie's camera, not take her to bed.

She didn't talk much about her photography business, usually blushing more than speaking when Brian pressed her to answer questions. When he'd asked what kind of photography she did, she'd answered with "portrait-type stuff, mostly". Not the whole truth. One look at her website and he'd discovered she did a lot more than take pictures of newborn babies and soon-to-be-married couples. Her website's gallery was full of commercial credits to go with the regular stuff. Corporate brochures, magazine ads, even some book covers. His girl had a hell of a lot of talent.

His girl. He had no right thinking of Cassie that way, but he did. The feeling had been growing since he first laid eyes on the sexy little pixie, and last night had cemented it. If the Italian was here modeling for one of her jobs, caving his smiling face into a wall probably wouldn't win Brian any points.

Didn't explain the box that had given him the smile, though. Could be a prop. Hell, if it was jewelry, it might even be the focal point of the picture, and *the guy* could be the prop. Now there was an image worth cracking a grin at. Still, he didn't like the idea of Cassie alone in her basement with a half-naked man. She was fit, for sure, and strong for her size, but that size was damn tiny. No match for an average Joe, and the guy in the driveway had been pretty damn buff. Good-looking too, in that slick, European way women seemed to fall all over.

Yeah, he had to get in the house, like, now.

So he'd knock and interrupt her appointment. Hopefully she wouldn't be *more* pissed at him. If he couldn't charm his way into the house, he wasn't above groveling. Whatever it took to make Cassie understand why he'd acted like a dick earlier, and keep her out of the Italian's clutches.

Noise from the basement drowned out the rap of his knuckles on the aluminum. A female cry of surprise made him grab the handle, ready to rip the door from its frame if necessary. Then a male voice and the unmistakable sound of moaning—very aroused, feminine moaning—drifted through the screen, knocking him back a good two feet. That's all he needed to hear.

Blood thrummed in his ears as he peeled from the curb. Had she jumped the first guy to cross her path because of the rejection at the gym, or was Cassie the type to bang two men within a twelve-hour period? Fifteen minutes ago, he wouldn't have believed either option. Now he didn't know what the fuck to think.

So much for the special chemistry he thought they had. Chemistry, hell yeah. But special—not even a little. He could've sworn he saw disappointment and hurt in her eyes earlier. And the night they'd shared, damn. All bullshit and games. To her, anyway.

CASSIE

Saturday night television sucked. Cassie stabbed at the remote, turning the screen black and thrusting the room into darkness.

Of course it sucked, Saturday nights weren't meant for wallowing, holding down the couch while snarfing an entire bag of potato chips. God, how many calories and fat grams were in that bag, anyway? She turned on the table lamp and smoothed the empty wrapper. Oh crap. Twelve hundred fifty calories, sixty-five grams of fat. She could practically feel her backside expanding across the couch cushions. Good thing she had that appointment for Tuesday. Brian had been a bit of a jerk this afternoon, but he was still a great personal trainer. He'd have those chips off her butt in no time.

Or, she could go to a club tonight and dance them off. Eleven thirty—early, by any decent Saturday's standards. She could be primped, dressed and on her way before the clock rolled over to Sunday. At midnight, though, the lineups would be insane. Unless she went to a club where she knew one of the bouncers.

Just because Brian didn't want a repeat of last night— which was extremely, ridiculously disappointing—didn't mean *everything* had changed between them. He'd casually dropped the offer to let her jump the line on more than one occasion. Time she finally took him up on that. And yes, if seeing her all clubbed-out caused him a twinge of regret for rejecting her earlier, that didn't hurt, either.

Forty minutes later, she was click-clacking across the jammed parking lot, trying not to twist her ankle—for the second time today. She turned the corner and found a mile-long line, as expected. A few men mixed in amongst dozens of females in varying degrees of slut-me-up. Cassie kept her eyes on the door, ignoring the voices who not-so-politely told her where to find the back of the line. Normally, she'd follow the rules. Not tonight.

"Hi there." She smiled up at the dark-haired doorman. His build matched Brian's for bulk, though he stood a couple inches shorter. Still, he flat-out dwarfed her, even in her three-inch heels. A good-looking guy, if you liked the monstrous, menacing type. Because unlike Brian, this man didn't smile down at her with a sexy combo of amusement and affection. He just...stared down.

"You got a VIP pass?"

"Um, not an official one."

"Being cute doesn't count." He flicked the air in front of him. "Back of the line."

The haters behind her jeered. Hey, he thought she was cute—that bought her another try, right? "I'm a friend of Brian's."

"You and half the ladies behind you, sweetheart."

At this, she glanced over her shoulder. Surely he didn't mean that the way it sounded. She looked up at him again and met a smug grin. Thought he'd struck a nerve, huh? "Maybe so, but did he tell all of *them* he'd let them in whenever they wanted?"

He crossed massive arms over an equally massive chest. "You really wanna play it this way?" He shrugged when she thrust her chin upward and nodded. "Your call. Name?"

"You're not going to go and get him, bring him out here?"

Cocky jerk shook his head and tapped his headset. "If he doesn't know you by name, you can join the rest of his *friends* in line."

"Cassie Johnson," she said, ignoring the cackling at her back.

He opened his mouth, clapped it closed and smirked. "Think I'll go old-school tonight."

She commanded her body not to fidget when he turned to pull the door open. Thumping bass spilled out into the summer night as he called to somebody she couldn't see.

Another thickly built guy wearing head-to-toe black

stepped outside to swap places. This one smiled genuinely, thoroughly checking her out as he did. "So, you say you're a friend of our hotheaded big man." Not a question, but rather a statement he found exceedingly entertaining. Great, another one.

"If we're talking about Brian Black, then yes." She agreed with big, absolutely, but hotheaded? Not the Brian she knew. Maybe that went with his bouncer persona. She certainly understood changing façades to match the job of the moment.

His gaze traveled from her low-cut neckline to her cherry-painted lips. "Well, if he's stupid enough to have forgotten you, I'd be happy to take his place as your friend tonight."

Bouncer number one reappeared, motioning her inside and saving her from answering. "Been here before?" he asked as she caught up to him several feet past the entrance.

"A few times, it's great."

He grunted. "Brian's working the floor. Enjoy." With that, her less-than-thrilled escort turned back toward the entrance.

She followed the pulse of music down the corridor. Near the end, she took a fortifying breath, then rounded the corner into the meat warehouse-turned-meat market. True, she'd been here before, but never solo. Alone amongst hundreds of gyrating bodies, many of which were fuelled by alcohol—a little daunting, but once she got on the dance floor, it wouldn't matter. But first, a drink to loosen her limbs.

A thirty-foot-long bar stood near the edge of the huge dance floor, serving patrons from all sides. She set her sights on the closest end and shouldered her way through the throng, reaching her goal with the barest minimum of good manners remaining. Stools didn't exist here. Get your booze and move it along, thank you very much. Cassie pulled a twenty from her tiny purse and leaned against the polished wood with the folded bill between her thumb and index finger. She chose her mark—an attractive twenty-something she pegged as a grad student at the university down the road—made eye contact and waved the money. When she'd been on the other side of the equation, she'd always gravitated to people with the cash at the ready, namely when the amount in their hand should accommodate a healthy tip. And here came the bartender, right on schedule.

"Money talks, right?"

Strong, tanned forearms swiped a rag across the bar in front of her. "What money? All I saw were gorgeous blue eyes looking at me."

"Nicely done," she said, and he laughed. "I'll have a Jäger Bomb, please."

"Going hardcore, I like it. But how about I mix you something that tastes better and won't make your pretty face numb?"

A bartender who didn't want to push an easy drink at her and move her out of the way—nicely done indeed. "Sure." She squeezed tighter to the bar to avoid an oblivious drunk on her left side. "Whatever you have in mind, I'm game."

"Words to get me through the night." He winked.

A quality wink, playful and sexy without a hint of creepiness. Here was a guy she would have gone home with not so long ago. She knew his type—easygoing and mildly adventurous in the sack. Like medium chicken wings—not too bland, not spicy enough to singe the senses. A good diversion for a night. But not this night. Not any night since she'd developed her Brian-fatuation.

The blond placed a tall shot glass in front of her and layered in melon liqueur, Baileys and Jägermeister. "Bottoms up."

She handed him the cash and lifted the glass. The aromas of sugar and alcohol filled her nose. She believed him that it'd taste good, but she bet the innocent-looking concoction still held the power to numb her face. "It's really pretty. What is it?"

"Loch Ness Monster."

"Ooh, sounds dangerous. Should I be scared?"

Another laugh as he placed her change on the bar. "Only if you have multiple sightings."

"Thanks for the warning." Cassie tipped her head back. Nessie floated over her tongue and rolled down her throat, setting off a mixed reaction. Happy taste buds at the entry point, focused channel of fire as the alcohol crept lower. She swallowed the last drop and shook her head. "Wow."

"Want another?"

"God no. I can only swallow one monster at a time."

"You're killing me here, gorgeous." He caught her hand as she pushed a generous, well-deserved tip his way. "Come back to my section for all your drinks tonight. I'll take good care of you."

"That's a sweet invitation, but that was it for me—I'm here to dance, not drink."

"Then just...come back."

Oh, it was *that* kind of invitation. "I—" The harmless fib poised on the tip of her tongue vanished when she caught sight of Brian in her peripheral vision, hovering over a curvy young blonde with hair that hung halfway down her back. Speaking of monsters, Cassie's green-eyed one reared its ugly head, higher and stronger than ever. She blinked her attention back to the bartender and smiled. "I will."

Chapter 5

BRIAN

WHAT THE FUCK. When Dave had come to tell him Cassie was at the door, dropping his name, Brian assumed—stupidly—she'd come to see him. He'd tracked her the second she walked through the archway, yet she'd headed straight to the bar instead of searching him out. Ten minutes later, she was practically holding JT's hand while the guy drooled on the bar in front of her, ignoring the rest of his customers.

Too bad Brian couldn't bounce the staff.

Maybe he wouldn't have to, now that Cassie had abandoned the bar. JT still had a smile on his face, the bastard. The night was young and the back parking lot was dark—Brian could straighten JT out later, if necessary. Make sure the only fluid JT gave Cassie came from a bottle.

The girl who'd latched on to Brian earlier kept chatting, following him as he trailed Cassie through the crowd. Bouncer groupies. Made no sense to him, but there were always a few.

He'd have to shake this one loose soon. When the opportunity to get Cassie alone appeared, he didn't need a tagalong.

"Wait up," a hand closed around his arm, "I don't want to lose you."

Stuff like this used to do it for him. Picking up a hot-and-ready female on nights he worked the club was pretty much a guaranteed thing. And they never wanted more. Hell, he rarely had to serve them breakfast, let alone court them. They just spread their legs, collected their alcohol-induced sex and cabbed it out of his life. The last time had been a month ago, and every stroke had felt wrong. Fucking a stranger and wishing it were Cassie had been the worst sex of his life. Unfortunately, it'd probably been pretty shitty for the woman in his bed too. He didn't even remember what she looked like.

One word and the attractive, slightly tipsy young woman at his side would jumpstart the old pattern. After hearing Cassie fucking that Italian guy this afternoon, he ought to take blondie up on her unspoken offer.

He bent his head to her ear so she'd hear him over the noise. "I'm working. Go find your friends. Dance, whatever."

Rum-scented breath wafted in his face as she pulled his head closer. "Will I see you later?"

Good question. "You might."

"I'd better," she said, nearly head-butting him in her drunken attempt at a sexy kiss.

Despite everything she had going for her, she did nothing for him. He let her finish her sloppy oral assault, then worked his way deeper into the crowd, putting as many bodies between them as possible.

Place was packed tonight. The hum in the air intensified the closer he got to the dance floor. The pounding pulse of the music. Adrenaline and endorphins rolling off the bouncing, grinding bodies. Picking out any one person between the flashes of light should be next to impossible, but he spotted Cassie immediately.

As it usually did, the crowd parted for him. One of the advantages of being built like a Highland warrior, as his mother had always described him. He found an open spot with a clear view of the dance floor and planted his feet in a wide stance. Folded his arms high on his chest and put on his bouncer mug. It might've appeared that he was working, but all hell could've broken loose in front of him and he wouldn't have noticed. He only saw Cassie.

Song after song played. Through all of them, she swayed, jumped and gyrated. Sang along to every word and smiled. Goddamn, that smile. Brighter than any of the spotlights that crisscrossed the dance floor. And he wasn't the only one drawn to it. First one guy, then another and another. She had no shortage of dance partners tonight. No surprise there. She moved alongside each of them in turn, never missing a beat. A couple of them lowered their heads to try to talk to her. They got a head shake. Turning down whatever they'd suggested. Now that part, he liked.

The DJ took things down a notch with a song made for sexy, close dancing. One of Cassie's admirers caught her arm in invitation. Again, she shook her head. Unlike the others, this guy wasn't taking no for an answer. Instead of releasing her, he pulled her toward him. Not only did he force her against his chest, he walked backward, moving them out of the central area. Like sand in a funnel, people filled their spot on the floor and folded in on their retreating path. Brian stretched to see over the sea of heads. No sign of the faux-hawk guy or Cassie. Fuck, where'd they go?

He pushed through the ever-thickening crowd. The club had to be over capacity. He could fix that, turf some idiots out the door—starting with the guy who'd dared touch Cassie against her will. Only that guy wasn't getting a polite escort out the front.

Then he'd deal with Cassie. What the hell was she thinking, coming here alone? Worse, dressed in a skirt that barely covered her ass, those fine legs of hers bare and finished off with fuck-me shoes? She might as well have had a neon sign over her head that read "cock tease". Shit. Blur had a solid rep for being the biggest meat-market in town. People came here to get loaded and get laid. That didn't excuse the bastard who'd dragged her off the dance floor, but it made his mistake more understandable.

"Trouble?" Craig, one of the other bouncers, asked when he emerged from the crowd.

"Yeah, possibly. Saw a guy drag a woman from the dance floor against her will. Can't find them now."

"Maybe you read it wrong. Maybe she's one of those chicks who gets hot from being manhandled, and now they're getting busy in a dark corner."

He'd flick Craig across the head for being a moron if they were talking about your average woman. But with Cassie, Craig might have it right. She'd certainly enjoyed their rougher play last night. Doing it with somebody else, though…

"Fuck, man, you look ready to pound somebody into next week. Maybe you should take a break, go out back and grab some air."

"Yeah, think I will." He buddy-slapped Craig, then headed past the bar. He'd been distracted enough when all he and Cassie had done was talk and flirt. Now that he'd been with her, his head—hell, his whole body—felt as if it'd been ransacked. He wanted her. He also wanted to throttle her. And when he thought of combining those two…it was probably a good thing they wouldn't be together again. She affected him too much. Brought all his hard edges too close to the surface.

He headed down the corridor that led to the restrooms and farther along, to the employee entrance. Typical of the later hours on a Saturday night, the ladies' room had a line stretching halfway down the hall. Also fairly typical, the few whistles and comments he drew from those alcohol-loosened females. He scanned the line for blushing cheeks that'd give away his catcallers and zeroed in on Cassie instead. He had about five seconds lead time before she noticed him. Long enough to note her downturned lips—a rare sight, and a huge change from how she'd looked while dancing. Not good.

"Having a good time?" he asked. The woman beside Cassie piped up as if the question had been directed at her, or the group in general. He didn't bother to acknowledge her. Didn't wait for Cassie's answer either. Not when it was obvious she was searching for words. Too out of character. "Come with me."

He half expected her to balk at the hand he offered. Instead she slid her warm fingers over his palm and let him pluck her from the line. Step one and he'd take it.

Near the end of the hall, he keyed in the code for the staff locker room and ushered her inside. Empty, as it should be this time of night. "Washroom's over there if you need it."

Her gaze followed the line of his arm to an open door, but she shook her head. And still said nothing.

"Not speaking to me, or did something happen with that guy from the dance floor?" That got her attention. The wide eyes staring straight up at him kind. "What'd he do?"

"He—it's okay, I took care of it."

Heat churned in his chest. "That answer's not even close to good enough. Tell me."

"He assumed I wanted to do more than dance. I let him know he was mistaken."

The rage worked its way higher, firing the tops of his ears and pounding a beat behind his eyes. "Wait here."

"Are you going to kick him out?"

"At least. Depends how many people are watching."

"Brian, don't."

The way she'd flung herself between him and the door almost made him smile. "You really think you can stop me?"

"Maybe."

"Think again." Cupping her tiny waist, he lifted her from the spot, took a few steps to the right and deposited her on the floor. "Stay."

Sneaky little pixie darted around him and plastered her back against the damn door. "I'm not your pet."

He crowded her. Curled his fingers under her choker-style necklace and tipped her face up. "If you were, you'd be better trained." Wrong time to think about Cassie naked and bowing to his wishes, but how could he not with her lips parted and her pulse beating like jungle music against his fingers? He had to let go, take a step back. "Go sit on the bench while I make sure that asshole got your message."

"It's packed out there, you'll never find him."

"I'll find him." He cracked his neck side to side. "Now move." Waves of short light-brown hair fell in her face when she shook her head. Again. Stubborn little thing. "Cassie. Out of my way."

"I don't want you to get in trouble because of me."

"It'd be worth it."

"Because you'd get to beat the crap out of somebody?"

"Call that a perk. Dealing with this asshole might make up for my stupidity earlier." Instinct took over and he stepped into her space again. "And then you'll let me take you home later."

"You want to drive me home?"

Cute. Very cute. "More than that."

"Oh?" She sent a different kind of heat through him when she flattened her palms on his chest, rocked her wicked little body back and forth against his bulging fly. "Decided you want another night with me?"

"Keep going."

"What, you're going to stick around and make me breakfast this time, instead of stealing my last orange and sneaking out the back door?"

Self-preservation screamed at him to remember what he'd overheard at that back door. Fuck it. She'd owed him nothing at that point. He had a shot at changing things and he was taking it. He caught her chin and held it. "I might make you lunch and dinner too."

The flirty smile shifted into something a hell of a lot rawer. Her hands slid down, nails dragging over his t-shirt. The buckle on his belt jingled. The sound of unzipping echoed between them, then her hand wrapped around his cock.

"Don't waste your testosterone on that idiot from the dance floor...save it for later, for me."

If she knew what he could do—wanted to do—with the testosterone coursing through his system, she'd run, far and fast. He wouldn't give her reason to run, he'd be careful. A hell of a lot more careful than he'd been with Leanne. He just needed to stay in control. Starting now, by getting back to work. But goddamn, that face. Eye-fucking him while she licked her lips. They could do without him in the club a few more minutes.

He found the bottom of her skirt and yanked it up. A tiny triangle of black lace disappeared between her legs. He shoved it to one side and curled his hand over her smooth mound, sinking two fingers inside her body.

She wiggled against his hand. Seared him with her eyes. "Make me." The words demanded, contradicting her whispered, begging tone.

"Make you what, move?" He lowered his mouth to her ear. "Make you come?"

"Yes."

A request he was more than happy to oblige. He caught her earlobe between his teeth. Bit it, making her gasp, then sucked it hard. The metal post from her earring dragged across his tongue, delivering a sting of pleasure. Like her teeth had given his cock last night.

He broke their contact with a half step backward. "Go sit on the bench."

"But—"

One finger pressed to her lips silenced her. He narrowed his eyes—his best shot at not cracking a grin at her adorable fucking poutiness—and tilted his head at the bench between two banks of lockers. Goddamn, if she didn't stomp over and plunk her cute, bare ass on the shellacked wood. How far would she let him take this?

He stepped between her legs, knocking them wider. Time to give her what she wanted. "Touch yourself."

Both hands moved to her pussy—one spreading her lips to expose her clit, the other rubbing it in small, firm circles. Fucking heaven and hell. Her head rolled to her shoulder, a deep-pink glow staining her cheeks.

"Do you want me to come, or...?"

Not quite asking permission, but damn close. "Yeah, but not yet." He slid his fist up and down his cock, getting harder every second her eyes devoured him.

The movements between her legs got jerky. She rubbed

faster, harder. Her mouth fell open, filling the room and his head with her sounds. She was almost there. But he wasn't done with her.

He forfeited the view and moved closer. "Suck me. I want to feel your sexy moan around my cock when you come."

She didn't just open for him, let him slide his cock in her mouth—she took him in greedily, gorging on his cock as if he'd given her the most delicious fucking treat of her life. Her eyebrows pinched together and her mouth clamped down on him, surrounding him with humming vibrations. Fuck. The tightening in his balls. The pressure building at the base of his cock. So close. Not yet. Not fucking yet.

Somehow, she took him deeper. Swallowed around him, the quick clutch of her throat pushing him over. "Fuck...so fucking good..." He gripped the back of her head and gave up control.

"Hey, Bri, you in here? Holy shit—sorry, man." As fast as Craig had opened the door behind them, he left, clicking it shut.

Fuck. Brian locked his knees to keep them from buckling. Cassie stared up at him, her perfect mouth still milking the last pulses of his cock, nothing but pure desire in those beautiful eyes. Caught in the act yet she didn't miss a beat. How'd he gotten so damn lucky?

"Come here." He pulled her to a stand. Squatted in front of her and took his time straightening her clothes, prolonging the incredible sensation of her delicate fingers in his hair.

"Are you going to get in trouble—oh god, you're not going to get fired because of me, are you?"

Of all the things she could have said, that was her question? He had to laugh. "No, not here, not for that." She looked away, but he'd already seen the frown. "Hey," he reached up and turned her face back to his, "Craig didn't see you." Whether that was totally true or not, he had no idea.

"I don't care if he did, it's—forget it." She shook her head, deked around him before he could stand.

Here, this time, he had options. He wouldn't let her slip through some door with things left unsaid. He snagged her by the waist and hauled her against his chest.

"You need to get back to work."

"The hell I do. It's what?"

"It was stupid. Nothing."

Call him a perverted bastard, he liked the way she twisted in his arms. "Look at me. I'm not letting you go until you tell me." And after that, he still didn't plan to, not in a big-picture way.

She gave in with a huff, staring up with stormy eyes. "Jealousy, okay? To which I have no right, but there it is. Now let me go."

Not a chance. The more she tried to break free, the more blood returned to his cock. "I want to talk to you, but you keep fighting me and I'm going to end up fucking you instead, so hard you'll feel like I'm still inside you two days from now."

"Okay." She froze, but if he read her eyes right, she was agreeing to the latter as much as to talking.

"When you look at me that way, I can barely think straight." He bowed his neck, pressed their foreheads together. "You have no reason to be jealous."

"I know, that's what I said."

"No, not like that." He blew out a breath. The staffroom at Blur is the last place he expected to spill his guts. "Cassie, you're it."

"Yay me, I beat out the blonde for pick of the night."

"What blonde?"

"The one hanging all over you, the one you were kissing. Ring a bell?"

The cling-on from earlier. Interesting. Apparently he wasn't the only one who'd kept eyes open out there. "She kissed me."

She aimed an exaggerated eye roll directly at his face. "That's original."

Much as he liked Cassie feeling possessive about him, this was some twisted shit. "You're jealous of some girl hitting on me—a girl who I walked away from, for the record—after what you've been doing?"

"I've been dancing off the fat grams from a bag of chips and kneeing a creep in the groin. You have a problem with those things?"

"Not those." Good sense screamed at him to keep his big mouth shut, forget the rest. "I stopped by your house earlier to apologize and explain about that bullshit at the gym. Went around back. You had company—and an open door."

The blood drained from her face and her eyes nearly burst from the sockets. Her bottom lip dropped and closed, more than once. But defend what he'd heard through that screen—not a word.

His mouth on the other hand, not so quiet. "Might want to lock up next time, or maybe you don't care who hears or sees."

Again, she strained against his arms. This time, with serious determination. "We talked, we're done here. Now let me go."

Fuck. Thanks to the hotheadedness he'd inherited with the red hair, they'd jumped tracks. Hell, they weren't even in the same station anymore. He couldn't let her go yet, not with things between them on the express train to can't-be-fixed. "I'm not done."

"Let. Me. Go." She wiggled and huffed until steam practically blew from her ears.

So wrong, smiling at her right now. Not his fault she owned the cute-mixed-with-sexy-fury thing. The madder she got, the more his anger seemed to fade. The harder she struggled to get away, the more he enjoyed holding her tight. He was definitely one fucked-up son of a bitch.

"You're hurting me."

The one thing in the world he couldn't handle hearing. He released her fast enough that she staggered to catch her balance. "Sorry." He dropped his chin, shook his head. Blindly found the doorknob and turned, pausing halfway through the doorframe without looking back at her. How could he? "I didn't mean to—" This time, he shut his stupid fucking mouth. Didn't matter that he hadn't meant to hurt her, just like it hadn't mattered when he'd unintentionally injured Leanne. "I'm sorry. About all of it."

CASSIE

"Crap, where is it?" The last time she'd checked her cell for any sign of contact from Brian, it'd been 3:30 a.m. and the darn thing had been tight in her palm. Now its ring tormented her from god-knows-where in the sofa. She sprang off the corduroy, kicking her chenille blanket to the floor in the process, and rooted furiously through cracks between the overstuffed cushions.

Found it, with half a ring to spare before the call redirected to voice mail. "Hello?"

"Morning there, gorgeous."

"Sam?" Nice guy, hot guy, but not the male voice she wanted to hear. "Um, how did you get this number?"

"Invasion of Brian's privacy." A smooth chuckle drifted through the phone. "He called me after his shift at Blur last night, massively pissed off, and ended up punishing himself with rye before passing out on my couch. When he was snoring like an old hound, I looked you up in his cell contacts."

"I can't believe he doesn't have it passcode protected." She slapped her forehead. Of all the stuff Sam had spilled, she chose to comment on Brian's phone. Good grief, airhead much?

"Oh, he has a code. I cracked it, pretty easily too. Like I said, invasion of privacy. I'm not above it if it's for a good cause."

Cassie squinted until the clock across the room came into focus. If Brian landed on Sam's doorstep after the bar closed, then drank until he passed out, Sam had to have been up at least as late as she had. How the heck did he sound so alert?

"I'm operating on five hours' sleep and no coffee, Sam. To be honest, I'm not even sure if this call is real, or part of some crazy dream."

"Grab a pen and paper, it's real."

She made her way to the kitchen. "Still not sure I believe you, but I'm ready. Go."

"Brian's fitness boot camp. Nine thirty at Victoria Park, near the pavilion. Damn Scot has one hell of a constitution, putting away so much booze, then getting up with the sun to train the masses."

"I'm way too tired..." From staring out the window half the night, hoping that damn Scot, as Sam referred to him, would appear. "Plus, I don't think he'd appreciate my presence."

KARLA DOYLE

"After what he said about you last night, Cass, especially after the rye kicked in, I can't think of much he'd appreciate more."

Things had gone from hot to disastrous in the locker room at Brian's second job. She'd obviously pissed him off by behaving like an immature, jealous girlfriend, and he'd retaliated by dropping the bomb that he'd seen her shooting Paulo and Beth having kinda kinky sex. Then he'd pushed her away —literally—and left.

She pressed the phone tighter to her head while tiptoeing down the hall. "What did he say?" After a few beats of dead air, she tapped the receiver and tried again. "Sam, are you still there—what did he tell you?"

"Sorry, had a beep. Our idiot boss looking for somebody to cover a shift since he can't call his favorite go-to guy on Sundays. As if it would kill Trevor Ritchie to work a few hours. Anyway. Let's just say Brian regretted some stuff. About you. And him."

Seriously, that's all he had to say? "Geez, Sam, don't tell me everything all at once."

"You know I can't tell you details, it goes against the code."

"Do guys actually call it that—the code?"

"Yeah, there's a handshake too. Look, get your cute little butt down there and make up with the giant dumbass."

"There's no making up, we're not...together."

"You sure about that? Like I said, he talked. A lot. Sounded to me like you're a great match—when one or both of you aren't being stupid."

Is that what Brian wanted—to be a couple? After what he'd happened upon via her back door, and how much it had obviously bothered him, was a relationship even possible? Maybe, since he already knew about the under-the-radar,

84

between-the-sheets side of her business, he'd get used to what she did. Maybe he wouldn't ask questions she couldn't ethically answer and he'd understand when she told him to steer clear of her house at certain times. Or maybe he'd end up like Lance, burning her because she'd trusted him.

"Is that a toilet?" Yet another laugh, this one totally amused. "Are we like girlfriends now, going to the can together?"

Oh crap, she'd hit the flusher. Stupid, distracted brain. She needed a save, and fast. "Women only do that at bars, Sam. I was grabbing a bathrobe and...my cat did it. One of his favorite tricks, the brat."

"Sounds like a cool cat. Catch him on video sometime and show it to me at the gym."

Great. Now she had to get a cat. A cat that knew how to flush toilets, no less. Shouldn't be too difficult, right?

"Shit, another beep from my boss. Wonder what he'll offer me this time so he can avoid a few hours' honest work. So, you're going to the boot camp, right?"

"I'll think about it."

"Don't think, Cass, do. See you around."

"Sure. Hey wait, why do you keep calling me that?" Nobody in her life had ever called her Cass, and she'd be happy to keep it that way.

Sam slid one last chuckle into her ear. "Passcode."

Chapter 6

CASSIE

DRIVING through the city took longer than expected. She reached the park at nine thirty-five, instead of twenty past, as she'd planned. Being late would make it difficult to slip into Brian's little band of boot-campers unnoticed. She found a spot on one of the side streets, grabbed her water bottle and hustled along the path, breaking into a jog until she reached the pavilion—and the fitness boot camp.

"Holy crap..."

Directly ahead, Brian's back. Beyond that had to be thirty or more women and a sprinkling of men, every one of them doing jumping jacks while Brian barked out a count—and he was already at ninety-three.

"Latecomer," a red-faced woman yelled, pointing straight at Cassie.

"Tattletale," Cassie muttered under her breath. She pulled the front of her baseball cap lower and tried skirting around the group to the back row. Too late, the entire lot of jumpers had zeroed in on her, and they were hooting like crazed people. This couldn't be a good sign.

"Not so fast there." Brian's deep timbre stopped her in her tracks. "You have to pay up."

Oh god, of course there was a fee. By the time she turned to face him, her cheeks burned something fierce and the one-armpit stress sweating had kicked in. Lovely.

He took the count to one hundred, then gave the trainees a break. "One minute rest."

A group sigh of relief went up from his minions. A few of them dropped exaggeratedly onto the grass. Brian ignored them, hooked one finger at her and reeled her closer. If he was hurting from a hangover, it didn't show. No bloodshot eyes or dark circles to give away the night Sam had outlined. If anything, he looked energized. And in gray sport shorts that showed off his muscular legs and a steel-blue sleeveless tee that accentuated his muscles and the color of his eyes, he also looked downright delicious. No wonder he garnered a huge crowd on Sunday mornings.

He folded his thick arms across his chest and stared down at her. "I didn't expect to see you here."

Not "this is a nice surprise", or, "glad you came". She could kill Sam for persuading her to do this. "I like to mix things up. But I left my purse in the car, so I'll go get it and be right back with some money." Yeah, right. Once she got to her car, she was so out of here.

"Hold it." He didn't touch her, didn't move a muscle. Nor did he need to. His voice alone glued her to the spot. "The first class is always free. No easy getaway for you, cutie."

"Then what was that comment about paying up?"

A wicked smile curled into place between that ginger beard and mustache. "Latecomers interrupt the flow of the routine. There's a toll for that."

She surveyed his students. Some were toned and fit, but most had a journey ahead of them before they hit that point. Whatever they could do, she could do. She lifted her chin and returned his cocky grin. "Name it."

"Ready for pushups," he called over his shoulder. Behind him, dozens of bodies assumed the standard position. "You'll be doing yours right here, in front of everybody."

"No problem." She shook out her arms. Clasped them behind her back to stretch her pectoral muscles, then hit the ground. "Drop and give you ten?"

"You're going to give me a hell of a lot more than ten." He chuckled. "But you're not ready to start yet." His feet left her field of vision. Some cheers—and taunts—rose from front of the pack. Next thing she knew, Brian had his hand wrapped around her shins, lifting her legs off the ground.

"What the—?" Her toes connected with a solid surface again, but they hadn't gone down in elevation. She craned her neck and saw the mammoth tire under her feet. Oh crap.

He knelt, tickled her ear with his breath. "Time to pay up." He straightened, giving her butt a hearty whack on the way. "One!"

By the fifteenth pushup, heat had spread across her chest and shoulders. To her left, the masses continued heaving their various weights up and down. Nobody quit. Nobody looked close to quitting. Neither would she.

"Seventeen…"

Boot-campers started falling off at eighteen. Not her. No way. Piece of cake, this.

"Twenty-three…"

Good god, her arms. Apparently Jell-O *could* do pushups.

"Twenty-nine…"

Her abs had officially caught fire.

"Thirty-one…who's had enough?" He laughed at the

mixture of groans that answered his question. "Too bad. Thirty-two…" He crouched beside her. "How about you—had enough yet?"

"Never." She only had enough breath for one word, and it seemed to amuse the hell out of him.

"Thirty-three…" A heavy palm spanned her back, applying less-than-subtle pressure. "Thirty-four…how about now?"

"You're a—"

"Thirty-five, and done. One-minute break."

This time, she joined her fellow victims in the communal sigh of relief. She collapsed onto her stomach, eyes closed, groaning as the grass soothed her scorching skin. Her baseball cap rolled off her head, letting more heat escape. She might not move from this spot for the duration of Brian's class.

"I'm a what?" he asked, tipping a bottle above the back of her head. Cool water dribbled down her shoulders and neck.

"Oh god, that feels good. I was going to say jerk, but now you're my hero."

"You should probably stick with jerk."

She mustered the energy to roll onto her back, catching one arm on his shin in the process. Forget the heat from the pushups, the sparks where their bodies touched were ten times hotter. She tipped her chin up, and yes, arched her back so her nipples made two points in her pale-blue tank top. "Do me again, you big jerk."

His eyes skimmed her body, then returned to her face. His fingers twitched on the water bottle. Instead of pouring it over her, or taking her up on her offer in some other, better way, he stood. Turned his back on her and boomed the next order of business.

"On your feet. Time to work the legs."

Sam had been way off-base, thinking Brian wanted her

here. For the next forty minutes, he put the group through a sequence of exercises that seemed as though they'd be a walk in the park, so to speak, but ended up being torture in the park instead. Through it all, he encouraged his trainees—except for her.

Oh, she got plenty of his attention. When he had them do long hops across the field, he reminded everybody else to keep their legs together. Not her. He made an example of her by securing her legs closed with a skipping rope. During numerous lengths of walking lunges, he strode alongside her, nagging her to take longer, deeper steps. He finally wandered off—when she met his expectations, presumably—only to return with a coil of thick rope, which he hung around her neck "for added resistance".

That rope later looped around her waist so she could run —a loose description of what she actually did—across the field while dragging the monstrous truck tire. Good god, the fire in her legs. Next, backward crab crawling. Modified back-rows using the rope slung over a low-hanging tree branch. Flipping the massive, heavy tire over and over until her muscles screamed. Alternating knee-raises while stepping up on the tire. She had no love for that damn tire. Not much left for the drill sergeant trailing her through every exercise, commanding her to tuck in, lift up, stretch out—and every-thing in between. They had to be nearing the end of this godforsaken hour.

Another boot-camper called him away to hold her feet for crunches. Cassie faked a cough to mask her laugh, though she could hardly blame the woman in neon spandex for finding an excuse to get Brian's hands on her body, even if it meant doing extra sit-ups.

Cassie used the reprieve to flop on the grass. She inhaled deeply, savoring the scents of lilies and fresh-cut grass, the sweetness of summer in general, before releasing it all in a slow, relaxing breath. Sunshine kissed her skin, creating spots behind her closed eyelids. Didn't matter that she was sweat-soaked, she welcomed the hug of the sun's rays as they gifted her with that sense of lightness that precedes sleep. Perfection.

"Hey," the toe of Brian's shoe nudged her waistline, "there's no napping at boot camp."

"Just enjoying my minute of rest." She cracked an eye open. The giant towering over her blocked her access to the sun, eliminating the need to squint. "What's next, slave driver, laps around the pond?" She blinked until the sunspots disappeared and he came into focus, looking massively sexy and more than a little amused. "What?" Oh crap. "I know... there's a toll for taking an unauthorized break. Let me guess, I get to *crawl* around the pond, dragging the tire, while you walk behind me, kicking my butt."

"Not today, but I'll keep it in mind for another time."

She bet he might—and he'd enjoy every minute of it. "Are you always this much of a taskmaster, or was today an initiation?"

"Does that mean you're coming back?"

"I'm considering it." She shuffled onto her elbows. "What the—where is everybody, and all your stuff?"

"Packed up. Why, you want another go at that tire?" He winked. "Everybody left fifteen minutes ago, while you were out cold." Now he was grinning ear to ear. "Don't worry, I didn't let them see you drool."

She waved a hand at him, forcing his gentlemanly side to grasp it and pull her up. "I do not drool in my sleep."

BRIAN

"I know." He should've released her. He didn't. Couldn't. Instead he pulled her closer. Not tight against him like he wanted, but damn near. She let him, but maybe that was because his hold on her tiny hand was gentle this time. "About last night—"

"I'm sorry."

"You're sorry?" Yeah, he drank too much at Sam's and the specifics of their conversation had blurry patches, but he sure as hell knew what'd happened at Blur, and it didn't require an apology from Cassie.

"You're still mad." The big eyes staring up at him lowered as she muttered, "I knew coming here was a bad idea."

Now he was really fucking confused. "Hey…" He nudged her chin up with his free hand. "You think I'm mad at you? Hell no, try turning that around. I'm the one who's sorry. I don't expect you to forget what I did, but I swear to you, it'll never happen again." That wasn't enough, but he plowed forward anyway. She'd come out this morning for more than a workout and he wasn't letting yet another chance slip away. "I want to see you again," he tried for a smile and hoped to hell he didn't look like a psycho, "and not just as your taskmaster."

"I'd like that, but…" If she chewed her bottom lip any harder, it'd bleed. Indecision swirled in the beautiful eyes staring up at him. "What about yesterday? Should we talk about it, or…would you rather not?"

His gut couldn't have ached more if she'd run him through with a knife. He deserved the pain for hurting her last night. But she was here, in his arms and still speaking to him, so he sucked it up.

"We can talk about anything you want, anytime you want.

Or we can—" How much of an asshole would he be if he asked if they could just move on?

"Accept that people aren't always perfect and hang out, have fun together?"

Forgiveness he desperately wanted, but hadn't dared ask for. "Sounds great."

"To me too."

He caught her around the waist as she did a cute little hop, throwing her arms around his neck. One hug and everything was right in the world. Didn't seem possible, but the proof was plastered against his body, and more to the point, trying to bust out of his chest. She'd given him a gift today and he wouldn't take it for granted.

He squeezed her tighter, dipped down to bury his nose below her ear. "You smell good."

"You must be hard of smelling." She giggled at his continued snuffling. "I'm sweaty from head to toe, I can't smell good."

"You do." Salty sweetness registered on his tongue as he drew it down her neck to her shoulder. With a hooked finger, he pulled the front of her tank top open, then lowered his head and licked between her breasts.

"Oh god, don't, I'm disgusting."

"Not even close. You taste good enough to eat." His cock had already picked up on the idea, and his athletic shorts did zero to hide his interest. He nudged her with his hard-on and nodded toward the nearby pavilion. "Let's go."

She glanced over, then up at his face. "There? And do what?"

"Pretty sure I just told you."

"You're not serious."

The lack of the word *no* in her answer worked for him. He slid his palms over her warm, bare legs. Lifted her and wrapped them around his waist. Torture for him, having her pussy pressed against his cock and knowing he wouldn't be inside her anytime soon. If she decided to return for more boot camp classes, he'd start bringing condoms with him on Sunday mornings. He could think of half a dozen places in the park where he'd like to fuck her, and multiple ways he'd like to do it. They might have to come back later.

Luck continued to smile on him, because the pavilion was empty. He carried her over, plunging them into deep shade compared to the brilliant sunshine beyond the shelter. The sense of darkness gave the hall a private feeling, despite its wide-open sides. Logically, he knew anybody walking by would be able to see them. Logic could take a seat in the back for a while.

He set her on a picnic table. Stood between her legs and cupped her face in his hands. "I've wanted to do this for over an hour." Her lips were soft and warm. Instantly yielding and eager as he crushed his against them, swept his tongue inside. It'd been less than twenty-four hours since he'd kissed her, yet too fucking long. And too dangerously close to losing this—losing her—for good.

Her tiny hands curled over his shoulders. She broke their kiss enough to talk without truly separating their mouths. "Only for an hour? I've wanted to do that since last night. I waited up for you, hoping you'd show up on my doorstep again."

"I wanted to, so fucking much, but I just—couldn't."

"I get it."

How could she, really? Cassie was so sweet and straightfor-ward, she had no idea what a man like him could do. *Had* done. That he'd needed to skulk away and punish himself for hurting her with his big, stupid hands. Put as much distance between his beastlike tendencies and her delicate body as possible, for her sake.

"Make me a deal?" she asked, tilting her head to catch his lowered eyes.

"Name it."

"No more walking away while things are all jumbled."

"That's it? You don't want to ask for something bigger, or more important?" He had to smile. Almost laughed. He'd expected her to ask for no more rough play or telling her what to do, sexually. "Okay, yeah, I can do that."

"You're smiling, but I'm being serious."

The little shove she attempted made it worse, in terms of the grin stretching across his face and the blood flow to his cock. "Sorry."

"This *is* important. We were friends before we got all, um," she glanced down to where the hard bulge in his shorts met the apex of her cut-offs, "friendly. I'd hate to lose that because of, you know…"

"Stuff that happens."

"Yes."

"Then I'll take that deal."

She lifted one hand from his shoulder and waggled it in front of him. "Should we shake on it?"

God, she was cute. And he was going to go to hell for tarnishing her halo, among other things. "I'd rather *you* shake on it—with *it* being my tongue." He went to his knees. Pushed the skimpy piece of gray jersey between her legs to one side and feasted his eyes on bare skin. "Commando. Nice. Convenient too."

"You can't do—*that*—now." She attempted to scooch away from his advancing mouth. "I'm sweaty from the workout."

"I've licked your pussy after it had a much harder workout

than this morning's boot camp, remember?" The fingers in his hair said yes, she did. "You tasted like heaven then, just like you will now."

"What about other people?"

"They'll have to find their own piece of heaven, I'm not sharing mine."

"You big jerk, you know what I meant."

He loved her giggle. That, and a growing list of other things about her, including her capacity for forgiveness and second or third chances. He shifted position so that one of his Nike cross-trainers sat squarely on the ground, his knee bent at ninety degrees.

"Put your foot up here, on my leg." No hesitation, no questions asked, she simply obeyed. He loved that too. "If anybody goes by, they'll think I'm tying your shoe."

She snorted. "Because a thirty-two-year-old woman can't do that for herself."

"If you'd rather tie your own shoe…" He swept his tongue upward, circled her clit a few times before sucking it between his teeth and making her moan. He pulled back, smiled up at her. "I can always sit back and watch you do it."

She shook her head. Bit into her juicy bottom lip. "I like the way you tie it."

"Single or double knotted?"

"Better stick with single."

That sounded suspiciously like skepticism. "You don't think I can do a double for you here?" Her little shrug said it all. Challenge accepted.

He kept one hand securely around the ankle positioned on his quadriceps. With the other, he spanned her opposite thigh. A bit of pressure and she opened wider. He leaned in, got his tongue under her clit and jiggled it back and forth, hard and fast. No teasing around the edges this time, straight to the prize.

Her hips moved with his rhythm, briefly, then slowed. Retreated. He switched to long laps with the flat of his tongue. Looked up to gauge what she needed—faster, gentler, harder? Her smile didn't hide her nervousness. Ah. What she needed wasn't physical.

One side of the pavilion faced the pond. Two sides had gardens blocking access. He darted his eyes to the fourth side. All clear. "Nobody's around to see."

"I know."

So it wasn't that. He drew back, kissed the inside of her knee, then along the inside of her leg. The closer he got to her center, the more the muscles in her legs tightened. He knew how to get her off and she wasn't worried about getting caught. That left one thing—he hadn't put her other concern to rest.

He pressed his nose to her thigh. "You smell so good. Like oranges and spice and everything nice."

"That's not how the rhyme goes."

"No, but it's how you go, and I love it." He kept his eyes on her face as he moved higher, right back to where he wanted to be. "Breathing you in is never enough. Now that I've had more, I can't go without. I need to lick you and suck you, because you taste as good as you smell."

"Sometimes, maybe."

"Every time." He dipped his tongue inside her, withdrew it and licked his lips. "Including right now." Another swipe along her pussy, this time suckling her clit at the end. "It's killing me not to lay you out on this table, press your legs wide open and bury my entire face between your legs for my own personal picnic. I'm hard as a rock and it's because of you."

Her eyes were glassy now. This time, when he focused his

attention on her clit, she tilted to meet him. As hungry for his mouth as his mouth was for her.

Above him, she moaned. Threaded her fingers through his hair. Her touch trailed lower, to his beard. "I love the way this feels, soft to my fingers but all rough when it's against the rest of my skin."

Fuck, she knew how to push his buttons. He shook his head, making sure his beard rubbed good and hard all over her thighs and pussy. She rewarded him by raking her nails over his scalp while pulling him closer. Yeah, that's how it should be. His hips thrust of their own accord. He feasted on Cassie like the starved beast he was, his fingers digging in where he held her, goddamn growling as he licked and sucked and nipped. No finesse, just fucking devouring her. If he didn't lose it when she came, it'd be a fucking miracle.

She gave a whispered, "Oh god, now—*now*", her thighs shuddering as she closed her legs around his ears while curling her body over his head. Her racing heart thumped its beat into his head. Ragged breathing heated his cheek as she whispered again, "Somebody's in the pavilion."

A slight turn to one side brought a lone man into sight. Late-sixties probably, quietly spreading a newspaper on one of the dozen or so empty tables.

"Shit." Subtly, Brian rearranged Cassie's shorts. Lifted his head level with her stomach. "Keep hugging me, he'll think we're having a couples' moment."

"*I* just had a moment, that's for sure."

He chuckled, wrapped his arms around her tighter. "Sorry I didn't get to tie that double knot for you."

"Single, double, I don't care. You can tie my shoes anytime."

"I plan to." Between Cassie grinding her hips against him and the sweet scent of arousal from her orgasm surrounding him, his hard-on didn't stand a chance of deflating. Another glance told him the man who'd joined them in the pavilion planned to stay awhile. Ready or not, it was time to go.

"Oh my," she said as he stood, eyes locked on his loaded gun. "Didn't anybody ever tell you it's rude to point?"

"The same rule applies to staring, cutie." And, much as he liked her eyeballing his cock, especially with that sexy glaze in her eyes, the attention wasn't helping divert his blood back to the rest of his body. He pulled her up, off the edge of the table and into his arms.

"Are we faking another couples' moment to get you out of here with a modicum of decency?"

"Nothing fake about it when I'm with you." The way she looked up at him right before throwing her arms around his neck was the best incentive not to fuck things up he could get —because if it wasn't love, exactly, it was close enough. He hugged her tight as possible without breaking her and nuzzled the top of her head. "Now how about getting me out of here with that decency you mentioned."

She nodded and giggled, turning inside the circle of his arms. "One human shield, at your service."

"You really ought to be careful what you offer." Especially to a guy like him. He nudged her ass with the hard reminder, making her giggle again as she started walking.

The man with the newspaper snagged Brian's peripheral vision. He'd abandoned the Sunday edition to watch them, and made no bones about nodding an acknowledgment at Brian now that he'd been caught.

"She looks happy, I guess that means your girl said yes?" the man asked from across the pavilion. "Nice to see some traditionalism still hanging in there, what with you down on bended knee and all."

Well, goddamn. The man thought he'd witnessed a marriage proposal.

Brian slid his arms tighter around Cassie's waist. Gave a squeeze. "Tell the man what he wants to know—did my girl say yes or no?" He smiled while asking, kept his tone light, but held his breath just the same while waiting for her answer.

"Yes. Without a doubt, she said yes."

CASSIE

Hard to believe the direction the day had taken. Cassie twirled her way out the back door, down the handful of concrete steps and onto the lawn. The grass tickled her bare feet as she practically fairy-danced to her garden. The backyard was due for mowing, but it'd keep. Brian might not mind her being a hot, sweaty mess—he'd certainly proven *that* in the pavilion—but she planned to be fresh as the daisies she was pinching from the flowerbed when he showed up for dinner.

An actual date. Hanging out, eating a meal together and talking, things people do—with their clothes *on*—when they like each other. Not that she had any problem with their spontaneous hook-ups. No woman in her right mind would turn those down, but as she'd gotten to know Brian the past couple months, she'd fantasized about having more than sex with him. And after the way he'd looked at her in the park earlier, the sweet things he'd said…gah.

She couldn't help being hopeful. He knew about her work, and though it'd obviously thrown him initially, he seemed willing to accept it. She didn't blame him for the gruff remarks he'd made and since apologized for. It's not every day you discover that the woman you've just gotten involved with gets paid to take pictures of couples having sex. Thank god he hadn't reacted the way Lance had—with greedy, over-interested enthusiasm—or she'd be shopping for a new gym instead of preparing for a romantic night with her very personal trainer.

She arranged the daisies in a glass vase, setting it on one side of the white-linen-covered patio table. Add a grouping of pillar candles in assorted shades of green around the base and, voilà. She stood back for a look. Pretty. Nicer than any of the restaurants she'd frequented in the past year—though on her rigid, self-imposed budget, that wasn't saying much. Brian had offered to take her anywhere tonight. His treat. When she'd suggested staying in, he'd pressed her against the side of his Jeep and showed her how much he approved of the idea by kissing her senseless. Best reward ever for being thrifty.

Cassie turned at the sound of said Jeep as it rumbled to a stop in her driveway. For months now, she'd seen Brian five-or-so times a week. Talked, joked and flirted. More recently, she'd seen him gloriously naked and enjoyed every solid inch. The familiarity didn't diminish a thing. A twister of butterflies whipped around in her stomach, raced higher to kick-start frenzied pounding in her heart, then zoomed to the top floor, making her lightheaded. Because, good god, look at him. In slow motion with the option to freeze frame, if possible.

As usual, the Jeep had no doors. The profile of Brian's body in the driver's seat, his biceps bulging as he grabbed the overhead roll bar, his long, muscular legs swinging out of the opening, gave her the jelly knees. She grabbed the back of a patio chair with both hands. Mentally instructed her bottom lip to come back up and join the top one.

"You look," his eyes did a deliberate, heat-inducing inspection, "amazing."

She had to glance down. The way he'd perused her made

her question whether she'd remembered to put clothes on after her shower. Yup, fully dressed. Tight jeans with a wide belt, topped by a form-fitting red t-shirt with pretty scalloped edging around its low-cut neckline. Patterned sneakers that'd cost five bucks at Walmart. Nothing fancy, but he didn't seem to mind. Go figure. "Thanks. So do you."

He smiled. "I brought wine."

"Great." Very date-like so far. She tilted her head as he leaned into the backseat. "So is your butt." Always, but the khaki cargo shorts made it mouthwatering. "And your back," she added as he straightened. Then turned. Was that even a real t-shirt, or black body paint? "Put chest, shoulders and arms on that list too."

He laughed, one low, easy chuckle. Closed the distance between them in a handful of strides. "If we're cataloging assets, I have a lot more to say about you than 'amazing'."

The canvas shopping bag in his hand thudded to the grass by her feet. He reached around her to place a bottle of red wine on the table, an act that trapped her between his massive body and the chair. The golden-ginger hair on his forearms tickled her skin. Forget the slow, normal, first-date stuff—she plastered herself to the front of him.

"You're like catnip. I want to rub my body against you and purr."

"I don't have a problem with that." His fingertips slid under the hemline of her top. "I like it when you purr."

"What about when I scratch?" She raked her fingernails upward, through his hair. "Or bite?"

His groan barely registered before he cupped the back of her head and tipped it. Not for a kiss. For access to the side of her neck, which he claimed with his teeth. Heat radiated from the spot and spread under her skin as she wiggled against him, desperate for more.

His palms skimmed her back. One snuck beneath her bra strap, the other dipped inside the back of her jeans in the only place an inch of space existed—right down the middle. He stroked the sensitive spot at the base of her spine, a teaser of what he could be doing if he had better access.

"I should've worn a skirt." She fumbled with his belt, one of the annoying kind that folded back on itself between double D-rings, practically requiring a user's manual. "So should you."

"I'll break out a kilt for next time."

What—whoa. "You're kidding, right?" Oh boy. Head shaking. "You'd wear a kilt?"

"I have, many times."

She planted both hands on his chest, stared up at him. Talk about hitting one of her fantasies squarely on the head. "Seriously?" A splash of color tinted his cheeks. Oh wow. Six-two, solid as a brick wall and blushing. Just like that, she fell a little more.

"Yeah. I was born here, but my parents emigrated from Scotland. To this day, my dad changes from his suit pants to a kilt the minute he gets home from work."

"That is so cool."

"Believe me, when I was a kid, and worse, a teenager, it was not cool. Used to embarrass the shit out of me. Wasn't bad enough I was the only red-headed giant in a small-town school, my dad wandered the neighborhood in a skirt."

"But you're okay with it now, obviously." The heat between her legs switched from boil to simmer. She slid her arms back around his neck, clasping her fingers together instead of playing rough. That'd keep. This—learning about Brian's life, his family, what made him *him*—was the other half of everything she wanted.

"I am. Even back then, I couldn't stay mad at him. At

either of them. I got lucky in the family department, they're great people. Very honest and accepting."

"They sound lovely."

He eyed her arm where it wrapped around his neck in a sweet hug. "And boring, compared to you fighting your way past my belt."

"I like talking with you. The belt can come later." Oh crap, that sounded bad. Bad, but really good, now that the picture had entered her head. Brian snapping a leather belt across her butt, the sweet heat it'd cause… Her face burned as he stared down at her, probably seeing all of her wicked wishes in her eyes. She licked dry lips and blinked to clear the image of Brian binding her wrists with his canvas belt from her mind. Not working, especially while pressed against his body, buzzing from pheromones.

The scent of charred food replaced Brian's soap and yummy manliness. "Oh crap—the chicken." She scrambled free of their clinch and dashed across the concrete slab. Dark-gray smoke seeped from every crack and hole, enveloping the top half of her ancient barbecue. A quick push on the handle and the lid flopped open with gusto. The whole unit rocked. The broken wheel that'd been precariously supporting the back of the stand shot across the patio. Brian's arm folded around her chest and yanked her backward, out of the danger zone formerly known as her grill.

"Holy shit," he said as the thing went down, the legs essentially folding in on themselves with the chunk of metal housing the grill—and the chicken breasts she'd marinated all afternoon—crashing on top of it all.

"I guess we're having salad for dinner."

"Anything's good if I'm having it with you." He planted a kiss on her head. "Stand back here while I disconnect the tank and get it out of the way."

"Oh god, I didn't even think of that." She grabbed his hand before it slipped free. "Don't get blown up."

"Not the kind of blown I had in mind for tonight, don't worry."

That grin—so naughty. He squatted, dealt with the propane tank so their evening didn't become truly explosive. Waited for the last flicker of flame to fizzle under the grill, then flipped the lid on the barbecue and stood.

"Closed casket, good idea," she said. God, his laugh made a lost meal and dead barbecue almost worthwhile. Seriously, what would she have done if the thing had done its implosion act when she'd been alone? Probably run into the house and buried herself in Photoshop work to avoid the issue altogether. Until the back of her house blew up, anyway. "Thanks for saving my bacon, even if I ruined your chicken."

"I'll take your bacon over chicken any day. And I'll get rid of the mess tomorrow, after it's had a chance to cool down."

"I can do it."

"I know you can—you're a capable, independent woman." He swiped his palms on his shorts once more, then slid one around her waist and hauled her close. "But you can be that and still let me take care of you."

Not a question of whether she'd *let* him take care of her, of course not. And boy, did that work for her—on multiple levels "Okay."

"Great. Thank you."

"Sure. Feel free to come back and lug my garbage can to the curb too. Thursdays, before 8:00 a.m. Don't be late."

"Noted." His hand slid lower to cup her ass possessively. "Anything else I can take care of?"

"The light bulbs are all good and none of my taps are leaky. Hmm." She tapped a finger on his chest and tried not to giggle. Or give too much credence to his offer, tempting as it was to picture him as the man of her house. "Do you do yard work?"

"I do." A smile tugged at the corner of his mouth. The wink that followed set fire to her panties. "But I know for a fact you don't have a bush that needs trimming."

Right now, she kind of wished she did, because the thought of Brian grooming her private parts to his liking gave her more than a little thrill. "And do you prefer your women," how to word it, "closer to nature?"

"First off, I don't have women. I have woman—and to be clear, that's you, cutie—until you boot my sorry ass off your property and out of your life."

Oh wow. Before she could come up with a response that wouldn't make him instantly regret his words, he dipped down and sealed her lips with a soft kiss. The tender touch quickly turned into a tangle of tongues. Dinner, what dinner? Thirty seconds of kissing Brian and she was back to struggling with his belt.

"Is this some kind of male chastity device?"

"Hell no. Just a mistake." He pushed her hand aside and got the buckles free. "Have at it," he said as he walked her backward, deeper into the yard.

"I think you're lost. My bedroom's the other way."

"Later. After I do some work in your yard." Her back connected with the old sugar maple near the far corner. "And we cover that closer-to-nature thing."

Chapter 7

CASSIE

THE SUN HOVERED above the treetops. Twilight was still an hour away, at least. A six-foot-high board fence bordered three sides of her property, but it wasn't without its cracks and peepholes, nor was it soundproof. Evidence of that carried from the nearby yards—the rhythmic snipping of garden shears, hip-hop music from the Baileys' pool house around the corner, the sound of splashing as bodies repeatedly jumped into the water. Surely all that white noise would mask any kissing—or other—sounds.

Brian circled her wrists with his thumbs and index fingers. Lifted them, turned them this way and that, inspecting her as though it was the first time. "You're so tiny, so delicate." He guided her arms to her sides, flattening the palms against the massive tree trunk. "If I ever forget that, even for a second, knee me square in the balls or poke me in the eye or something."

"That'd be a mood killer."

The intended joke died when he pulled back, straight-faced. "I'm a foot taller and probably have a hundred pounds on you."

"You won't break me."

"Fucking right I won't. And I won't hurt you either."

He'd taken another step back. Fine, she'd put the space to good use. On her knees. "Here's the thing about that. You know that saying, 'hurts so good'?"

"Cassie…"

"I happen to agree." Down went the zipper on his shorts. "And so do you." She freed his cock from black boxer briefs. Curled her fingers around his rigid shaft and slid her fist up and down. She brought it to her lips, scooped the bead of pre-cum away with her tongue, then took the engorged tip between her teeth.

His nostrils flared as she increased the pressure. His hand moved to the back of her head, urging her to take more. Exactly what she wanted to do. But not too easily. She resisted his control by scraping her teeth along his length as he sought entry into her mouth. Strong fingers fisted in her hair. Immobilized her while he thrust, fast and mercilessly, burying his cock deep in her throat.

Oh god, yes, like that. She pinched her eyes closed, focused on breathing through her nose. A couple more seconds and she'd be past the initial gag response, ready for him to own her mouth as long as he wanted.

"Shit, *shit*." He staggered backward, taking his cock and her balance with him. Wildness ruled his features. His jaw clenched, his lips thinned to a straight line. The worst, though —his eyes, hard and full of storms.

From her position on all fours, he looked more massive than ever. A broody giant holding his cock protectively. She'd be lucky if he ever let her near it again. "Are you okay?"

"Not even fucking close."

"I didn't mean to hurt you." She shook her head. "I mean, obviously I wanted you to feel it, but—" This was not going well at all. "I didn't think I bit hard enough to…damage it. You. I'm sorry."

"Christ, stop apologizing to me."

What was she supposed to say to that? Not I'm sorry—again. She lowered her eyes. If she kept them there long enough, maybe he'd leave her alone with her humiliation. Or not, since his shoes were headed toward her, not away.

A pair of lightly tanned knees entered her field of vision. "You keep getting it wrong." A hooked finger caught her chin and lifted until she met his eyes. "You didn't hurt me, and you have nothing else to apologize for, either. I'm the one making the mistakes in this relationship."

"Relationship?"

"It might be if I stop fucking things up. Come here." Hands linked, he helped her to her feet. "I'm going to be straight with you. All at once, like ripping off a Band-Aid. When I'm done, you say go and I'll go. Back to the way things were before I showed up on your doorstep in the middle of a rainstorm, with my promise never to touch you again. You say stay and I'll agree to whatever terms work for you."

"Sounds ominous…with a side of promising."

He leaned in for a soulful kiss. "Just in case the promising part doesn't work out."

"Points for sweetness awarded." At least he smiled at this joke, even if briefly.

"I had every intention of being nothing but sweet tonight. Courting you with conversation and making love to you by candlelight. Then I went and forced my cock down your throat, practically bringing tears to your eyes."

"No, it wasn't—"

Brian brought their joined hands to her lips and shook his head. "You've seen, more than once, that I can be a selfish prick. Stupid hot head has gotten the better of me plenty of times. I'm not a bully but I am a brute at the core." He squeezed her fingers, stared down at her with an earnestness that made her want to hug him. "I can and will control the brute, keep him away from you. Be that sweet guy who kisses instead of biting. But…"

"But?" Nope, he didn't budge, physically or verbally. Time for a nudge. She turned their hands until she had access to his fingertips. Kissed them all lightly, then sucked one into her mouth. She swirled her tongue around his finger. Bit it the way she'd done to his cock—the way that made him take control. Fiery passion danced in his eyes as she let the digit slide free. "Tell me the rest, tell me the *but*."

"But give me a taste of rough and raw and I have to fight not to get lost in it. To give in to my possessiveness. And it's so fucking strong with you. If I had my way, I'd tattoo my name on your pretty little body as a warning to anybody who dared look too closely, and a reminder to you exactly where you belong. Then I'd keep you so incredibly well-fucked you wouldn't have the time or energy to look at another man."

At some point during his speech, her bones must've dissolved, because she'd utterly melted against his big, hard body. "Stay."

"There's more."

"I don't care. Tell me after I'm so well-fucked the only thing I can do is lie there and listen." God, his laugh. How could one simple sound make her heart jump and her body ache with need? She slid her hands up his arms, over his wide, round shoulders. "Stay."

"Staying."

"About those terms…"

"Name them," he said, his face pressed to the side of her neck.

"I want it all. You, just like your beard—soft and rough, sometimes one, sometimes the other, sometimes both at once." Maybe that was asking too much. Maybe it didn't make sense.

A line of kisses and the soft tickle of ginger made her shiver. "Soft enough?" he whispered in her ear.

"Yes."

He dragged the underside of his beard down the column of her neck, creating delicious friction, nipping as he went. "Rough enough?"

"Not even fucking close," she said, attempting—and failing in a massive way—to mimic him. But he laughed again, and that sound gave her as many sparks as the scrape of his bristles.

"How about this?" He clamped his teeth over the tender spot near her collarbone. Shook his head a little for extra sting.

"Still not enough."

"Cassie…"

"You said you'd agree to my terms, and I want all of you…including the brute." A growl rumbled along her neck. She tipped her head farther, pulled the sleeve of her t-shirt aside, baring her shoulder and the top of one breast. "Give in to it. To me."

His fingers curled around her waist. He used his power and size to back her up to the maple before she'd registered their first step. "Take your pants down to the knees."

"I guess that's a yes to my terms."

No acknowledgement, unless a raised eyebrow counted. Intensity and amusement played across his face. He released her to cross his arms over his chest, making muscles bulge and pop out all over the place. Half a foot separated them, enough space for her to move away if that's what she wanted. Maybe he was testing her. Bossing her around to see if she'd change her mind.

"I'd suggest we shake on our agreement, but I don't think my old patio set can take the kind of strain we put on that picnic table in the pavilion."

"How about this tree, think it can take it?" His hand thudded against the trunk. He kept his eyes locked on hers as he ran his palm up and down the old maple, skimming the side of her body along the way. "What about you? This bark's pretty rough—it's going to hurt when it digs into your soft skin, and it will dig in, because if you're brave enough to take those pants down, I'm going to let the brute fuck you any way he likes."

Her cheeks burned. She shifted foot to foot, acutely aware of the satin teasing her nipples, the tight jeans pressing against her clit. "I'm ready for him."

His jaw ticked and his eyes darkened. "Then get those pants down, now."

She scrambled to obey, fingers trembling as she fumbled with the buckle. The wide belt had been a chore to fit through the belt loops and the stiff leather made undoing it harder yet. "New belt, it needs breaking in."

"I'll keep that in mind." One corner of his mouth lifted—from reading her mind, no doubt—when her hands froze in their efforts. "Here. Let me."

She nodded, swallowing a mouthful of cotton as he took over the job. But he didn't pull the strip of leather free of the belt loops. Didn't order her to bend over so he could use it to paint stripes on her ass. He just separated the metal buckle from the opposite end, one-handed her button open and slid the zipper down, all without looking away from her face.

"Take off your bra."

"Okay." Hands shaking, she reached around for the clasp. Then the hem of her t-shirt.

"Just the bra. Keep the shirt on."

She slid the straps down her arms, clearing each wrist in a wholly unsexy manner, then pulled the white satin bust-enhancer out of one sleeve. "And there goes my artificial cleavage."

"You've got something better—perfect nipples. I like seeing them poke through your shirt. Like at the gym when you wear that light-purple tank top, or the white one. Those tops don't hide much. Did you know your nipples get hard when you're working out?"

"Really...I had *no* idea." Batted eyelashes, along with feigned innocence, did the trick. The sound that came from his chest was part chuckle, part growl. And oh god, was it hot.

Beneath the thin red fabric her nipples tightened. Like a good hussy, she arched her back to make their condition more visible. Her breath caught when he lowered his head. The words *bite me* hovered on the tip of her tongue. All that came out of her mouth was a choked cry of frustration as he grazed the cloth-covered nubs in passing.

He crouched before her, his mouth level with her open zipper. "Pants are coming down now. Last chance to get away." Above him, she shook her head. "No? Good." He gathered her jeans, belt and panties in his fists and pulled the lot down to her knees a heck of a lot easier than the skintight jeans had gone up. "No," he said when she lifted one leg to step out of her pants. "This is where they stay."

"But I won't be able to open my legs," she wiggled in demonstration, "or move."

"I know." His smile bordered on feral. He grabbed both ends of her belt and yanked, squeezing her legs closer together, then fastened the buckle above her knees. "Comfortable?"

She didn't know how to answer. What he'd do to her if she said the wrong thing. God, she didn't even know what the wrong thing was. Would he make it tighter if she said yes? Freak out that he'd hurt her if she said no? The opposite?

"Remember the other night, on my couch, when we talked about the moon?"

His eyebrows pinched together for a few seconds. Then they rose. The light-bulb moment as the safe word she'd chosen clicked into place. "I remember."

"I don't see the moon, but I promise to let you know if that changes."

Clear blue eyes met hers. He nodded. Serious moment over, he returned his attention to her belt and ratcheted it a notch tighter, forcing a squeak from her mouth. When he looked up, all wariness had vanished. "Comfortable?" he asked again.

There was no mistaking the change in his voice. This time, the question came from the brute.

BRIAN

"It's a little tight."

Five minutes ago that answer would've had him scrambling to free her. Apologizing, hating himself. Running for the hills and a forty-ouncer of therapy. Now that Cassie'd all but given him an engraved invitation to cross boundaries and push limits—*their* limits—her complaint registered with a completely different part of his brain. The part he'd warned her about. The part that'd been clawing its way closer to the surface since their first time together. Then there was the effect her words had on his cock. Little. Tight. Hell yeah.

He ran his hand along the top of her jeans. Still room to slip two fingers inside. The belt was snug, yes. Enough to throw off her balance, probably. But cut off her circulation —no.

One hand on her soft, warm skin, he pressed her backward, against the tree. With his fingers spread, his hand practically spanned her waist. So damn tiny compared to him. He slid his thumb lower, along the line of her pussy. Not breaching, just tracing. Up and down, with enough pressure to tease her clit inside its hiding place. Her hips rolled forward with each pass. Entreating him to give her more, and fuck, did he plan to.

He skated his other hand under her t-shirt. Cupped one breast, strummed the nipple to a rock-hard peak, then moved to the other breast. "I love these." Her soft moaning changed to whimpering when he abandoned her nipples. Cute. Fucking sexy too. "I hate giving them up too, but I need both hands down here." He curled his fingers around her hips, used his thumbs to pull back her silky, pink skin and expose her clit. "Fuck, this is beautiful. I know you're the photographer, but I'd like a picture of this—your pretty clit, all swollen and waiting for me."

"Take one."

Holy Christ, she'd let him?

"But you'll owe me." Bold words in a shaky voice. Testing the waters, maybe?

As if she needed to barter to get something from him. He was already so head over heels he'd do anything she wanted. How she couldn't see that boggled his mind.

"You got it." He reached into his back pocket and pulled out his iPhone. With its camera, he snapped a picture of her face, looking down at him. "That's a keeper. Now for this one..." He angled the phone's lens lower, exposed her clit with his thumb and index finger and leaned in for a quick taste. Mistake. Her scent filled his head, sent what felt like a gallon of blood rushing to his cock. One lick wasn't going to cut it. "Fuck the picture."

The phone bounced off his thigh, onto the grass. He held her by the hips and dove in, tongue first. So wet and warm. The sweet taste that was uniquely, deliciously Cassie exploded on his tongue. He suckled her clit. Lapped at it and circled it, took her to the edge. Above him, she made the soft moan-gasp sound that meant she was about to come. Not yet. He scraped his teeth across her clit as he released it. Teased a finger inside her, then two. Stroked into her nice and deep while teasing her clit with the lightest touch of his tongue.

"Please…make me come."

Yeah, now he was ready. He sucked her clit into his mouth. Devoured it. Strapping her legs closed prevented him from burying his whole face between them. He'd do that later. And then do it some more, because having her thighs locked around his head while she writhed against his face made him harder than just about anything.

"Please, yes, oh god, that…" Her legs shook under his palms. Hips thrust forward to meet his tongue. Fingernails raked the back of his head, delivering a sting as she pulled him closer.

His cock pounded its protest against his fly. Yeah, all of her responses did it for him. The nails she wasn't afraid to use. Her voice. The way she begged and demanded at the same time. And god fucking damn, her *everything* when she came.

He didn't wait for the last waves of her orgasm to end, instead steadied her with one hand, pushed to a stand and shoved his clothes out of the way. Nudged his cock between her thighs.

"Condom," she whispered.

"Shit. Right. Don't fall down."

She grabbed the tree in a backward hug, holding on as if her life depended on it. He wanted to fuck her harder than a beast in heat, but she was still the cutest thing he'd ever seen. When she licked her lips at the sight of him rolling on the condom, cute disappeared. Now she was nothing but hot, sexy woman.

He gripped her hips, held her still against the maple. Slid his cock between her legs again. Slick heat welcomed him. And her eyes, fuck. If he looked in those big blues a million times—and he hoped to—he'd never get tired of them, of the honesty, willingness and desire in them. "Now you're mine."

"Prove it."

Exactly what he planned to do. And did, in one solid thrust that made them both groan. He braced one hand on the tree above her head and snaked the other under her shirt. Rolled her nipple between his fingers as he pulled out, then thrust inside her again. Then again and again, until heat swirled at the base of his cock and his pulse pounded in his ears.

Sandwiched between his body and the tree, Cassie panted and moaned. Clawed at his ass. Either trying to rip him to shreds or drag him deeper inside her. He didn't fucking care.

"Harder…"

An invitation he wouldn't refuse. He thrust upward with enough force to lift her, making her gasp. "Fuck…" Too late to hold back. He pushed deeper, pinned her to the tree with his cock buried to the hilt as he came.

"Can't—breathe…"

Everything twitched as he pulled out—cock, leg, arms… heart. Cassie clung to his shoulders while he removed the condom and tossed it aside. "Going up, hold on."

She squealed as he hoisted her over his shoulder. Her

sneakered feet toed a beat against his front, but the hands seductively exploring his back and the top of his ass told him the assault on his kidney was halfhearted, at best.

"Where are you going?" she asked when he passed her bedroom door.

He had to chuckle at the disappointment in her voice. "Bathroom." He turned into the room and gently lowered her to the ground. He knelt before her, unbuckled the belt from her legs and pulled off her shoes. "Step out of these pants."

"*Now* you want me to strip?"

"Yeah, I'm a fucked-up bastard. You didn't figure that out just now?"

"No." No more giggling, just a soft tone that matched her touch as she slid her fingers through his hair. "You seem pretty perfect to me."

"So do you." More than she could imagine. He pushed the pile of denim aside. Ran his hands up and down her smooth, silky legs, then stood. "Turn around, put your hands on the sink." Christ, the way she looked at him before she obeyed. Totally trusting. "And don't try getting away from me."

"Okay." Her reflection stared at him, eyes roaming all over his face and body.

Unbelievable. He'd fucked her so hard against that tree it'd turned her pretty ass cherry-red. Left her with scrapes in a couple of spots. Yet she had that look in her eyes, the one that said she was ready and willing to go another round, for whatever he had in mind.

He leaned in, closer than he needed to, and grabbed a facecloth from a basket on the vanity. "You smell so good." Not just to his nose, his cock agreed. He pressed its length along the crack of her ass, nuzzled the spot below her ear. "I don't think I'll ever get enough of you."

The little temptress backed up, embedding his stiffening

cock in the valley between her reddened cheeks. "I'm good with that."

He could take her right now, as rough or soft as he wanted, and she'd let him. More than that, she'd love it. Tempting. So fucking tempting.

Hard as it was to do it, he pulled back. They were both hopped up on endorphins, but it wouldn't be long before she crashed and her backside stung like a sonofabitch. Taking care of his brutish handiwork took priority. Condolences to his cock—it'd have to wait.

He kissed her neck gently while soaking the cloth with cool water. "Remember what I told you about escaping."

She jumped at the first touch of the compress. "Holy crap, that's cold." It didn't take long before her head lolled forward and she sighed contentedly. "I take that back, it feels great."

"I bet. You're sporting quite a bark burn from that maple."

"Totally worth it." She peeked back at him, her shy smile a complete contrast to the woman who'd dug her nails into his butt and begged him to fuck her harder only minutes earlier. "What kinds of trees do you have in your yard—maybe we should, um, do some comparisons."

Might as well put a bow around his heart and hand it over to her right now. "No yard, I live in an apartment building. But I know a trail with some ancient black walnut and chestnut trees. Not one of those civilized paths with the level asphalt and conveniently spaced garbage cans. This place has real terrain and not much human traffic."

"A hardcore hiking trail?" She beamed, and it lit up the entire room. "I'd love that, with or without the bark burn."

"So would I. Guess we have a date for next Sunday—a hike and possibly some wilderness sex. After I've run you through boot camp in the morning."

"Sounds perfect."

Shit, and he thought he couldn't fall any further in one day. Wrong. "But that's next week's plan. Tonight, I'm going to finish taking care of your pretty little ass, then I'm going to take care of the rest of you. I hope you don't mind being serviced all night long."

"It'll be a hardship, but I'll tough it out."

"That's my girl." Presumptuous—maybe. If she wasn't his after the way they'd connected out back, he'd keep working until she was. He shifted slightly, holding the compress on her bark-burned backside while reaching around to prep a second, freshly cooled cloth. "Long arms for the win," he said as her eyes tracked his movement.

"I like that you're big." A pink blush flooded her cheeks. "I didn't mean your—you know."

Both of them looked down at his *you know*.

"Not big enough?" As if commanded, his cock stood a little taller. Good boy.

"Oh god, yes. It's fine. Better than fine. I love it." So long, pink cheeks, hello, red.

He couldn't have held back his smile if he tried. "I don't think I need to tell you the feeling is mutual." He hung the damp cloths over the faucet, caging her while he leaned in, temptingly close. "I'm going to get some food ready for us, because if I stay here one more minute, I won't be able to resist showing you exactly how mutual that feeling is."

CASSIE

Alone in the bathroom, Cassie turned her back to the mirror and looked over her shoulder. Brian hadn't exaggerated when he said she had bark burn. Her butt went from bright pink to red at the tops of her cheeks, with a few souvenir scrapes to show for their backyard adventure. She touched one of the scuffed areas gently. Ooh, tender. The redness wouldn't last, but the memory would. Always. Maybe she'd get lucky and their relationship would stick too.

The skintight jeans weren't going back on, that much was certain. She peeled off her last remaining article of clothing, did some freshening up, then slipped into her short robe. The satiny fabric soothed her hot spots. No regular clothing would feel this good against her sensitive skin. Besides, this robe had served her well that first night.

She cracked the bathroom door and listened, then followed the noise to its source—the kitchen. Brian's back greeted her. If he heard her approach, he didn't let on. Her bowl of salad was on the counter to his left. The end of her wooden chopping board was visible under his arm, but not whatever he was slicing and dicing. He scooped a handful of something pale from the surface and tossed it into the salad.

Crumpled butcher paper sat on the counter. Must've been from the bag he'd brought, because she never bought anything that came wrapped that way. Too pricey. He didn't seem like a man with expensive taste, but really, she had no clue. For all their conversations over the past couple months, he hadn't given up much information. Mostly, he'd asked questions about *her*. In hindsight, they'd both avoided spilling a lot of personal details. She'd certainly had her reasons, but what were his?

She wanted to know everything. Time to give up lying to herself where Brian was concerned. She'd take a *strictly for fun* relationship with him, but she longed for much more. A couple minutes of watching him in her kitchen, looking as if he belonged there, and that longing swerved into the dangerous territory of wanting to share her life with him. Too quick to trust—that's how Nana had described her on more than one occasion. Nana was right.

She shook her head. Her heart was a goner, that was a given. If he crushed it, she'd recover eventually. But that'd be all she'd lose. Anytime she had the urge to hand over her spare key, she needed to remind herself of the devastation Lance had caused with his betrayal. Brian had stumbled upon her secret the other day, but until she knew him a lot better, she had to be cautious. Panties down, sure, but with her guard up.

"Hungry?" he asked without turning.

"Always."

He laughed, obviously catching the insinuation she'd intended. Emboldened, she tipped her chin up. Donned her best authoritative voice.

"Shirt off, please. I'd like to ogle my beef while he cooks for me." There, she'd done it. Verbally claimed him. Sure, her heart might jackhammer out of her chest and splat onto the white-tiled floor, but what the heck.

Another laugh, and still he didn't turn. Just set the knife aside and peeled off his t-shirt, tossed it over his shoulder at her and went back to work.

Oh god, what an incredible back. Beautifully broad across the shoulders, tapering to a trim yet manly V at his waist. Rippling muscles left to right, top to bottom. And his tattoo. She'd only gotten glimpses of it by candlelight. Done entirely in black with dozens of twisting, intertwined lines, it spanned most of his left shoulder blade. The Celtic tree of life, he'd told her when she asked. Now that he'd given her a tiny glimpse into his upbringing, it fit perfectly.

She drifted over and stood behind him, traced the looping lines that both circled and became the tree. "How old were you when you got the tattoo?"

"Thirty."

"Just last year?" She leaned on the counter beside him, as close as she could get without hindering his food preparations. "I expected you to say eighteen or twenty—after you realized how awesome your Scottish heritage was, or something."

"The tattoo is more...personal." He continued chopping cheese into small cubes. Didn't smile, didn't frown. Didn't expand on his answer.

"Okay, gotcha. Next question. What're you doing to my salad?"

The knife went down again. He wiped his hands on a dishcloth and angled his body toward her. "Adding stuff. What do you mean, gotcha?"

"You'd rather not tell me about the tattoo. Message received, moving right along."

"I'll tell you anything you want to know, but there are some things you may wish you didn't know, once they're out."

"Sounds ominous."

Those massive shoulders shrugged. "I've made mistakes."

"Who hasn't?"

"What's your biggest mistake?" he asked.

"You always do this—turn the questions back on me."

"Do I?"

"Your sexy beard doesn't hide your smile, so you know."

"Maybe I should grow it bushier."

"Don't you dare, it's perfect the way it is." She reached out and stroked the short dark-ginger hairs, running her thumb over his full bottom lip in the process. The beard, his mouth, every other part—all exactly right. She plucked a cube of cheese from the cutting board and popped it in her mouth, buying a smidgeon of time to organize her thoughts. "My biggest mistake was trusting my fiancé with something I should have kept private."

"Private from the person you planned to spend your life with? I wouldn't get serious, let alone married, if the relationship couldn't handle full disclosure."

"I found out the hard way that it couldn't. I won't put myself in that position again."

He crossed his arms over his bare chest, making muscles pop out all over the place. "Commitment and marriage are off the table for you now?"

"God, I hope not. But I plan to be a lot more careful before I put on a ring again."

"I feel the same way." His stance relaxed and he reached into the shopping bag for more packages. "Though I've never gotten to the ring stage with anybody. Thought I was on the way there once," he tilted his head toward his back, "but I ended up with the tattoo instead of wedding plans."

"I'm sorry...but I'm not." She smiled at his chuckle and pilfered a slice of cucumber from the salad, savoring its refreshing coolness on her tongue while she watched him prep baguette slices with a creamy cheese mixture, spices and smoked salmon. "Tell me about it?"

"The tattoo, or the almost-fiancée?"

"Either. Both. I'll take whatever you're willing to give."

He abandoned the lemon he was zesting and faced her. "That's what scares me about being with you. You make me want to give you—fuck, all of me. The good, the bad and the worse than bad. I have to force myself to hold back."

"Don't." She released the tie on her robe. Her nipples tightened to hard peaks as his eyes swept over her exposed breasts, then lower. She stepped closer, slid her arms around his waist, her entire body coming alive when their skin connected. "I want all of you. No holding back."

He tucked a piece of hair that'd escaped her barrette behind her ear, then stroked her cheek. "I might hurt you."

"If so, I'll cry myself dry, then pick myself up and move on. I'm small but resilient."

"Of that I have no doubt. But that's not how I meant. I might *hurt* you, physically."

God, the apprehension in his eyes. "We talked about this. Is it the bark burn on my butt—is that what has you worried?"

"That's nothing compared to what I could do. What I have done…to the almost-fiancée."

She didn't want to know, but had to. "What did you do to her?"

"Strained her rotator cuff. Tore the long head of her biceps. Caused her to miss the most important competition of the year."

"How?" Her voice had been reduced to a squeaky whisper.

He let her go and stepped back, curling his palms over the edge of the counter. But he never took his eyes off her face. "You sure you want to hear this, the details?"

"No. Tell me anyway."

"It was my birthday. She'd had a few drinks at dinner and they'd made her extremely tipsy. Leanne rarely drank, and never while she was training for a pageant. Her next competition was only two weeks out at that point, so she was pretty fucking lean."

Instinct compelled Cassie to close her robe. She'd seen pictures of Leanne online. Leanne was a national fitness champion. Tall, beautiful in a classic, European way with a ten-out-of-ten body. Hearing Brian remember how amazing it was made the bottom drop out of Cassie's stomach.

"Leanne and I had the health and fitness stuff in common, but our preferences in the bedroom were very different. I'd accepted things as they were, but she knew my appetite was still there. So that was her birthday present to me—a night of sex, my way."

That was a visual she didn't need—Brian and his ex, naked and full-throttle fucking. She hugged herself. Swallowed a mouthful of bile that'd snuck up her throat. She'd heard this much, might as well get the rest over with.

"How did you—damage her?"

"Cassie…"

"Tell me."

"Bound her arms behind her back. I must've put too much strain on them. On the right one, anyway."

Yes, Brian liked things a little rough, but Cassie couldn't imagine him actually hurting his partner in the act. It didn't fit with what she'd experienced. How many times had he asked if she was okay, if his actions were too much? There had to be more to the story.

"Were you drunk too?"

"Fuck no. I've had a no-sex-while-under-the-influence rule since I broke a guy's wrist while arm wrestling after a bunch of pints, years ago. Realized then how easy it is to forget my strength."

Strong and determined, but controlled—exactly the kind of man she thought he was. Something definitely didn't jibe. "I don't believe you hurt her."

"The police report would convince you."

"What?" No way could she have heard him correctly.

"Two days later, the cops showed up at my work. Not Iron Works, another gym. Quite the scene, being handcuffed in front of a club full of members and my boss. I was arrested for domestic violence."

"Oh my god, *what?*"

He shrugged, the casual gesture in conflict with the stress on his face and the tight grip he maintained on her countertop. "Nothing in Leanne's statement was a lie, it was just... skewed. I took advantage of her while she was under the influence, coerced her into a scenario where she couldn't defend herself."

"But you didn't coerce her—she initiated it!"

"But I did take advantage of her. I should've known better than to accept her proposition. Leanne isn't like you...she didn't *want* what we did that night, the way you do. Fuck," he pounded a fist against the laminate countertop, "that didn't come out right."

She wanted to go to him, hug him, calm him down. But her feet didn't move an inch. "I understand. And you're right —when we're together, I want everything we do as much as you. Maybe more."

His snort was laced with self-loathing. "Not possible."

"My body is smaller than yours, but my desires are just as big."

They stared at each other for an eternity of minutes. Brian broke in the end, blowing out a long breath while shoving one hand through his hair. "Bottom line, I should have controlled myself with Leanne a hell of a lot better than I did. I hurt a woman, period." He raised his head. Locked on to her eyes. "I couldn't live with myself if I hurt you."

This date had certainly careened into serious territory. While the topic of the conversation was horrible, his straightforward honesty, the way he owned his behavior and took responsibility, was incredible. After what he'd said about only getting married if the relationship could handle full disclosure, his confession hit even closer to the heart. He'd trusted her with his biggest mistake. That had to mean something.

"What happened after the arrest?"

"Lost my job, obviously. Broke up with Leanne, also obviously."

"Did you dispute the charges, defend yourself, legally?"

"No."

Okay, now she was mad in addition to being moved. Taking responsibility was one thing, absolving his ex-girlfriend of her involvement altogether was another story.

Cassie stomped across the room and planted herself in front of his massive frame. Stabbed him in the meaty pec with her index finger. "You had consensual sex with your girlfriend and it may have gotten out of hand. It was an accident, not —not—"

"Assault? Yeah, legally, it is. As it should be."

Looking in his eyes was too much. He'd been accused of being a monster and clearly, he thought the label fit. She pressed her forehead to his chest, slid her arms around his waist. Squeezed her eyes shut when he didn't return her embrace.

"You won't hurt me. I know it."

Above her, he sighed. He kissed the top of her head and blanketed her with his thick, warm arms. "If I do, I'm going to have my balls cut off."

"I don't think that's an option in our penal system." She blinked up at him. "Not that I'd ever do what Leanne did. I wouldn't. Anything that happens between us stays between us."

"If I ever give you more than a tanned bottom or a hickey, you *will* report me. As for the balls, I'm sure I can find any number of guys willing to castrate me. Hell, there'd probably be a lineup of people—male and female—willing to pay for that opportunity."

Did he really think that? There was so much she didn't know about him, his past. In time, hopefully she'd know it all.

"You're not so tough, you know. I'm pretty sure I could take you if I tried."

He whooped and lifted her off the ground. Spun and plunked her on her sore butt, next to the cutting board. He stepped between her legs, cupped the back of her neck and seared her lips with a kiss that left her breathless. "You already did. I'm completely at your mercy and I wouldn't want to be anywhere else."

Chapter 8

CASSIE

UNSURPRISINGLY, no leftovers remained from their dinner. A man Brian's size put away a lot of food, and with the chicken lost in the demise of the barbecue, and nothing to replace it in her house, it hadn't been the most filling meal ever served.

The additions Brian had made to her tossed salad—cheese cubes, chopped nuts, the last of her on-hand veggies—elevated it from side dish to entrée, even though it left her fridge next to bare. She could get used to having a resourceful man in the kitchen. And when he'd pulled the toasted rounds topped with goat cheese, salmon and lemon zest from the oven…she'd almost asked him to pack a bag and move in.

She tossed the cloth napkin on her empty plate, crossed her ankles atop Brian's knee and leaned back as comfortably as the rigid lawn chair permitted. To the west, peach and amber streaked the sky as the sun dipped below the horizon. Twilight's glow wrapped around Brian, bouncing off his hair and creating a warm aura that made it even harder not to stare at the handsome hunk of male who just might be her boyfriend.

He turned his amazing smile on her—one that'd melt her panties, if she had any on—then leaned forward and tugged her chair closer, directly across from his. The action tented her legs. Down slid her robe, to her hips. The July evening was warm and windless, yet she shivered. Goose bumps rose on her arms, matched ten times over by her nipples poking against the satin. Mischief sparkled in the eyes appraising her. Gently, he stroked her calves, the sensitive spot at the back of her knee. Higher, up the inside of her thigh, until his hand disappeared under the edge of her robe.

"Mmm, dessert," she said as his fingers parted her flesh and found her clit.

"Exactly what I was thinking." His chair's legs scraped the patio. On his knees in front of her, he repositioned her— thighs spread, one foot resting on each of his wide shoulders. His face disappeared between her legs, his tongue replacing the teasing touch of fingers. No teasing now. He suckled her clit, pushing her closer to the edge with each flick and swipe of his tongue.

"Please…" She arched, desperate to take his thrusting fingers deeper. He added another and she groaned at the fullness. Still wasn't enough. "Touch me everywhere."

A growl rumbled against her clit. She whimpered in complaint when he withdrew his ministrations. He looked up at her, eyes dark and hungry, while moistening his smallest finger.

"Say it again."

"Touch me everywhere."

"You can do better than that. Tell me what you want."

Trapped by his eyes, his massive body and her wanton

needs, she whispered, "I want your fingers inside me—fucking my pussy and my ass while you make me come."

"With pleasure." His lips touched down first, then tongue, then fingers sliding into her pussy. Then a single digit pressed against her ass, circling its way inside oh so slowly.

"Oh god, more…" And more she got. Sensations crashed together as his pinky pushed in all the way. So good, the teasing taste of fullness. Later, she'd make him give her more than this. He'd hold her hips and ease his cock inside. She'd take every thick inch of it, beg him to fuck her ass deep and hard.

The sweet buzz of climax tugged at her. She rolled her hips against his tongue to get more pressure. The top of his head shook and bobbed as he took her to the edge only to torture her by easing off, over and over.

"Stop teasing…make me come." She threaded her fingers through his soft, short hair and forced his face tighter to her needy clit.

Like a starving man he licked, sucked and bit her. God yes —that was it. She tipped over, bucked and clawed and pushed her pussy against his face.

"No more." She attempted—unsuccessfully—to wiggle free of his clutches. "Too sensitive." His laugh vibrated through her core, and just like that, her sated feeling melted into desire. "Take me in the house…so you can *take me* in the house."

"On it." He scooped her out of the chair and into his arms. Skirted the pile of dead barbecue parts and took the stairs of her back stoop two at a time.

They hadn't turned on any lights before heading outside to eat, and only a few weak rays of sunshine filtered through the west-facing windows as he carried her through the house. The dim lighting didn't keep her from admiring his profile.

Straight nose, high cheekbones, strong, square jaw. So many words described him—handsome, masculine, beautiful. And another one—photogenic. The crappy pictures she'd snuck with her cellphone had proven that.

"Remember by the tree, when I said you'd owe me and you agreed?"

"For the picture I *didn't* take, yeah."

"That's on you. Not my fault you didn't take advantage of your end of the deal."

"Oh, I took advantage." He turned into her bedroom, hitting the light switch as he did. The grin on his face—pure wolfish. "If you've forgotten, I'd be more than willing to refresh your memory."

"Sorry, no trees in my bedroom. And my belt's in the bathroom."

"Don't need any props." He deposited her on the bed. Crawled over top of her, linked their hands and stretched her arms above her head. His lips grazed her forehead, eyelids, the bridge of her nose, then found their way to her ear. "Have everything I need right here."

"You have to stop doing that."

"Kissing your neck?" he asked as his mouth traveled lower, to the sensitive spot near her collarbone.

"God no, never stop that."

"Then what?"

"Saying romantic things to me."

"You have something against romance?"

"Yes, actually, I do." She tilted her head, in part to grant him better access, mostly to avoid looking into his eyes during her admission. "Romance is dangerous. And when you talk to me that way, I want more days like this. Making dinner together and endless sex and other dangerously romantic stuff. I am a woman, you know."

His head lifted enough for her to see the twinkle in his eyes. "Oh, I did notice—though I'm always up for a refresher of that fact."

"*Brian.*" God, he was bad. And so very good. The man should come with a warning label—guaranteed to spike hormone levels while causing dreams of white dresses and fancy, tiered cakes. "Brian."

"Cutie," he said, pseudo-mimicking her serious tone.

"Stop with the sweet talk, or I won't be able to help myself, I'll fall even more."

"Good, because I'm already there."

She angled for a better view. Smiling—he was smiling at her, the sweetest, most romantic smile. The kind she could totally picture at the top of a tuxedo. Oh crap. "You're still doing it."

"I've warned you about my lack of control."

How did he do that—take her from horny to sappy to giggling, all in the course of minutes? Talk about lack of control—she's the one who had it, big time. For now she was going with it. If he broke her heart, she'd pick up the pieces.

"Back to our deal, the part where you owe me."

"Right." He released her hands to prop his weight on his forearms. He fiddled with the barrettes restraining her hair, worked them free and tossed them aside so he could play with her short, unruly waves. "What did you have in mind?"

"I'd like to take your picture." Merely thinking about getting Brian in front of her Canon had her heart racing. "Not with my cell phone, I mean really take your picture, in my studio. Tasteful shots, don't worry."

His eyebrows rose at her closing statement. "No naked pictures?"

Of course he'd ask that after what he'd seen of Paolo and

Beth's photo shoot. "That's not what I had in mind…though I wouldn't say no if you wanted to drop your kilt."

"My *kilt?*" The bed shook with his whooping laughter. When he finally caught his breath, his eyes shone with the almost-tears that accompany absolute amusement. "Okay, cutie. You tell me when to be here with my skirt and I'll try not to break your camera."

As if that'd happen. With his looks and physique—not to mention his kilt—these would be amazing pictures. She could already see them in her mind. So good, she could probably sell them as stock photos, maybe even as exclusives, if he was interested in making a bit of extra money.

"I look forward to seeing your studio. Watching you work."

"What?" She couldn't have heard correctly.

Oh god, no.

His words from their argument in the staffroom at Blur replayed in her head. *You had company—and an open door. Might want to lock up next time, or maybe you don't care who hears or sees.*

She'd assumed he'd meant the Mancusos' erotic photo shoot. What if he hadn't?

"Hey, you're pale as a ghost. Shit, I'm probably squashing you." The safety and heat of his body vanished as he rolled to his side, leaving her far more vulnerable than she'd been any of the times he'd fucked her. "You okay?"

She nodded a lie she'd never pull off if she used words. "Just confused. I thought you'd already seen my studio. You didn't go down to the basement when you were here —before?"

"Like when you were hiding from me the first night? No. You gave yourself up before I took the second stair."

"I guess I did, didn't I?" She smiled, but it had to be weak.

Concern flickered in his eyes. He curled one strong arm

over her waist and tugged her as close as possible to nuzzle her hair and whispered in her ear, "I have an idea that'll put the color back in your pretty face."

Sex, yes. That's what this had to be about. Not falling in love, not frivolous dreams of wedding dresses and happily ever after. Those had been dangerous enough when she thought Brian knew about her specialty photography. How stupid she'd been, assuming he'd discovered her secret and had no questions about it. For a photographer, she was pretty damn blind.

"Come on, I'm going to run you a bath. You can relax. I'll clean up from supper."

Perfect domestic bliss, exactly what she couldn't afford. "Forget the dishes. How about a shower instead—then you can join me. You know, wash my back, hold me while I bend over to pick up the soap…"

"You drop the soap a lot?"

"I will if you're standing behind me."

BRIAN

Whatever had her worried a few minutes earlier seemed to have disappeared. Gentleman be damned. The prospect of slippery shower sex with Cassie had blood roaring through his veins, all of it headed to one location.

His feet hit the floor and he hauled her up with him. Hands cupping her sweet ass, he steered her toward the bedroom door. "To the shower it is."

"Wait," she threw on the brakes, "I need to grab condoms."

Not one, but plural. That worked. She let out the world's sexiest shriek when he smacked her ass as she moved toward the nightstand. Probably stung, given the earlier encounter with the maple tree. She bent to open the drawer, causing her robe to ride up, exposing the smiley curves of her cheeks and a hint of the bark burn he'd tended before dinner. He adjusted his stance to accommodate the growing hard-on. Part of his brain screamed *sick fucking bastard*, but he pushed it away. Cassie didn't think so. She welcomed that side of him. Got off from it, as he did. A few days together and he couldn't see himself fucking another woman, ever.

"Ready," she said, waving a fan of packets at him. Two steps in his direction, the phone rang. She ignored it, and by the time the condoms were within reach, the old-school answering machine picked up.

"Hi, Cassie, this is Trevor Ritchie, the owner of Iron Works."

And there went the condoms as Cassie darted for the phone by her bed. "Want me to grab it before he hangs up, in case it's important?"

"No—it's not for me." Shit. Definitely should've gotten around to this conversation during dinner.

Trevor's voice continued through the speaker, slick as ever. "The club is due for updated promotional shots for the website and fall print campaigns, and your work comes highly recommended. I'd like to discuss my ideas with you over dinner. My treat, of course. You can reach me at the club, or on my cell. The number is—"

"Fucker," Brian muttered, drawing Cassie's attention.

"Were you the one who recommended me—is that how you knew the call wouldn't be for you?"

So much for their hot shower. He sat on the bed and pulled her onto his lap. "As for the recommendation, it wasn't me and I doubt there was one, period. I'm not saying you don't deserve the job—I've seen your website, you definitely do. But I think Trevor's looking for a guaranteed way to get you on a date. You caught his eye the other day. You were barely out the door before he started asking questions about you. He's used to getting his way. About everything."

She shivered in his arms. "He gave me the creeps. Did you puff up and growl at him like you did with Sam?"

He snorted. Yeah, he'd done exactly that the day Sam was taunting him by flirting with Cassie. "Wish I could have. Trevor's an asshole, I'd love to flatten him."

"But you can't because he's your boss. I get that."

Not entirely, she didn't. "More than that. He's the only guy who'd hire me after the domestic charges. When Leanne had to withdraw from the CBBF Fitness Championships, she almost lost her biggest sponsor. The only thing that saved her was the cause of her injuries. That kind of thing is big news in the fitness community. Most clubs wouldn't even take my résumé, let alone give me a chance to explain."

"So your boss knows…everything?"

"As in, *how* I gave Leanne the injuries? Yeah. Not something I want out there as public knowledge, but it was either divulge the circumstances or let my sole potential employer assume I beat her up. The lesser of two evils, unfortunately." What he wouldn't tell Cassie was how Trevor smiled through the story. Brian would forget that part of the conversation himself, if possible.

"Well, he gave you the job, so he gets credit for that. If he truly wants to talk business, I'll take my portfolio to his office. And if he pulls any more of his creeptastic moves on me, I'll tell him I'm spoken for."

"I told him that when he asked about you. He doesn't care, he said as much."

"You told him we were seeing each other and he said it didn't matter? What kind of person is he?"

"A lazy, disrespectful sleazebag, but," and this was where it got tricky, "I didn't tell him *we're* together. I couldn't, still can't. No romantic or intimate contact with members—a condition of the contract I had to sign when he agreed to hire me. That's why I didn't ask you out months ago, and every day since."

"And why you acted like a jerk to me at the gym the other day?"

"Yeah." That, and having overheard her fucking the Italian guy, but he wasn't taking on that conversation tonight. "I should have told you right away. I hate secrets—they always come back to bite you in the ass."

Cassie scrambled off his lap and pulled the tiny robe tighter. Subtly, she put distance between them. Didn't take a genius to figure out what she was doing—especially since she'd left the condoms on the bed. He could hardly blame her for needing space after everything he'd unloaded on her tonight. Fuck, it was a miracle she still wanted him at all.

"How about you take that bath and unwind—alone—and I'll head out, give you time to yourself."

"Okay."

The single word knifed him. He stood, weighed his options and consequences. Fuck it. He crossed the room and cradled her face in his palms. "I'm not leaving without kissing you good night."

"You'd be in trouble if you did."

Exactly what he needed to hear. He caught her bottom lip between his teeth and gave it a small tug. A reminder. Then he met her mouth full on for a long, deep kiss. The kind that made her whimper when it ended.

"Yeah, me too," he said, taking a necessary step back. Without it, he'd already have her pinned against the wall with his hand under her robe.

"When will I see you again?" she asked.

The simple question felt like first prize. "Tomorrow."

"I guess I can wait that long."

Goddamn, her smile could keep him going for days. Only it wouldn't have to.

BRIAN

Time was such a fickle bitch. Went too fast when Cassie was around, dragged painfully slowly when she wasn't. Didn't help that he hadn't heard from her since leaving her house last night, or that his boss had chosen this afternoon to hang around the gym *and* make comments about the "hot little number" he had plans for.

Once, to shut Trevor the fuck up, Brian had come close to telling him to stuff the conditions on his employment contract and keep his hands—and mind—off Cassie. Brian had gotten as far as Trevor's office door, the words "there's something I'd like to discuss with you" out of his mouth. Trevor had waved him in. Before Brian had had the chance to spill the rest, Trevor dropped *his* bomb—a new contract was in the works, one that included a ten-percent stake in Iron Works and the option to buy a larger share in the years to come. Guess he'd be keeping his relationship with Cassie under wraps awhile longer.

"You look like shit." This from Sam as he strolled behind the front counter to liberate a post-workout protein bar from the gym's packed display rack.

"That'll be three bucks."

"For the bar or the insult?" Sam grinned and stuffed the second half of the supplement bar in his mouth. He aimed, tossed the crumpled wrapper into the trash can and crossed pumped-up arms over his chest.

Few people had stood beside Brian after the Leanne mess. His parents, his brother. As far as friends went, Sam was it. The guy had even stuck his neck out and put in a recommendation with his boss—now their boss—at Iron Works. Let Sam think he was sticking it to that idiot Trevor by snagging free bars and shakes. Brian would toss the cash in the till later. He owed Sam that and a hell of a lot more.

Sam swallowed, then grabbed a bottled water from the fridge and took a long swig to wash the chewy mass down. "So, how'd it go yesterday?"

"The boot camp? Great turnout, getting more people every week. Thirty-four bodies at ten bucks a head."

"More people every week, huh? That mean Cassie showed up?" Another grin when Brian slowly nodded. "Good. And you're welcome." He pushed off the counter and made his way to the members' side of the front desk. "Do you remember all the stuff you told me Saturday night?"

Brian snorted. "I wasn't *that* drunk, Jacobs." Total bullshit and they both knew it.

"Whatever. Look, I've been telling you not to go for anything with Cassie because you could lose your job over it, and I'd hate to see you in that position again. But after listening to your rye-loosened lips for a couple of hours, I've changed my position. Go for it, man. Be happy. Just be careful."

The hair on the back of his neck bristled. "I won't hurt her."

Sam shook his shiny bald head while reaching over the counter to cuff Brian, an act only a select few could do and live to tell the tale.

"Not what I meant, dumbass. Be careful Ritchie doesn't

find out. It might be wise for Cassie to switch gyms if you're going to do the couple thing. Have you told her yet—about the lame conviction and the stupid contract you signed?"

Trust Sam to say exactly what he meant. The women he dated didn't always appreciate that quality, but Brian did. Honesty beat the hell out of pussyfooting around and lies any day.

"Told her everything last night."

Now Sam nodded. "Explains why you look like you haven't slept in two days."

"Nice. Thanks."

"Anytime." Sam hoisted his backpack onto one shoulder. Drained the water bottle, crushed it and tossed it, basketball-style, into the recycling bin. "Sounds like she might be a keeper. Don't fuck it up or I'll kick your ass."

BRIAN

All night long the damn door opened and closed. Members arrived, exercised, hit the tanning beds, ordered shakes, signed up for training, bought supplements and exited the gym. Every time Cassie didn't walk through the door, Sam's threat replayed in Brian's head. Looked as if he had an ass-kicking coming to him.

The place was empty by eleven forty-five, so he started the cleanup process. No point in spending any extra minutes here tonight. Sam was right, Brian hadn't slept much on the weekend, and the few hours he'd had the past two nights were the toss-and-turn variety. Tonight probably wouldn't be any better.

He got the cleaning caddy and headed for the mirrored

wall on the east side of the weight room. An idiot scowled back at him. He sprayed glass cleaner on his reflection and wiped harder circles than necessary to do the job. Pain, that's what he needed.

Fuck the cleaning for one night. He tossed the bottle and roll of towels into the bucket. Cracked his neck side-to-side and grabbed the hundred-pound dumbbells. He dropped onto a flat bench and planted his feet on the floor. Slowly, he lowered the weights until the plates touched the sides of his chest, then pushed the dumbbells back up, banging out twelve reps with ease. More weight required. He swapped the hundreds for the one-twenties and returned to the bench. The burn kicked in on the fifth rep. By the eighth his chest and triceps protested. Yeah, this was what he needed. He grunted and pushed out two more before letting the weights thud to the floor.

"The sign on the wall says, 'please do not drop the weights'." Cassie looked down at him, the ends of her short, slightly mussed hair falling forward, brushing her cheek and begging to be tucked behind her ear.

"Are you going to turn me in?"

"No, your secrets are safe with me."

A promise laced with double meaning, he was sure of it. Had to be a good sign. Plus, she was here.

She bent and wrapped both hands around the bar of one dumbbell. "Oh my god, this is heavy." Her eyes bugged when she read the number on one end. "This thing weighs more than I do—and you were benching *two* of them?"

"That's only two-forty, and I weigh two-fifteen. A man should be able to bench his own weight, minimum, and a hell of a lot more with the straight bar."

"So you wouldn't have a problem benching *me*."

"Not at all." He positioned his hands a little wider than his shoulders, palms up, and winked. "Get on, I'll prove it."

"I was kidding."

The idea of holding her this way, showing off for her, gave him a rush. Now he needed to get her up there—and after her stubborn performance at the boot camp, he knew how to make it happen. "I wasn't. But if your abs and legs aren't strong enough to hold your body straight…"

"You did not just say that." Her purse hit the floor and she stepped closer, a little wrinkle forming between two perfectly shaped eyebrows. "How do you want me—front or back?"

His grin at the blush on her face had to stretch ear to ear. "I want you every which way, but for this exercise, I think you'll be most comfortable facedown." The reverse would probably be better for him, but he wasn't about to give up watching her face as he lifted her. The parts of her sexy body he'd get to paw didn't hurt the deal either.

He brought his hands down to chest level. Tentatively, she settled the weight of her upper body on one of his palms.

"A little to the left…"

For a second she shimmied, giving him a handful of t-shirt-covered breast. Then it clicked, or more likely, his face gave him away. Didn't matter, really. The chastising set of her lips sent more adrenaline through his veins—and more blood rushing to his cock. Bench-pressing with a boner. Should be interesting.

"Do I even need to ask what part of my body goes on your other hand?"

"Only if you want me to talk dirty to you."

The little vixen rocked her pelvis side-to-side, brushing his fingertips. "Tell me which body part to put on that big, sexy hand."

Getting in on the dirty talk, huh? Fine by him. "Your

pussy." Christ, she had to go and lick her lips while looking at him with fuck-me eyes. All right, he'd up the ante. "Your bare pussy. Lift your skirt and take down your panties."

"Can't quite do that." The purple-flowered skirt went up, up, holy-fucking-hot up. "No panties."

"Give it to me." Warm, soft woman descended on his splayed palm, perfectly positioned for his pinky to graze her clit. He'd be lucky to get more than one rep. "Whenever you're ready, lift your legs and lock them as straight as you can."

This would take strength on Cassie's part as much as his. Her legs rose and her body stiffened above him.

"Ready."

Weight-wise, pressing Cassie was nothing. Balancing the lopsided distribution of her weight, not having a decent grip, the distraction of holding his hot little girlfriend above his head—not so easy. But doable. He drew a breath and pushed up from his chest.

"Oh my god, you're doing it." She shrieked. Wiggled. Almost caused him to drop her headfirst onto the gym floor.

"Told you...no problem." He grabbed more air as he lowered her, huffing it out as he pressed her up a second time. And then a third, just to hear her fucking adorable squeal. "Time to get off now," he said as he brought her down the final time. He caught her arm as she reached for her purse and shook his head. "Unless you're getting a condom from that bag, put it down."

"What?"

Oh, the wheels were turning behind those pretty eyes now. "That's right. I said time to get off and I meant it. Now park it on a bench, right at the end, so I can make good on my words."

"Not here—we can't. If we get caught, you'll lose your job. I was stupid to let you do what you did."

He stood, caught her hips and yanked her against the part of his body that didn't give a rat's ass about her good sense. "I'm going to turn off the cameras and lock the doors. When I get back over here, I want you on that bench, ready for me."

The purse hit the floor. Two delicate, talented hands cupped him, cock and balls, through his work khakis. "How do you want me," down went his zipper, in snuck her fingers, "face up, or ass up?"

Christ. He hadn't even thought about the second option. He slid one hand up her back and curled it around her nape as he brought his mouth down onto hers. She opened for him, let him take control without giving up one ounce of her spirit. As it always was with her. He broke the kiss, her frustrated, turned-on moan sending another gallon of blood to his already aching cock.

"Show me that sexy ass."

Eyes never leaving his, she slipped from his arms. She knelt at the end of the weight bench, gathered her skirt around her waist, then pressed her breasts to the vinyl. "Like this?"

Hell yes. "Don't move. Going to lock up and wash my hands so I can touch you all over."

"Hurry."

Not something she had to tell him. If it wouldn't make him look like a desperate, horny idiot, he'd sprint across the gym right now. Fuck it. Let her see that's exactly how she affected him. He jogged around the equipment, took care of business and jetted back.

"You were quick."

"Words no guy wants to hear."

She giggled. Smiled. Snagged yet another piece of his

149

soul. "And I doubt *you* ever have. I certainly have no complaints."

"Good. I'll try to keep it that way." He dropped to his knees behind her. Such an incredible ass…he'd never get enough. He smoothed his hands over it before sliding two fingers between her legs. One touch to her clit elicited a soft moan that made his cock jerk. "Gym doesn't open until 5:00 a.m. How many times do you think I can make you come in five hours?"

"More than I can take." She arched toward his touch, hips moving in rhythm with his circling fingertips.

He used his other hand to free his cock. Stroked it for relief and got the opposite. Cassie's fluttering eyelids and parted lips, her breathy moaning as she got closer to coming, the way her hips moved so damn temptingly…fuck.

"So fucking hot—have to put a condom on before I fuck you bare." Something he wanted to do so badly he could almost feel it—how wet and warm she'd be around his cock, the sensation of her skin hugging his, nothing separating them. Latex sucked. Always had, always would. Necessary and smart, yes. Every time he was with Cassie, though, he resented the barrier more.

"Feel free to be quick about *that*."

He snagged the packet from his wallet and ripped it open. Damn near dropped the condom in his hurry to get the fucking thing in place. Her obvious amusement at his fumbling might've been emasculating if it'd come from another woman. With Cassie, it only made him want inside her more.

He smacked her sweet ass, the crisp sound punctuating the air in the high-ceilinged room and making heat curl at the base of his cock. No more giggling from his girl, only a sigh that made his cock and heart swell simultaneously.

"Again, harder."

No worrying anymore, only doing. Giving in to what they both craved. He brought his palm down on her other cheek, then again on each side, bringing a fresh pink glow to her fair skin. "The things I want to do to you…" He flattened his hand over her tailbone. Slid his thumb down the valley of her ass and pressed it against her tight ring. Christ, the low, needy sound she made. The way she tipped to meet him. "I'm following you home tonight, and when we get there, I'm going to lay you out on the bed and fuck you again." He breached her with the tip of his finger. "Right here, in your pretty little ass."

"God yes, I want that." She wiggled to get more and he was happy to oblige—to the first knuckle. Enough to hit all her nerve endings but keep her hungry for more, later. Her hips rolled against his hand. Her lips separated and soft, sexy gasps slipped out, filling his head. When she snuck a hand between her legs, those soft sounds got a hell of a lot rawer.

A man could only take so much. He angled his cock, found her very welcoming entrance and pushed inside. "I lied. Won't last long."

"Me either," she whispered.

All rhythm went to pot when she started to come. Didn't fucking matter. Fire licked at his balls and raced up his shaft. He grabbed her hips and pounded into her. One final thrust buried him deep inside. His pulse rang in his ears as he unloaded for what could've been forever.

He collapsed over her back, hugging her to the bench, face buried in the hair behind her ear. "I'm not letting you go."

"That's going to be awkward when the gym opens."

He knew she was playing. And he loved that about her, only this time he was serious. Call it sappy or hokey, but with Cassie everything fit. The only way he'd give that up was if she walked away. Even then, he'd chase her. He might be in control during sex, but she had the real power. He couldn't think of one thing he wouldn't do for her. Shave the beard he'd had since he was eighteen, give up pants for a kilt 24/7, get down on one knee with a ring... Yeah, he was done for. Tonight, when he had her soft, naked body in his arms, he'd tell her exactly what he meant about not letting go.

CASSIE

Brian hadn't responded to her playful comeback. He placed a sweet kiss at the base of her neck, then lifted his giant body off hers. Was he angry she'd joked off his comment? Of course she'd known he was serious. Hence the reply. She couldn't do serious with Brian. Wanted to—oh, with all her heart, she wanted to. But knowing how he felt about secrets, plus what he *didn't* know about her body of work... She had to keep things casual. Keep Brian away from her business and by default, out of her heart.

She settled her skirt into place while he tucked his cock away and zipped up. He hadn't taken his eyes off her, but he hadn't spoken either. Not quite a fight, but not altogether right. Even when they'd been gym friends and nothing more, things had never been awkward between them. Flirty and occasionally nervous, but never uncomfortable. She wasn't about to let it become that way now.

"I'll help you clean and stuff so we can get out of here." She snagged a feather duster from the caddy of supplies, put one hand on her hip and bent over to mock-dust the weight bench that—thanks to them—now required much more thorough cleaning. "Pretend I'm your maid or one of your subordinates. Put me to work, order me around a little." A smile ticked at the corners of his mouth. Now she was getting somewhere. "The sooner we get started, the sooner we'll be in my bedroom where you can tell me what you really want me to do." Mischief flickered in his eyes. Much better. "So, what'll it be, boss?"

Two steps and he stood behind her. Not touching her, yet lighting her up just the same. "You'll do whatever I say?"

"Oh yes. I'm a very good minion." This was how it should be between them—spirited, fun, spontaneous. Temporary. She pushed that last bit far to the back and focused on the way his eyes shone as he looked at her. As if she were the only woman in the world. Crap, maybe she shouldn't focus on that either.

He lowered to his haunches in front of her to grab a spray bottle and rag, but the way he kept his eyes on her face, the significance such a pose *could* have—her heart dared to flutter in spite of the threats she'd made against it all day long.

"Wipe down the seats and benches?" She needed a purpose, and fast. At his nod, she snatched the cleaning supplies and put three pieces of bulky equipment between them. Not nearly enough of a buffer if she was going to resist him. Heck, three cities wouldn't be enough, the pull was so strong. Watching his muscles bunch and flex while he wiped the mirrors ten feet in front of her didn't help her feeble resolve.

"Tell me about your photography business."

"What?"

His eyes caught hers in the mirror. Caught and held. "From the beginning. Was it a hobby that turned into something bigger, did you stumble into it accidentally, or was it all planned and executed on a schedule? I'm curious. Fascinated and impressed too."

"Don't be. Impressed, that is. I'm just a run-of-the-mill, small-time photographer. One of many taking advantage of a steady hand and halfway-decent eye. Don't get me wrong, I love what I do. I've had a camera in my hand since I was a teenager and that's all I've ever wanted, career-wise, to take pictures. I'm lucky I get to pay the bills that way, but nobody's banging on my door, begging me to leave my life behind and move to Paris or New York to shoot magazine covers. I'm nothing special."

"I've seen your work online and I disagree."

Product shots, engagement photos, a mish-mash of other respectable work—those were what he'd seen. She was tempted to show him some of the boudoir pictures she'd taken, see how he reacted. None of the truly explicit stuff, and nothing that showed the identity of the subjects—she wouldn't make that mistake again. That's how Lance had blackmailed her, by copying her files and threatening to expose her clients. Bastard. Lance was proof that sharing sexual proclivities didn't mean two people had the same code of ethics. The more she fell for the dreamy ginger giant staring at her in the mirror, the more she needed to remember that.

"Who put the camera in your hand, your parents?"

"Indirectly." She wiped a couple more benches before catching sight of his raised eyebrows in the mirror. Might as well tell him, get the inevitable pitying over with. "They died when I was fifteen. Icy roads, jackknifed tractor trailer." She shrugged, then turned her back on the mirror. Quick and simple, that's how she preferred to share this part of her life. "I lived with my grandparents after that. On my sixteenth birthday, Nana gave me my first SLR camera, along with a set of car keys and a roadmap. She told me to go out and take pictures of life instead of holing up in my room and avoiding living. So I did."

In the course of those few sentences, Brian had ditched cleaning and come up behind her. Big arms wrapped around her. Like a fool, she gave in to the security and sympathy of his embrace, turning in the circle of his arms.

"Your nana sounds like a strong, smart woman. Like you."

No pity. That was a first. Cassie smiled against his warm, solid chest. "She's pretty amazing. Seventy-nine and still kicking my butt when necessary. If I end up with half her wisdom and backbone one day, I'll be lucky."

"I'd like to meet her."

"She's not some sweet, shriveled old lady who knits and sips tea. She's…formidable."

Laughter rumbled in his chest and he squeezed her tighter. "Now I *have* to meet her."

God, what was she supposed to say to that? After bailing her out of the Lance mess, Nana hadn't suggested Cassie give up her non-mainstream business. What she had done, however, was warn Cassie not to get emotionally involved with anybody so long as she "led a life that required secrecy". Cassie could tell herself this thing with Brian was strictly sex all she liked…Nana would take one look at them together and know Cassie was head over heels.

"On the topic of family," he loosened his hold to lift her chin, "I dumped my Wednesday shift so I could have dinner with mine. Come with me."

Not a good idea when she was trying to keep her heart in check. "I'm, um…"

"Booked up with appointments?"

Right there, he'd offered her the perfect out. So why was her head moving back and forth, instead of up and down? "No, just nervous."

"No haggis with neeps and tatties, I promise."

"I don't even know what that means."

"Traditional Scottish meal. Heart, liver and lungs, ground up and mixed with spices and stuff, then cooked in sheep's stomach, that's haggis. Neeps and tatties are mashed turnip and potatoes, normal enough."

Haggis, in particular, sounded nasty. Then again, there'd been a time she felt that way about butt plugs. "Is it good?"

"Not always. But when it's done right, yeah."

"So it's like sex."

Laughter burst from deep within his chest and rang in the open, quiet space. "Now I'll think of you whenever I eat that meal." His hands trailed up her arms to cup her face. "And if I'm a lucky bastard, you'll be sitting beside me every time."

She didn't need to taste them. Haggis, neeps and tatties were officially her favorite foods.

Chapter 9

BRIAN

THE KEY WASN'T EVEN in the lock when Brian noticed the BMW at the side of the building. The interior light flicked on briefly, showing it was occupied, as was his waist, since Cassie had her arms wrapped around it from behind. If Trevor's windows were down—and they probably were, given the incredible weather tonight—he'd heard her giggling too. If there was a way out of this where he still had a job tomorrow, he couldn't see it. Shit.

He spoke over his shoulder, as low as possible. "We have company. My boss is parked over to the right, in the shadows. He's looking straight at us."

"Oh my god, Brian. Wait—I know, act as if I'm throwing myself at you and you're trying to politely shake me off."

Executed well, they could probably pull that off. What he needed to know was whether they should try. "This isn't how I wanted to do this," he mock-fumbled with the key, still talking at whisper volume, "but I'm crazy about you. I don't want to hide it or lie about it, and I'm willing to take the heat for breaking the rules if you feel the same way." She hadn't moved since he alerted her to Trevor's watchful eyes, but at his words and his question, her body tensed against his back. Shit. No turning back now. "When I pull this key out, I'm turning around and putting my hands on you. Kiss me and I come clean to my boss, no regrets. No kiss means you're not sure about us and we play it off like you suggested."

The deadbolt clicked. Metal slid across metal as he withdrew the key. When he turned, he might as well've been standing in quicksand, it was that hard to do. Cassie's arms dropped to her sides. He cupped his palms over her shoulders and looked into her eyes. Her lips trembled, but they didn't come up to meet his. Damn it. Damn it to fucking hell.

"Sorry if I led you on, Cassie. I like you, but there's no *us*." Fucking irony.

"I'm sorry too, we could've been good together." Glassy eyes, downturned lips, regretful tone. She ought to switch sides of the camera because she was one hell of an actress.

The only response he had for this insanity was a grunt.

She clutched her purse and took a step backward, severing contact. "Sorry for…the mistake. See you around." And then she was gone. Speed-walking toward her car, almost at a jog. She cursed uncharacteristically when her keys clattered to the asphalt, the string of soft-spoken obscenities carrying through the still night air.

He wanted to laugh. To call out to her, say something that'd make her laugh in return. More than that, he wanted to march over there and pin her against the door of her Ford and demand she change her decision. None of this "we could've been good together" bullshit—they *were* good together. They were fucking amazing together. Instead, he watched her taillights disappear down the road.

"Interesting night."

And now for more fun. Brian shoved the keys in his pocket —though there was still a huge chance he'd be handing them over any minute—and turned to face Trevor where he leaned on the hood of his BMW. "That it was."

"I was on my way home from a date and thought I'd drop off some paperwork you might be interested in."

Again with the fucking carrot. Brian wasn't jumping for it this time. Not tonight, not in this mood. "I got last month's sales and expense reports in the email tonight, but thanks anyway."

Trevor's slimy smile glinted in the half light as he weasel-walked to where Brian stood his ground. "Not that boring shit. Your new contract." Trevor slapped a palm on the glass of Iron Works' front door. "The one that gets you a stake in this baby…if you follow the rules."

Aka, if he remained Trevor's lackey. Fuck that. "I bust my ass for this place and you know it."

"True. But the rules, big guy. You broke the terms of your employment tonight." Brian's silence only made Trevor's smile widen. "You should've turned out the lights before you fucked the hot little photographer. Not that I blame you for wanting to watch that piece of ass while you smacked it. Bet it had a nice glow by the time you screwed her."

Son of a fucking bitch. Brian stepped closer, crossed his arms high on his chest and stared down a couple inches at his soon-to-be-former boss. "Despite what you saw or overheard, Cassie's still a friend. One more word and I'll—"

"Heel, boy, or you're out on your ass." Trevor twirled his key ring on his index finger and waited until Brian did exactly that—heeled like a desperate fucking puppy—before saying another word. "Fact—you breached your contract. You owe me."

This wasn't going to be good. "And?"

"You've had your fun with your *friend*, Miss Johnson, and sent her packing. Now I want a crack at her."

"Sloppy seconds don't seem like your thing."

"I can wait until she showers." Another despicable grin. "Maybe I'll head over to her house now and see if she needs a shoulder to cry on…or somebody to wash her back."

Brian's fists clenched and released, clenched and released. If Ritchie didn't shut his trap, Brian would be facing more assault charges, and this time he'd enjoy the hell out of earning them.

"On second thought…" Trevor pocketed the keys to a vehicle that cost more than Brian made in a year. "I'll wait a couple days. Until her sexy little ass has had time to get its normal color back. I'd like a blank slate to play with. And while I'm waiting, I want you to make nice with your friend and encourage her to accept my dinner invitation. Feel free to point out all my superior qualities."

That'd take two seconds, one for each syllable in the word *money*. "And if I do this, suggest Cassie go out with you, I keep my job and get the new contract?"

"Greedy. See how alike we are? This is why I want to bring you on as a partner. But no. After I get my date and I'm convinced she's giving me a real shot, not going along to save your ass, then you get the new contract." Trevor clapped Brian's upper arm as if they were best buddies. "If I don't have plans with Cassie by the weekend, you're fired. Enjoy the rest of your night."

BRIAN

He didn't expect her to answer. Hell, he wasn't even sure why he was on her front step, knocking.

Until she opened the door.

"I'm still crazy about you." Yeah, that was why.

"I won't be the reason you lose your job."

Close enough to what he'd hoped to hear. He stepped over the threshold. Hands on her waist, he backed her up to the wall, kicking the door closed behind him. They'd been here before. The difference—this time he didn't hesitate. He tugged the belt from her robe, drank in the sight of her naked body as the satin fell open and slowly slid his hands over her soft, warm skin to her face. No power outage to hinder the view this time. Big blue eyes blinked up at him, overflowing with everything she wasn't saying.

"You should've kissed me."

"I wanted to, but—"

He stopped whatever argument she was about to give him with his lips. Then it was all good. Her mouth submitting under his. Her hands around his waist, one under his shirt, the other heading into the back of his pants. The soft moan of pleasure she made when he pressed his body hard against hers.

He gave up the sweetness of her mouth for her neck. Kissed his way down the slender column to her shoulder, then her breasts, giving each nipple a long, equal turn in his mouth. So perfect. He could spend all day enjoying them—softly kissing, teasing with nips and pinches, biting until she arched and writhed and dug her nails into his head. Barely an hour since they'd fucked and he was dying to get inside her. Claim her. Leave no doubt in her mind how he felt about her—about them.

"Brian…" she whispered as he worked his way lower, past her bellybutton.

From his knees, he looked up at her. Her eyes, Christ. Didn't matter if she said the words or not, she was in as deep as he was. Had to be.

He parted her with his thumbs, exposing her clit. "Tell me this is mine," he said, sealing his mouth over top.

"God yes, all yours." Her hips arched off the wall. "Only yours."

Those were the words he wanted to hear. The way he intended to keep things. He sucked her clit between his teeth. Flicked and suckled it until she grabbed his head and pulled him closer, bucking against his mouth and panting above him.

She wiggled, tried pushing him away. He knew this move, how sensitive she got after she came. This time, he held fast, stilled her hips with his hands, tongued her with long, slow passes. Took her down from her orgasm without letting her go. Couldn't. He needed more. More of her sweet-spicy taste, more of everything that made her *her*.

"Mmm…" Her fingernails raked through his hair. "Take me to bed now. Please."

"Nothing I'd rather do." In a damn smooth move if he did say so, he stood and scooped her off her feet. Kissed her while walking. Kept kissing her as he laid her on the bed. Was still kissing her as he unzipped his pants.

"Let me do it," she whispered into his mouth. She slipped out from beneath the cage of his arms and dropped her robe, an act that brought him promptly to his feet for a better view. Delicate fingers caught the bottom of his t-shirt and rolled it up—to a point.

"I'll help." He took over with the shirt when she couldn't reach any higher. "I love how pint-sized you are."

"Gee, that's a sexy description."

"Maybe not, but the subject of that description is incredibly fucking sexy."

"That's better," she said, taking his pants and underwear —along with his resolve to behave more like a gentleman— down with one good yank.

He stroked her cheek, the side of her neck, then cupped his hand over her shoulder. A little light pressure and lower she went. Cassie naked, on her knees, fondling his balls and stroking his cock—only one of the sexiest images he'd ever seen. And the most beautiful.

She circled the base of his cock and angled it out from his body. Her skilled tongue darted out. She scooped the bead of pre-cum, hummed as she licked her lips. Then he was in her mouth, sheathed in slick warmth, all the way to the root. He wanted to watch, loved watching her work his cock, but let his head fall back and his eyes close instead. Sweet suction and the tug of her lips drew his balls up tight. Set fire to his groin. The scrape of teeth over the ridge of his tip pushed him temptingly close to the edge. He fisted a handful of her hair. In his head, he pulled her off, told her to stop so he could make love to her. In reality, she moaned and sank down his length again. Christ, too good.

"On the bed," was all he managed to ground out.

The picture she made crawling across the top—damn. She leaned over the far edge, reaching for the bedside table. Give him strength. She dipped into the drawer, the move arching her back and tipping her ass up irresistibly. He'd promised to fuck her there. By the items she'd tossed over her shoulder toward him, she expected him to follow through.

He corralled the condom and lube and joined her on the deep-red duvet. He smoothed his free hand down her back, over the curve of her ass. "So soft. I could touch you forever and still want to do it more."

"I'm okay with that."

"You're going to have to be," he tucked a wave of hair behind her ear, "because I don't plan to let you go."

"And if I try to get away…" she said, creeping forward while peeking over her shoulder.

He closed a hand around her ankle. "I'll make sure you don't."

The little vixen kicked free, landing a heel in the middle of his quadriceps in the process. Wanted to play, did she? Fine by him. He'd even give her a chance to get away—a small one, anyway. He pretended to lunge for her. Tracked her as she giggled and scrambled off the bed, then deked sideways to snag her by the waist.

"Back to bed with you." He walked them toward the mattress, bending en route to collect her robe from the floor.

"What are you doing with that?"

"With the robe, nothing." One-handed, he shook the satin tie free. "This, on the other hand—or should I say hands—is another story."

CASSIE

A slow, spreading, you're-all-mine-now smile curled his lips. This was it. He intended to bind her and fuck her…in the ass. A charge of raw sexual electricity rippled through her, top to toe, the majority of those sparks concentrated between her legs. She shifted, needing to alleviate the building pressure. Her thighs slicked against each other. Evidence of how badly she did *not* want to escape drifted up, filled her nose. Brian's as well, from the flare of his nostrils and the dark hungriness in his eyes.

She glanced down at the thick rod pressing against her hip. Oh god. That was not going to fit where he planned to put it. Where she'd given him permission—no, practically begged—him to put it. The thought of him trying had her squirming in his arms. Half trying to get away, half desperate for him to get on with it.

"Easy now..." His words tickled her ear. Settled her, made her rub against him like a happy kitten. "Let's try this again..." A sound smack warmed one half of her butt. One big arm reached in front of her and swept pillows to the floor. "On the bed, ass up. Stretch those arms and pretty pink fingernails straight above your head."

Had she answered? All she knew is that she did as instructed. The duvet was cool against her skin. The crinkle of crisp percale echoed in her head, quickly replaced by the throbbing pulse of her heartbeat when Brian's hand slid up her back and along her outstretched arms. Soft satin encircled one wrist, then the other. Far enough apart that she could swivel each freely. Tight enough that she couldn't pull her hands through.

"Good," he said, slipping a finger between her skin and the material. Not a question posed to her, simply a verbal confirmation for himself. He straddled her hips, smoothed his hands over her body, massaging the tension from her muscles.

But relax—no. Not possible with his hard naked body atop hers. She tipped her hips, inviting him to slide between her legs. And he did. Up and down, never pushing inside.

"Please..."

He pulled back to don protection. Or so she thought. He shifted on the bed, stretching across its width to poke around in her nightstand. Between her prone position and his massive back, her view was blocked.

Without his touch, her nerves about their impending activity jangled back into place. "I already got the stuff."

"Just want one more thing." The drawer closed and he

resumed his position astride her hips. Whatever he'd gone searching for, he must've found.

She twisted her neck to see, to no avail. "What is it?"

"Something good." The foil condom packet ripped. A second later, the cap on the bottle clicked open. Cool beads of lube trickled down the valley of her ass as the lid snapped closed. His fingers slid inside her pussy, then out, moving lower to her clit. He rubbed just enough to make her crazy. The moment she pressed her hips down on his hand, he withdrew it. "Soon, baby, soon." Two fingers, already slick with her juices, dragged through the trail of lube. Made small circles over his true, intended destination. Then he was inside her, cock sheathed in her pussy, a single digit in her ass.

"Yes...more..." More she got. More of his cock as he moved inside her. More of his touch as he added a second finger, then a third, setting fire to her nerve endings. Still not enough, she wanted his cock there, stretching and filling her. Making her burn. She drew her bound hands under her chest, using them to lever her bottom higher. "More. Please."

"I'll give you anything. Everything." His fingers and cock withdrew, left her whimpering at the emptiness. "Tell me what you want."

"Fuck me," she whispered.

His chest covered her back, his arms wrapped around her shoulders and head. Protective yet dominant—soothing her and turning her on simultaneously. His lips grazed the sensitive spot behind her ear. Made her shiver in spite of his large, hot body trapping her.

"Fuck you how? Say it. Exactly what you want me to do."

"I want you to..." Oh god, oh god. Her heart kicked into a frenzied gallop against her ribs, beating so hard he probably felt it through the mattress. "Brian, I-I..." No other words came.

"I only want what you want, baby. Ever. I just want to be with you."

Fear, desire, need—she couldn't name the feeling welling in her chest, they'd become one inseparable, overwhelming thing that only he could satisfy. "I want you to fuck my ass, to own every part of me and never let me go. I—" Oh god, it'd happened. She loved him. She shouldn't, but heaven help her, she'd fallen. "Please."

He pushed into her pussy again. Rained soft kisses on her neck while reaching beneath her to draw her arms out and extend them above her head. He pushed up from her back, dragged rough palms over her curves, stroked a finger back and forth through her lube-slicked valley.

"Such an incredible body, I love looking at you." His cock slid free. Traced the path of his finger, then nudged her rear opening. A gentle push and he breached her by a fraction of an inch. "Fuck, I love being inside you. Can't wait to get inside you." He rocked while he eased in and out, so, so slowly. "Breathe. Trust me to give you everything you want."

"I do." She exhaled and let her body go boneless.

"That's my girl." He groaned as he pushed deeper. "So fucking tight—making me crazy, I want inside you so bad."

Her body was on fire, screaming at the invasion yet desperate for him to give her more. All of him. She wanted to tell him. Demand he fuck her fully. Claim her hard, so she'd feel his presence for days, if not forever. All that escaped her lips was a low moan as his balls slapped against her.

"I wish you could see this, your sexy ass taking all of my cock. Your arms tied up for me, the way your lips part when I do this…" He eased back and stroked deep inside her again. Growled and did it again.

"More…god, harder."

"Fuck, Cassie, don't tempt me. You feel too good—I can't—have to go easy."

She clenched, a move that squeezed his cock, making him suck in a strangled breath. "No easy. Give me what I want—to be yours."

One hand spanned her lower back. "You *are* mine."

God, the possession in his voice. Sparks raced to her nipples, her clit. She wiggled, trying to find some friction. He grunted and took another deep stroke into her, driving her needy clit against the folds of the duvet. Enough pressure to tease her higher. Not nearly enough to get the job done.

Whirring sounded from behind. The thing from the drawer—her multi-speed bullet. He slid the vibrator into place between her clit and the bed. Oh god, yes. If she didn't already, she'd love him just for this.

He pulled all the way out, laid a resounding smack on her backside before thrusting back in, fast and hard.

Her guttural moan topped the sweaty slapping of skin. "God, again, all the way out, I love it when your cock pushes inside."

"You're killing me." Again, he withdrew, and again, he filled her in one forceful thrust. "And I fucking love it."

"Yes, like that...*harder.*"

"Christ." Both hands landed on her back, one above the other. He pressed her to the bed. Pushed faster, deeper inside her. "Fuck, can't stop, too good."

Each thrust ground her clit onto the little bullet, pushed her closer. He bore down on her, fucking her like a wild animal. Owning her. Shattering her into a million shining, aching pieces. "God yes, oh..."

He all but roared. Teeth clamped on the back of her neck as his body shuddered on top of her.

She couldn't get air, but didn't tell him, though. Didn't want him to roll off or walk away. Not ever.

Still connected in every place possible, he caged her, taking the bulk of his weight on his forearms. "I need you to breathe, baby." He tugged the end of the satin tie, freeing her hands, then snuck a hand under the heap of their sweaty bodies to scoop away the bullet. "There, better."

"Thank you."

"My pleasure, every single second of it."

"Don't leave," she said, grabbing his hands when he shifted away.

He dealt with the condom, then settled half alongside, half on top of her. Possessive. Protective. "Told you, that's not going to happen." The soft-rough combination of his beard brushed her upper back. He kissed along her shoulder, paying extra homage to the spot he'd claimed with a bite. "I left a mark." His fingers skimmed down her back. Lower, tracing the red ovals that matched his hard grip on her hips from Friday night. "Fuck, here too. You've got bruises, baby. From me."

"Good."

"Good? I hurt you. That's not good."

"You've never hurt me. I swear."

His body tensed and his jaw ticked. "Your body has proof of the opposite. I need to get control."

"Don't you dare." She shook her head and snuggled in closer. "I love having a reminder of you on my skin."

His body tensed and his jaw ticked. "You've got a few, from the looks of it."

"Even better."

"Cassie…"

She pulled back enough for their eyes to meet. "Stop worrying. I promised you the moon, remember?"

"I do."

God, his smile. All for her. She curled into his neck again. "I love the things you do to me. I—" She caught her tongue in the nick of time. Two usages of "love" already. She was in dangerous territory, especially with her emotions running high and unchecked. "I don't want anything to change."

He hugged her tighter, nuzzling the top of her head. "It'll only get better."

If only that were true. Between her secrets and his work troubles, they had so much stacked against them. Maybe too much. "Can you let me up? I need to use the washroom."

"Yeah, of course." He shifted off her, watching as she stood. "Here, you might want this."

The tie to her robe. She caught the end he offered and pulled, only to be tugged off her jelly legs and back onto the bed by the handsome, grinning force at the other end. "Um, this isn't the way to the washroom."

"You told me never to let you go."

"I didn't mean it literally." Crap, she'd walked right into that confession.

"Glad to hear it." One hand cupped her breast. His arm curled around her and dragged her tight to his body. "Your heart's racing."

"I'm—" Truth or evasion? With how completely honest he'd been about every corner of his life, she owed him the same, even if it broke her heart in the end. "I'm scared."

"Of?"

"You losing your job because of me. That's what I planned to do at the gym tonight, then what I tried to do when your boss saw us—end this." She angled toward him. Under her palm, his heartbeat thumped along lazily, the perfect pace to accompany the gentle eyes looking into her soul. "I know what I *should* do...and yet here I am, selfishly jeopardizing your future." There, truth. Not the whole truth, but her hand was on a hard pectoral muscle, not a stack of bibles.

"I'm not going to lose my job."

"Your boss bought the scene where you pushed me away? You think we can pull off sneaking around if I steer clear of you at the gym?"

At the mention of Trevor Ritchie, Brian's eyebrows drew together and his eyes narrowed. "Yeah, he believed that I dropped you. But I still broke my contract conditions. He saw us together."

"You mean…"

"Yeah." The Adam's apple bobbed in Brian's throat. "Through the glass in the front doors. He saw me fucking you. Saw all of it."

"Oh my god."

"I'm sorry. If I could go back and change things, I would." The corner of his mouth ticked up. "I should've taken you around the corner and bent you over the preacher-curl bench instead. Perfect height for spanking and out of view of all windows. Maybe next time."

"Brian!" The mattress jiggled from his laughter. If he could make light of the situation, maybe she hadn't screwed him out of his job, literally. "What now? I should probably switch gyms, to be on the safe side."

A sweet intensity replaced the twinkle in his eyes. He toyed with the piece of hair that kept falling over her face, tucking it behind her ear, his fingers lingering on her cheek. "You'd do that?"

"Of course I would. I'd miss ogling you every day while I'm working out, but if you're fired from Iron Works, I won't have you to look at *and* you'll be unemployed." And he'd hate her, which would tear her heart out.

"You don't need to switch gyms."

By the clenched jaw, there was more to it. "But…?"

"Trevor offered me a deal that'll let me keep my job and give me the sliver of Iron Works he's been dangling in my face for six months."

"That's great news." She wrestle-hugged him onto his back. The kiss she planted was met with tight lips. "It's not great news?"

"Yes and no. Yes to what I'll get out of the deal. No to what that scumbag wants in return."

"What does he want?"

"He wants you."

Chapter 10

CASSIE

IN HER LIFETIME, Cassie had made some mistakes where men were concerned.

A month into the eleventh grade she'd given up her virginity in the backseat of a restored '69 Mustang to a boy who'd promised she was *the one*. Only she wasn't. Len got back together with his former girlfriend before the tenderness between Cassie's legs had eased. Mistake number one, tagged as Len Schneider.

College and her twenties spawned a few more regrettable moments. The doozy in her life, though—at least to this point —had been Lance. The Lance era in general, but the weekend when she'd let him pressure her into trying drugs ranked high on the list. One trip. It'd loosen their inhibitions and take their sexual relationship to the next level, he'd claimed. Oh the bullshit she'd believed from that asshole. High on ecstasy, she'd then given in to his longstanding wish for a threesome. Lance's choice for their third—a female intern from his rotation at the hospital. Threesome only loosely described what'd happened. More like authorized infidelity and forced voyeurism. Not so much fun, watching her fiancé with another woman, even with chemical euphoria running through her veins. And it hadn't smartened her up any either.

The testosterone and trust combo had never worked out for her, yet here she was at Iron Works, about to toss them into the figurative blender. And once again, she was justifying her impending stupidity in the name of love.

She stopped in front of the building and took a fortifying breath, finger-checking her barrettes while she exhaled. Nervous habit, it's not as if she wanted to look her best. She'd chosen the drabbest, ugliest thing she owned, a shapeless plaid dress that made her look frumpy and flat-chested. Anything to lessen her appeal. Though, when she'd modeled it for Brian earlier, it certainly hadn't turned *him* off.

Brian. She sighed, one of those over-the-moon sighs that hopelessly in love women made. He needed her help. And help the man she'd utterly fallen for? Call that a no-brainer. She'd signed up on the spot, even though helping involved making friendlier than she'd like with his horrible, creepy boss. Once Brian's job was secure, she'd tackle her own. Work on building her photography business strictly in the blinds-open areas.

That's how it had to be if she wanted a shot at the fairy-tale. Yes, the logical part of her knew Brian wasn't Lance, but every time she considered simply talking to Brian, telling him about the very confidential side of her work, Lance's reaction, his deceit, choked her speechless. So she'd quit. Without those jobs, there'd be a lot less income, but she'd have nothing to hide. No more worries, rational or otherwise, about what *could* happen if Brian knew her secrets. The secrets were her past.

If they could get through this Trevor mess, happily ever after with Brian might be her future.

The massive man who made her heart flutter and her body sing smiled when she stepped through the heavy door. Not the full-face grin she'd fallen for months ago and now had the pleasure of seeing at intimately close range, but enough to give her strength for the chore ahead. Though her instinct was to smile back, she schooled her face into a more appropriate expression. He'd fucked her and sent her packing last night, or so his boss believed. For now, that's how they had to play it.

She raised her eyebrows in question. A subtle head tilt toward the offices told her what she needed to know. Trevor was here. As expected, since she'd called him this morning to arrange a meeting.

"Hey." Brian's voice halted her just shy of Trevor's door. "I'll be right here."

Thank god. She nodded, raised her fist and knocked, shuddering when he called her in. This was a business meeting with a potential client. With any luck, Trevor would see her in the grandma dress and have second thoughts about wanting that date. If not, she was really going to need Brian as backup.

As soon as the office door closed behind her, Cassie's mouth kicked into sales mode. "Thanks for the opportunity to pitch my work. I brought samples of promotional shots and the resulting media for a variety of businesses—"

"Whoa, slow down. Save something for our dinner meeting."

And there went the bottom of her stomach.

"I've done my research, had a good look at your work online. It's safe to say the Iron Works job is yours, Cassie." Trevor raised his index finger when she opened her mouth to jump in. "I'm not much of a desk-pusher, I'm only here because you called. We'll discuss details over dinner. Are you free tomorrow night?"

"I'm busy tomorrow. Any other night will be fine." No way was she giving up time with Brian to do this ugly deed, even it was going to get her a nice, legit project.

Trevor leaned back in his chair, a smile so slick it couldn't possibly be genuine sliding across his thin lips. "It'll be better than fine. Our dinner date is going to change your life."

Good god, the conceit. She forced a smile and focused on thoughts of the future—the exposure she'd get from the Iron Works job, the money it'd bring in, the freedom to be with Brian, publicly, after she'd given Trevor what he wanted…only that last bit curled her stomach so badly, she almost lost the veggie pita she'd had for lunch. She and Brian had danced around what Trevor might've meant when he'd told Brian he "wanted a crack at her". The possibilities were nauseating. Surely Trevor wouldn't expect her to sleep with him. And if it came to that—having sex with Trevor to secure Brian's career —would she do it?

"You know what, let's make it Saturday. The best chefs always work weekends. I'll make a reservation and pick you up at five thirty."

"Saturday, sure." Merely shaking his hand made her skin crawl. "Where are we going, so I know what to wear?" Also so she could call ahead to ensure they had a well-lit, non-cozy table.

"Don't worry about dress code. Whatever you choose, I'm sure to be the envy of every man in the place."

Sweet words she refused to acknowledge, given the source. "I'll see you Saturday."

———

CASSIE

She'd had to juggle appointments to free up her Wednesday evening. Now, thanks to her current client's *third* pee break, Cassie was officially behind schedule. Brian would be here to pick her up any minute. She couldn't exactly push the pregnant lady out the door, but if she and Brian were going to be late to his parents' for dinner, it should be for more exciting reasons.

"Cassie, I'm here." Brian's deep voice filtered down the basement stairs.

"Oh crap," she muttered, skirting the seating area to catch him before he descended. "I'm finishing up with a client, shouldn't be too long."

"Is it okay if I come down?"

"Um, no…hang on a few." This wasn't an explicit shoot, but Debra had been dressed in her bra and pants for the last hands-on-the-belly shot. Movement caught Cassie's eye. Debra had exited the washroom, shirt on, face flushed and eyes wide. "Don't worry, he'll wait upstairs until we're done."

"We're done now." Debra's head shook like a bobble-head doll in the hands of a rowdy two-year-old.

"There's no rush to finish the shoot, honestly. Let's take a look at the images we've got and figure out what we still need."

"Whatever we've got will have to do. My water broke. It's baby time."

"Oh my god, Deb, that's wonderful…" Oh no. In conversation, Debra had told her she had a few more weeks to go. "You're early. You need to get to the hospital." Cassie darted for the cordless phone on her desk. "Who do I call—Richard? An ambulance? Somebody else, or should I take you?"

"Relax, you're stressing more than I am." Debra laughed,

hands sliding over her big belly. "This is baby number three, which practically makes me an expert at this labor gig. I texted Richard from the bathroom, he's on his way over. Pretty sure the baby'll keep cooking until we get to the hospital."

How could Debra be so calm about the impending delivery? Thinking about what it entailed had Cassie's gut—and lady parts—clenching.

Debra bent half over, clutched her belly and moaned. "Not another one…"

"Lie down before you fall down."

"No way," Debra said, breathing through the end of a contraction while eyeing the white sofa. "I'm not getting baby juice all over your fancy couch."

"It's leather, the baby juice will wipe off. Come on." No amount of tugging on Debra's arm budged her. "Geez. You're strong for a woman in a delicate condition."

"Delicate?" Debra snorted. "Honey, I'm toting an extra fifty pounds. Nothing delicate about that. You wait—one day you'll know what I'm talking about."

Kids were part of her happily ever after dream, but seeing Debra in this state made Cassie's ovaries shrink in on themselves, with no sign of baby lust. "What are you doing now?"

"Going upstairs to wait for Richard." Debra turned on the second step. "Unless you want to photograph the birth on your prop bed?"

"I think the hospital is a better choice than my studio, but if you want me to go with you to take pictures, I will." Even though it'd mean canceling on Brian—he'd understand.

"Honey, you're an amazing photographer, but I really don't need pictures of *that*."

Oh thank god. "If you're not going to rest while you wait for Richard, at least let me help you."

"If this," Debra's hands did a sweep of her body, "falls on

you, you'll be flattened. You're worse than a nattering mother, you know that? Stand back and let me climb the damn stairs."

"Not without help." Cassie eyed the stairwell. Had to be done. "Brian, we could use you down here."

He was on the landing before Debra could haul herself up another step. And good god, he looked delicious. Cassie had teased him about wanting to see this, and there he stood, wearing a tan kilt, black boots and t-shirt, putting her imagination to shame.

"On second thought, maybe I should watch some of your next photo shoot while I wait." Debra turned her head toward Cassie and mouthed, *Holy shit*.

"Brian's not here to pose for me," Cassie said as he carefully sidestepped Debra and took the position behind her, for safety. "Though I wouldn't mind if he did."

"You're the new boyfriend?" In spinning to get a better look, Debra wobbled and nearly lost her balance.

Good thing Brian was right there to steady her. "I am." His hands stayed on Debra's lower back and arm, gently supporting her as she resumed climbing. "The newest and the last, if I have my way."

This time Debra's laugh was more of a girlish giggle. Cassie didn't blame her for falling victim to Brian's looks and charm, especially today. As they reached the back door, Richard appeared on the stoop, grinning ear to ear at the sight of his wife. The absolute adoration Richard had for Debra, even in her much-enlarged state, struck Cassie straight through to her core. Another example of enduring true love she'd had the good fortune to document in images over the years. Her eyes left the blissful couple and settled on Brian. Maybe it was her turn for a happily ever after. God, she wanted that.

They followed the repeat-parents-to-be out. Cassie waved

as Richard helped Debra into the passenger seat of a minivan. "Call me when you have news."

"Will do." Debra stuck out her hand, raised in a thumbs-up.

"Pretty sure that was about you," Cassie said as the van drove away. Now that she had him alone, looking the way he did, all bets at getting back on schedule were off. "You're wearing a kilt." Not the traditional tartan kind, but jaw-droppingly sexy, nonetheless. "I didn't know they came in plain colors like that."

"They do. They're utility kilts. I have a couple others like this, plus the old-school clan colors for special occasions."

Sparks skittered up her arm when Brian closed his fingers around hers and led her back inside the house. "I'm going to need to see those."

"That means you'll be joining me for more family stuff then, because that's usually when I haul them out."

The suggestion sent a thrill through her body. He wanted her with him at family events, had stated his desire to be her last-ever boyfriend. Things felt so good right now. So hopeful. The sexy photo business was over. All she needed to do was get through one evening with Trevor. She could do that. Look at the prize waiting for her once she did.

Ack, waiting. She dropped his fingers and started for the stairs. "Sorry, that client-going-into-labor thing threw me off schedule. I'll be ready to go in a couple of minutes."

"No rush. For you, I'll wait as long as it takes."

His eyes told her he meant the words in a bigger way. How soon was too soon to tell him how *she* felt? Once his horrible boss had signed Brian's new contract and she'd informed all her private clients about her decision, she'd have nothing to hide. That's when she'd tell him. Until then, she'd keep on showing him, every chance she got.

"You okay?" He stepped closer to stroke a finger over her cheek. "Worried about your client having her baby?"

"No—I mean, yes. But no." Cue airhead moment. "Yes, I'm okay. No, I wasn't thinking about Debra. I was thinking about you and…us."

"I like the sound of the second part."

"So do I." She bit her lip as her cheeks warmed. "Want to come down with me while I put things away and shut off the lights?"

"Yeah, I'd like that."

"Great." No point in being nervous, there was nothing down there he shouldn't see. No nude photos hanging on the walls. No kinky props lying around—those were tucked away in a cupboard. When they reached the bottom, she did a wide one-arm sweep of the basement. "So, this is my studio, such as it is, currently."

"Nice. A lot bigger than I expected. Is it okay if I look around?"

"Sure." She patted him on his kilted butt and left him to it. She'd used two cameras for Debra's pregnant-mama sitting, so she set about removing memory cards and lenses, packing the pieces away in protective cases. His arms closed around her waist, making her jump a little—and tingle a lot. Good call, inviting him down here.

"I realize that I have no frame of reference, but I'm impressed. This is where you take most of the pictures, in front of this big white cove thing?"

"A lot of them. With the correct lighting," she tipped her head at one of several umbrellas, "I can virtually eliminate shadows, or control them."

His beard rasped her neck, his breath on her skin raising her nipples inside her sleeveless blouse. "Keep talking. I like hearing about your work."

Oh yes. Proof of how much he liked it was lined up against the crack of her ass. She rolled her hips against the hard ridge, making him curse softly into her ear. "I—" She whimpered as his hand pulled up the front of her skirt and slipped inside her panties. "I have backdrops I can roll down if the shot calls for it, but—" Oh god, two talented fingers had her clit in a ready-to-come sandwich.

"But?"

"But, um, with commercial work, the background is often…often…" Her knees buckled, but she didn't fall. Not with Brian's thickly muscled arm holding her in place while he tortured her by increasing the friction between her legs.

"The background is often what?"

"Added in later by graphic artists." The words tumbled in a near-incoherent stream as she strained to get more pressure where she needed it.

"Cool," he said, withdrawing his hand before she crested over the edge. "Show me something else."

"But—aren't you going to—I didn't—"

"I know." He chuckled and turned her in his arms. "Neither did I, cutie."

"I'd be happy to fix that for you. Is it true what they say about men who wear kilts?" The twill reached his knees, but she got her hand underneath easily enough. Yup, nothing but fine, bare buns under there. She dragged her nails around his hip, smiling victoriously when he moved back to grant her access to his cock. "I'm going to lobby for you to wear these more often." She pumped his erection with a tight fist. "I'm a fan of this easy access to my favorite toy."

A deep laugh filled the room. "Is it now? I've seen the contents of your nightstand drawer."

"I don't need any of that stuff," time to go for it, tell him, if only a little, "as long as I have you."

He smiled as if she'd given him the best compliment ever. Bent and kissed her, claiming her again. Soft lips, firm control. His tongue danced with hers. A palm on her behind brought her forward, crushing them together, trapping her hand and his rigid cock between their bodies.

Maybe this would be a good time to point out she had a bed in her studio. Or tell him to bend her over the end of the couch. Up against the wall would do nicely too.

"Are you ready?" He breathed the question into her ear, making her shiver.

"God yes."

"Then let's get going." A hearty smack on her behind and he stepped away, leaving her gaping like a goldfish.

"That's it? What about…you know."

"Later." He followed up with a wink. "Worth waiting for, don't you think?"

Oh now she got it. He wanted to play the tease-you-until-you're-frantic game. No problem—two could play at that. "I can wait. Oh, and I hope you like the color blue." Because that would be the state of his balls before this game ended.

BRIAN

Ten minutes into the half-hour drive to his parents' house, Cassie unfastened her seat belt. Given how long it'd taken him to convince her to ride in the Jeep with the top and doors off, and the way she'd white-knuckled the roll-bar when he took the corner onto the back road, something had to be up. He looked her way long enough to see the mischievous smile decorating her full lips. Oh yeah, something naughty was definitely going through that pretty head.

"It's going to be a hot one today."

Innocent chitchat? He'd bite. "I like the heat. You?"

"Mmm-hmm. The hotter things get, the better."

He had to chuckle at that one. The blush on Cassie's cheeks gave her away—this conversation had zero to do with the weather.

Today her nails were painted a Caribbean blue. Nice, especially in contrast to the white shirt, whose buttons they were flicking open one by one. She pulled the ends free from her skirt. Reached inside and unhooked a skin-colored bra, pulled it out one armhole and tossed it aside. She slid the sleeveless shirt off her shoulders, letting it pool around her elbows. Not fully topless, but fully fucking sexy. Hell, she could wear anything—or nothing—and he'd get hard just from looking at her.

A prime example was yesterday, when she tried on the ugly dress from the back of her closet. She'd even put on granny panties. Giant, god-awful underwear he could hardly believe she owned. And what'd he done? Laid her out on the coffee table, pushed the cotton briefs to one side and tongued her 'til she came on his face, then pinned her arms to her side and fucked her hard enough to move that huge-ass piece of metal and glass a foot across the floor. Today's exercise in abstinence and patience was one stupid fucking plan.

Christ, was it ever. Cassie turned under her refastened seat belt, facing him with a coy grin and very pert nipples. Sexy. Adorable. Totally destroying him and he loved it.

If he thought he couldn't get more distracted, he'd thought wrong. She dragged those blue nails all over her skin, leaving faint red tracks he wanted to trace with his tongue. "That's hot. You're hot." He spread his legs to accommodate his expanding cock. "I love your nipples."

"You mean these little things…" She caught each one

between her thumb and index finger and pulled, stretching them and making herself moan.

"Yeah. I'm pulling over so I can do that."

"Oh no, you're not." She cupped the objects of his attention, hiding them from view. "Some things are worth waiting for, don't you think?"

"Fuck." Burned.

"I'll assume that's a yes. Time to move on." She'd obviously studied his kilt some, because she reached across and found the opening in the time it took him to blink.

"Cassie," he hissed as she stroked him while arranging his kilt to her liking. She slipped the shoulder belt under her arm so she could lean over. He knew what to expect, but when she lowered her head and sealed her lips around his tip—holy fucking hell. He was going to drive into the ditch and kill them both.

Up and down she worked him. Her tongue flattened against his shaft, her cheeks hollowed from suction, her teeth scraped the head, nice and rough, the way he liked. So good. Air hit his dampened cock as she let him pop free of her mouth.

He cupped the back of her head before she could right herself. "Not so fast, you're not done down there." Thank god they were alone on the rural road. Gave him leeway with the lanes while he met her eyes. Defiance—yeah, it was there. A hint of it, ringing the giant pupils that told him how badly she wanted to give in, give him what he wanted. What she wanted too.

Little pixie dropped a closed-mouth kiss on his tip, then slipped out of his grip. "Later."

If they were at home, he'd have her on her knees for that, sucking him until he couldn't take one more second. But this was a different game. One that made him laugh out loud, despite the heat she'd stirred at the base of his cock. "I look forward to later."

"So do I." She picked up her bra and twirled it, but made no move toward covering up.

Taunting him? All right, then. "There's a little farming town ahead. We're going to pass some houses, a gas station and a couple of stores. You're going to make their day."

"Oh crap." She hurried to refasten her bra and shirt, finishing the job as they slowed for the residential area. "Thanks."

"You're welcome." The town boasted one stop sign at the main crossroads. The Jeep rolled to a full stop and he leaned across for a taste of her juicy pink lips. "The warning was mostly selfish, though. I'm not interested in sharing you with anybody, not even gawkers at a distance."

Her smile wavered as he accelerated. Once they'd cleared the town, he took a longer look in his peripheral vision. No more playfulness. She stared out the windshield, but he doubted she saw any of the trees overhanging the road or the fluffy clouds in the brilliant blue sky. Not with the faraway expression she wore.

"What's going on in there?" he asked, stroking the soft, loose waves of hair by her temple. Under his fingers, she shook her head slightly. "Come on, tell me." Her eyes were wide as ever, beautiful as always, but definitely unsettled. Shit. "Did I do something? I'll try to fix it, whatever it is."

"It's what you said about not sharing me."

Not the answer he'd expected. At all. "Is this where I find out you're into three-ways?"

"Oh my god, no. No, no, no."

"Good."

"Really? You don't have some secret fantasy to have two women at once?"

The question made him squirm a little, so he used the moment to settle his kilt back into a respectable position. "Pretty sure all heterosexual men have had that fantasy." In his case, he'd done more than fantasize, he'd lived it. A couple of times. "But I'm past mine. I love watching you get off—fuck, I get hard thinking about the way your eyes glaze over and your mouth falls open when you come—but the idea of anybody else taking you to that point, even another woman, makes me want to smash things."

"What if it was the other way around? You wouldn't like to watch me eating some hot chick's pussy?"

This had to be a test. "No."

"And you wouldn't like permission to fuck another woman, maybe from behind while she sucks my nipples and I rub myself off?"

Stupid, traitorous cock, rising to the suggestions coming out of Cassie's mouth. Casually, he placed a hand over his lap. "Definitely not."

"Because I won't do those things for you." She crossed her arms over her chest. "The day I'm not enough, turn around and walk away."

The words were directed at him, but the tension beneath them came from somewhere else. Somebody else. And from the bits and pieces she'd told him so far, he had a good idea who.

"Hey," he closed a hand over her thigh, "I'm not him. I'm never going to be him."

Her head fell back against the seat and turned his way. "I know that. I do."

He slowed for the bend that rolled into his hometown, catching her hand for a squeeze once they'd cleared it. "For the record, the same goes for me. I won't give you permission to be with another man. The only other cock that's getting near you while we're together is the artificial kind."

"What about Trevor?" she whispered, not looking at him. "Ow, Brian, my fingers…"

"*Fuck.* Sorry." He dropped her hand and administered the death grip to the wheel instead. "Whatever happened in that prick's office, whatever he asked for, tell me now." Stupid, selfish ass. He should never have agreed to let her *help* with his boss.

"Nothing happened. He insisted we discuss details of the Iron Works job over a nice dinner. He didn't touch me or demand anything, but he's so," her hands wrung in her lap, "pervy. And after what he said to you about wanting a crack at me…what if that means sexually? What if he expects more than a conversation and dinner?"

The leather-wrapped steering wheel squeaked under his grip. Yeah, more was exactly what Trevor had in mind. Brian knew it because Trevor had all but spelled it out. Trevor wouldn't rape Cassie—he'd expect her to willingly open her legs for him on Saturday night. Brian had essentially pimped out his girlfriend to the scum of the earth. For a job, for fuck's sake.

"He'll give you the gym project. Have the dinner meeting, thank him up and down so he knows how important he is, then leave—alone. I can wait in the parking lot if you're worried." And he *would* wait, even if she declined, just to be sure.

"That'll satisfy him enough to save your job?"

The options in front of him sucked. The truth would be like pressuring her to get naked with Trevor. A lie was, well, a lie. He didn't deal in those.

He decelerated at the edge of town. Focused on the familiar

houses and hundred-year-old maples that lined Main Street. At Young Street, he hung a right, then another right onto Smithson Avenue. Half a block up, he parked in front of the two-story of his childhood and killed the engine. He released his seat belt and faced her. Time up, he needed to answer.

"It might be enough, it might not." He cupped her soft face. God, she was perfect. Beautiful, sexy, talented and *his*, damn it. "It's only a job. And the conditions I agreed to for that job are my fault. I don't regret breaking the terms to be with you, regardless of what happens."

Her seat belt clicked free. She shimmied as close as the Jeep's bucket-seating would allow and wrapped her arms around his neck. "I really want to make out with you right now. Do you think anybody's watching?"

One glance toward the house confirmed what he would've guessed. "Definitely. Dad's in the driveway, Mom's staring at us through the front window." He dropped one hand to her leg, then snuck it up the middle of her skirt and under the strip of material between her legs. "But don't let that stop you from climbing onto my lap and sticking your tongue in my mouth."

"Brian…" She wriggled and bit into her bottom lip. "Stop that."

"I told you I'd make you come later. It's later." He eased two fingers inside her while working her clit with his thumb. "And you're so wet, I know you want to. A little one, before my dad gets to the Jeep. You've got about ten seconds."

"Oh god, seriously?"

He laughed as she scrambled backward in her seat. "I underestimated, you probably had eighteen seconds."

"You're horrible," she said, then, "I'm not all hot-and-bothered looking, am I?"

"You're perfect, baby." He leaned over for a kiss before she could protest. "Come meet the family."

CASSIE

Dinner with the Blacks. Easy peasy, they seemed like nice people. A little in-your-face, but in a well-meaning way.

Angus, Brian's dad, had gathered her into a massive bear hug as soon as she stepped out of the Jeep, lifting her off the ground as if she were a child. Compared to him, she was built like one. Angus and Brian were on par for height at six-two, the older man's shoulders as wide as his son's. The ginger hair and beard must have been part of the DNA too, though Angus' was longer on top and on the chin.

Wedged between the two giants, she'd been shepherded into the house to meet Brian's mom. That'd been a surprise. Especially after seeing Angus, she'd expected a tall woman, one with long hair and a sturdy frame. She couldn't have guessed more incorrectly. Cassie was almost eye to eye with Fiona Black. Almost in that Fiona was shorter by an inch or two. She had short, spiky hair a shade darker than Cassie's. Honestly, Fiona looked more like she could be Cassie's mother than Brian's. Maybe that should've given her the willies—the possibility that Brian had a mama complex—but instead she had a warm, comfortable feeling in her chest. And when Fiona had embraced her, she'd felt utterly at home.

A rather large glass of wine later, Cassie was making herself very at home on a cushy bench seat in Fiona's kitchen, staring out the window at Brian and his dad. "Is this normal behavior for them?"

"Pulling on the old stump? That's part of their bonding

routine."

"Pulling?" A resounding *thwack* came through the screen as Brian forced his dad's knuckles against the weathered wood for the third time in a row.

"Pulling—arm wrestling."

"I've never heard it called that."

"Brian's never taken you to the pub on match night?" Fiona raised a dark eyebrow at her, then went back to peeling and chopping. "Probably didn't want to show off too much. He's my modest, unassuming boy. It's the other one who's full of himself."

To hear Brian referred to as a boy made Cassie smile. But Fiona was right, he was modest and unassuming—except when they got naked. "Is your other son coming for Angus' birthday dinner?"

"No, he had to work. Modeling for some la-di-da menswear ad at the harbor, as much as that's working. Enough about Ian. Ask Brian to take you upstairs later and show you his trophies."

She pried her eyes from the show out back to look at Fiona. "He won trophies for arm wrestling?"

"Among other things." The last potato plopped into the pot of water. Hands on her hips, Fiona turned and gave Cassie another arched eyebrow. "How long have you known him?"

"A few months."

"The way he talked about you on the phone and how he looks at you, I assumed it was longer."

"It feels longer." It felt like the beginning of forever.

"That's good." Fiona wiped her hands on a towel and came to stand beside Cassie for a view of the men. "Nobody believes in simply falling in love anymore. Always overanalyzing and planning and worrying, instead of following the heart where it wants to go. You're in love, dive in. That's what I did with Angus. Plenty of bumps along the way, but I wouldn't want anybody else."

Sometimes it wasn't as easy as Fiona's philosophy, but Cassie wasn't about to argue with the petite matriarch. "Thank you for the advice."

A small but sure hand curled over Cassie's shoulder. "I hope you take it. I've waited a long time for another woman in this house to balance out three Blacks' worth of testosterone." When Cassie looked up at her, Fiona nodded. "Family rule. Once they moved out, I told the boys they can only bring home women they're planning to keep. I don't want to get attached to anyone they're not invested in." Fiona patted her shoulder. "You're the first, my dear."

What should she say to that? "I hope I'll get to keep you company in the future."

"Me too," Fiona said with a final pat before wandering toward the oven.

Another crack of bone on wood drifted in from the yard.

Cassie grimaced as Angus wiped a smear of blood from his hand. "I'm not sure how this is bonding. Brian should give his dad a rest."

Fiona's songlike laugh filled the kitchen. "Oh, darling. Good thing Angus didn't hear that. And you wait, you've not seen anything yet. After dinner they'll have the axes swinging, seeing who can chop wood fastest."

Her panties might burst into flame watching Brian wielding an ax, especially while in a kilt. "Would it be okay if I go out there to watch?"

After a peek at whatever delicious-smelling thing she had cooking in the oven, Fiona linked arms with Cassie and nodded toward the back door. "Wait 'til you see what happens when they've an audience."

Chapter 11

CASSIE

AT THE SIGHT of their women setting foot on the patio, both men peeled off their shirts. Chests puffed out, shoulders straightened and biceps flexed none-too-subtly.

"See what I mean about testosterone?" Fiona tipped her head close to Cassie's. "Give them a wave or such, watch how ridiculous they get."

Fiona was clearly a troublemaker of the best kind. Cassie already adored the woman.

"I can do better than that." She left Fiona in a deck chair, her pulse picking up the closer she got to the stump. She'd intended to kiss Brian, but now that she was standing before the men, she had a better idea. "Happy birthday, Angus," she said, stretching to plant a chaste peck on the man's cheek. "I love your kilt."

Oh, the whooping that rose from that yard. She'd been to wedding receptions less noisy than the laughter from these three people.

"I like this bonnie lass of yours." The twinkle in Angus' eyes matched his son's. "I think she wants to see me kick your arse." The older man winked, dropped one elbow on the stump and crooked his finger at his son. "Lefts. Come on, boy, let's pull."

She wouldn't have thought it possible after watching Brian repeatedly best his dad minutes earlier, but when it came to left-handed *pulling*, he didn't stand a chance against Angus.

Over and over, Angus pinned Brian, hollering, "Match!" loud enough to be heard throughout the neighborhood.

They'd set up again, Brian saying, "Ready, go", and the cycle would repeat.

Adirondack chairs were meant for relaxing, but she'd only used the edge of hers since returning to the patio.

"You look a bit pale, darling," Fiona said with a chuckle. "Did you think he was invincible?"

"Pretty much." Each time Angus smashed Brian's hand against the wood, Cassie cringed. "He won't be able to train clients if he can't grip the weights."

"Guess he ought to call it quits, then...though I've never seen that happen. Stubborn, those Scotsmen."

The next match must've hurt like a son-of-a-gun because Brian shot a string of curses at his dad while shaking off the pain. Angus' response was to laugh and call Brian a bunch of names Cassie'd never heard, but could guess the meaning of. Enough was enough already.

She pushed up from the chair and marched across the grass. "Why don't you two quit? Come sit and talk for a bit before dinner?"

"Quit? Not I." Angus folded meaty arms over his chest and raised a thick russet eyebrow at Brian. "How about you, boy—ready to admit defeat?"

She stopped Brian before he could answer, wrapping her hands around the bulging muscles in his arm and urging him to her level so she could whisper in his ear. "I need your hands in good working order later."

The fun-loving sparkle in his eyes turned hotter. He slid his hand around her waist, pulled her tight against his body, squeezing the air from her lungs with a startled whoosh. "I give. You win."

Whether he was talking to his dad or to her, Cassie wasn't sure. Nor did she care.

"Fiona...you were right," Angus called across the yard. "The boy's in love." A hearty smack landed on Brian's back, then Angus ambled off to join his wife.

And hadn't that just put the two of them on the spot. Even more so when Angus collected Fiona and disappeared inside the house.

"I really like your parents."

"I'm glad. I see them as much as possible. I'd hate dragging you along if they irritated you."

Her heart did a little dance in her chest. "Not at all, they're great."

"And they're right." His hands roamed up and down her back, one staking a claim under the curve of her butt, the other much higher, cupping the back of her neck as he looked into her eyes. "I'm in love with you."

BRIAN

He'd said it. Not the way he'd imagined it going down, and definitely not the place. To hell with planning a moment with candles and soft music, it'd felt right. The only thing that'd make it more right would be Cassie returning the sentiment.

Not quite what he got, but the "Oh, Brian" as she threw her arms around his neck and the frenzied pace of her heart hammering against his chest were close enough.

He pressed his face to her neck and inhaled. "You smell so good. I'm tempted to take you behind the wood pile and have a taste." On cue, his cock thickened and shifted to a north-pointing position.

"Take me to your old room instead. Your mom did say you should show me your trophies."

"Oh, I've got a trophy to show you." He scooped up his t-shirt, grabbed her hand and headed for the house.

"Where're you going—the food's almost ready," his mom said as they breezed through the kitchen to the stairs.

"Cassie wants to see my trophies."

"Well, don't take too long," came the warning from down-stairs. "And wash up before you come to the table."

His hands, yes. Anything else that got *dirty* while they were up here, no way. He loved Cassie's scent on his skin. In his beard. Anywhere and everywhere he could get it.

The floorboards creaked in the same places they always had as he steered her along the narrow upstairs hall. A collage of family photos dressed the wall on their left, catching her eye and slowing her step. "Keep moving," he said, giving her ass a smack. "First door's mine. In you go, cutie."

"Wow, this room is all bed." Cassie's eyes roamed the trophies and plaques on an overhead shelf as her hand trailed along the navy-blue comforter on his old queen-size.

The door clicked behind his back. "When you're a six-foot-two fifteen-year-old, you warrant something larger than a twin."

"I guess so." She pushed down on the mattress, a cheeky smile tipping her lips. "Ever sneak girls up here to try it out?"

"Don't I wish. You met the people downstairs, right? Even if I'd managed to get somebody past the guards," he tossed a nod toward the door, "there's no lock. They're all about full disclosure. Made jerking off an adventure, never knowing who might open the damn door."

Her smile turned to a giggle. "You poor thing."

"Yeah, now it's on you to help me make up for missed experiences."

Her eyes dropped to the front of his kilt, then to the door, then back to his face. "There's still no lock."

Small room that it was, he had her trapped within seconds. "Long as the springs don't squeak too much, or you don't scream too loud, we should be fine."

"Should be?"

"On the bed, ass at the edge, with your skirt to the waist." And up she went, as directed. Fuck, he loved it when she obeyed. Of course, he also loved it when she acted like a feisty, defiant brat. Being with Cassie defined win-win. He hooked the sides of her black string-bikini panties and pulled. "I'll take these." In the cargo pocket of his kilt they went. He spread her legs with his hips, went to his knees and looped her soft, warm thighs over his shoulders. "And I'll take this." One lick and his hips jutted forward automatically, seeking entrance to a prize that wasn't available—yet. "You taste so fucking good." Another swipe of his tongue had her arching to meet his mouth. "That's my girl, press your pussy against my face."

His girl did exactly that. Opened wider, tilted for him. Seared his skull with the tracks of her nails.

"Hey." His dad's deep voice accompanied a single, solid thump that rattled the paneled wood door. "You're not married yet. You've got sixty seconds to get to the table."

"Shit."

"Oh my god, did he *hear* us?" She skittered off the bed, yanking her skirt so hard she probably lengthened it several inches in the process. "I need my underwear."

He pulled the t-shirt over his head. Gave the raging hard-on tenting his kilt a shove to one side. Cassie's eyes tracked every movement. Still glassy and dilated from her almost-orgasm. Hungry looking. As a test, he stuck his hand down front and adjusted his cock some more—a mistake since he needed it to go down, and touching himself while watching her tongue slide along her bottom lip was definitely having the opposite effect. Christ.

"My underwear," she said again, this time in a raspy whisper that made his balls roil with heat.

"Are mine now." This time, when he snagged her hand to tow her along, she didn't follow as willingly.

She leaned into him from the top stair. Whispered in his ear, "Do I smell like sex? Are they going to be able to tell we were doing stuff?"

Hell yes to both, but she'd go six shades of red if he told her. No lying, though. That left evasion. "My dad'll probably say something in hopes of embarrassing me. You should be good."

"There's that *should be* again."

He chuckled, took the last step down and led the way into the kitchen, Cassie tucked behind him. His mom rolled her eyes and his dad grinned widely enough to look borderline maniacal. They weren't mad, not really. Just being their normal, in-your-face, controlling selves. When in their house, follow their rules—even if he was a thirty-one-year-old man.

CASSIE

Miracle of miracles, they hadn't gotten caught with Brian's face between her legs, or worse, had Angus come to the door a minute later. Though both Brian's parents gifted her with knowing looks after settling at the table, they didn't say one word.

Then the meal started. Since it was Angus' birthday dinner, they were having his favorites, Fiona explained while serving the first course. No salad for a man like Angus. Its replacement in the appetizer category—Scotch eggs. Hard-boiled eggs wrapped in sausage meat, rolled in seasoned crumbs, then pan-fried in oil. Delicious, but dear god, her arteries…not to mention how all that saturated fat would find its way straight to her butt.

"Have another." Angus pushed the tray her way.

"I'd better not, or I won't have room for Fiona's amazing-smelling dinner."

Angus scooped another egg and demolished it in two quick bites. "Aye, you'll want space for that. Makes the best haggis you've ever tasted, she does."

Beside her, Brian coughed. No haggis, he'd promised. Uh-huh.

"Brian told me about it. He said it's delicious, I can't wait to try it."

"Try it? Is this your first time—a virgin, are you?" The way Angus said virgin, the word had about six Rs in the middle.

At this, Brian chuckled. Beneath the tartan-covered table, she knocked her knee against his. His eyebrow rose in challenge. So she did it again.

This time, his quick, strong hand clapped over her leg. And not just to still her knocking knee. His fingers caught the hem of her skirt and worked it upward, the corner of his mouth curling higher with every inch of skin he uncovered.

He wouldn't…

Oh god. Yes, he would. She lowered her eyes to her plate, focusing on pressing crumbs between the tines of her fork rather than the finger gently stroking the crease between her legs.

"Brian, get the Glenlivet and four glasses." Angus crossed thick forearms on the table and leaned toward her, the casual move demanding eye contact. So much like his son. "You drink whisky, don't you?"

"I do now."

Laughter rang up around her. As loving and kind as her grandparents were, their house had never been filled with fun moments like this. Sitting in this kitchen, being immersed in the easygoing warmth that seemed to come so naturally to all three Blacks, the future she'd always dreamed of unfolded in her mind. This was it, in bold, living color. In tartan, actually.

By the time Fiona stood to clear the table—a job she refused to accept help with—two glasses of whisky had joined the haggis, neeps and tatties in Cassie's belly. The third glass went down easier and faster than its predecessors. The glass was half empty when Brian cupped his hand over the top.

"You okay?" His close, softly spoken words tickled her ear. "Dad's whisky's strong stuff, careful it doesn't sneak up on you."

"Too late," she said on a giggle. "You're going to have to drive."

"Not a problem. I'll even put the doors on so you don't fall out."

She leaned into his shoulder and whispered, "I wasn't referring to the Jeep."

Angus snorted and pushed back from the table.

Okay, so maybe she hadn't quite whispered. Oops.

"You're drunk." Zero accusation, just a smile.

"Not *too* drunk." She snuck her hand into his lap, under the flap of his kilt. Wrapped her fingers around his cock and slid her fist up and down the rapidly swelling shaft. She knocked the twill aside with her wrist. One glance at his lap and her mouth was watering.

"Careful." Despite the warning, he didn't stop her ministrations, merely pulled the tablecloth over her tugging fist.

"Spoilsport."

He leaned in close. "Wait until I get you past the town limits. There's a tie-down rope in the back of the Jeep that now has your name on it."

The tingling in her core had nothing to do with the alcohol loosening her limbs and lips. Images of Brian binding or restraining her, fucking her hard against the metal of his Jeep, or—

"Who wants dessert?" Fiona asked, snapping Cassie from her X-rated thoughts.

"I do. I've been waiting for dessert all day." Brian's eyes darkened as Cassie dragged her nails along his hard length.

"Good thing I made a double batch." Fiona plunked a big bowl in the middle of the table.

As if magically summoned, Angus reappeared from wherever he'd gone and dropped onto his chair. "Ever sampled a Tipsy Laird, Cassie?" The twinkle in his eye belied his innocent tone. "One mouthful and you'll be addicted."

"No, but it looks delicious." Under the table, she used her thumb to spread a bead of pre-cum over the head of Brian's cock. "I love thick, creamy treats."

Brian exhaled sharply, his cock pulsing in her hand. "Guests first around here. Cassie, you're up." The conniver winked victoriously as she was forced to trade his handle for that of the serving ladle.

The Tipsy Laird looked like an innocent trifle. One bite revealed this version had something Nana's had not. Something with kick. "What's in this, sherry?"

Angus snorted as if affronted.

"Drambuie, darling," Fiona said between mouthfuls. "Speaking of, want a nip?"

"Of course she does," Angus threw in before Cassie could answer. "Brian, get the ladies a couple of fresh glasses."

A little shuffling of his kilt and Brian stood, kissed the top of her head and fetched the goods. A couple minutes later, a half-filled tumbler of golden liquid landed next to her bowl.

"Sláinte," Fiona said, raising her glass—then draining it.

"Um, cheers," Cassie said, following suit. She coughed and sputtered as several ounces of amber devil cut a hot groove down her throat. Dear god, these people were trying to kill her. And by the laughter bouncing around her head like a pinball in a lit-up machine, they found the process hilarious.

"Shame your brother couldn't be here to meet your lass." Angus spoke from two feet away, but his voice sounded more like a muffled echo.

"Just as well. He'd have monopolized her all day, talking shop."

She turned her head, attempted to focus on Brian's smiling face, but he kept swinging back and forth. She wanted to ask why he was moving around so much, but between the pre-dinner wine, Drambuie and the three glasses of Angus' whisky, her tongue seemed to have disintegrated.

"Aye, you're probably right. Good boy, big ego. Thinks he's world famous already." Angus nudged her shoulder. "You must see that a lot in your line of work."

The room careened wildly as she turned to look at Angus.

"Fiona, show Cassie a picture of Ian."

"Here's our vain boy." Fiona slid a framed photo across the table, requiring yet another change in Cassie's heading.

She blinked and took a breath. Focused on controlling the hand reaching for the wooden frame. Had it. She pulled it in for a look. A handsome, dark-haired man stared up at her from the picture. A familiar man. He wore a long-sleeve t-shirt in the photo before her, but she knew what was underneath, had photographed every hard—very hard—naked inch of him.

Meat, potatoes, sponge cake and booze rolled over in her gut. "Oh god, I'm going to be sick."

CASSIE

The digital clock slowly coming into focus read 5:50. She lifted her head and regretted it instantly. "Ugh, I'm in hell."

A soft chuckle sounded beside her. The mattress dipped as he shifted, then Brian's large, warm hand stroked her head. "Probably feels like hell, but you're home. I packed you into the Jeep after your stomach eased up. Figured you'd rather wake up in your own bed."

"Thank you." The return trip from his parents' was nothing more than a few choppy moments of awareness. With each blink, pieces of what'd come before it trickled into the front part of her brain. "I made it to the washroom before I puked—oh, thank god."

"Yeah, you did. You were in there a while. You kept saying, 'whisky is the devil'."

"It is."

"Nah, it just requires conditioning. It won't hit you as hard next time."

"No next time." She buried her face in the pillow to stifle a sob. There wouldn't be a next time for whisky because there wouldn't be a next time at the Blacks. There wouldn't be a next time for anything with Brian.

The framed photo changed everything—that part of the evening was crystal clear. She'd thought giving up the explicit photography jobs would be enough. That if she parted ways with those clients, she could keep all those contacts and their activities safely hidden in locked files, never to be seen or heard from again. Brian wouldn't need to know about that part of her life. She wouldn't have to worry about how he'd react, or worse, the potential fallout from his knowledge should they part ways down the road. One look at the picture his parents had innocently shown her and that road had ended on the spot. Of all the people her alter ego had photographed, the only one that mattered now was Ian Black.

"Hey," a gentle touch coaxed her face in his direction, "don't cry. I'm here. The worst part is over, trust me."

She pushed his hands away before clutching her temples to tamp the stabbing pain. "I'm sorry."

"Shh, no apologizing. I've been there, I don't know anybody who hasn't." The soft touch on her hair resumed. "This'll probably sound crazy—and not help your hangover— but my dad was proud of you." He chuckled while gently massaging her spine with his knuckles. "My mom cuffed him for that statement, by the way. She said to tell you to come back soon. She likes you a lot, they both do. How could they not when I feel the way I do?"

She groaned and stuffed her face back into the pillow. Every sweet word made it worse. Made the inevitable harder. "You should go."

"No, I shouldn't." He pulled a blanket over her when a silent sob racked her body. "Try to get some more sleep, I'll be right here."

Puking had drained her physical strength and energy. Brian's never-ending attentiveness had eroded her emotional walls. If she let him stay now, she'd have to say goodbye in the light of day. The first rays of dawn already peeked through the bottom of her window. She had to do it now.

She turned on the pillow to face him. Tried to look through him, rather than at him. Even in the dim lighting, she could see the warmth in his eyes and smile. The love.

"I'd like to be alone...I'm a mess."

"I'll take care of you."

"I don't need you to take care of me." The *need* part of that statement was true. What she wanted was another story, and no longer mattered.

He propped on one elbow and lorded over her in his dominant yet endearing way. "What if I need to take care of you?"

"This isn't your fault."

"I wasn't talking about the hangover."

"Neither was I." Sunlight inched its way up the window. Plenty of light to see Brian's eyebrows draw together and his jaw clench. She swallowed despite the desert in her mouth. "You should go."

"If that's what you want." Seconds ticked by as he waited for a response she couldn't give. He swept his thumb over her cheek, tucked a piece of hair behind her ear—killing her bit by bit, even though he couldn't possibly know it. "Call me later."

"Okay." She bit back tears at the soft touch of lips and beard on her forehead. Later had a lot of meanings.

KARLA DOYLE

BRIAN

"You don't look so hot." Trevor clapped Brian's shoulder. "Rough week?"

It was as if the motherfucker knew. And he could, to a point. Brian had checked the member logins for the past four days—the bastard might've done the same. Cassie hadn't scanned in once. She also hadn't called. Not really. The single, brief voicemail telling him she needed space and time to think sure the fuck didn't count.

"Yeah, actually, it has been rough. Some of us have been working our asses off, assembling equipment, dealing with broken tanning beds, contacting members about a recall that came down the pipe for one of our bestselling testosterone boosters. And you've been out of the club why?"

"Listen to you, mister almost-a-partner, demanding to know how I'm contributing to the team."

The words *you're not* licked at Brian's lips, but he swallowed them. Instead, he made normal, human conversation with a couple who approached the front desk inquiring about group strength-training classes. Unluckily for Brian, Trevor stuck around until they left.

"You're bouncing tonight?"

"Yeah." If the asshole was looking for passes to jump the line, fuck that. Brian tipped his chin at Trevor's suit pants and tailored shirt. "Might want to downgrade the clothes if you're heading to Blur. You'll sweat your bag off dancing in those."

"Oh, I'll be sweating tonight, but it won't be from dancing, and it won't be while I'm dressed. On that note…" A flick of the wrist had Trevor checking his Rolex. Or more likely, demonstrating he owned one. "I'd better head out. Wouldn't

206

want to keep Cassie waiting." He walked away, but turned to face Brian before pushing through the doors. "Don't worry, I won't do anything you wouldn't—or haven't."

Brian watched Trevor walk away. "He lays a finger on her, I'm going to kill him."

"I don't think it's his finger you should worry about," Sam said as he drifted behind the counter and snagged his usual bar from the rack. He tore into the wrapper and dusted off the protein bar within seconds. "Am I in some bizarro world—aren't you gonna tell me I owe three bucks?"

"Eat all the fucking bars you want. After tonight, it won't matter to me."

"Oh shit. Man, you've got that look in your eye." Sam knew better than to put a hand on him right now, but there it was, around his elbow.

"Watch the desk for me. And let go of my arm before I break your hand."

"You do not want to follow your boss and beat the hell out of him in front of Cassie." The hand lifted, landing on Brian's shoulder in a subtler gesture of restraint. "At least wait 'til later tonight when it's dark, he's alone and you've had a chance to hunt down a ski mask."

Some of the urgency to maim subsided. Hard not to relax around Sam—he had that effect on people. "What's with you being the voice of reason all of the sudden?"

"Guess I'm going soft in my old age."

"You're twenty-eight."

"Exactly." He gave Brian a good-natured shove that didn't move his buddy an inch. "And I'd rather not celebrate the next ten birthdays by visiting you in the pen."

Brian snorted. "I'd get more than ten for what I have in mind."

"Listen. Whatever's going on with Cassie and this timeout

she called, I doubt it involves getting naked with that asshole. Trust her to have a business dinner and walk away. Plus, watching her turn Trevor down in the middle of Barolo around seven o'clock could be fun, right?"

What the hell? His eyes snapped to Sam's face, now sporting a wide, pearly grin. "Hack his phone or his email?"

"Email, which happens to be synced with his planner. You're welcome."

BRIAN

Seven bucks for a domestic beer. Plus tip. Fucking robbery, yet the place was packed. Forget health and fitness, he was going into the restaurant business. Brian lifted the bottle to his lips and let the icy lager cool his throat. No amount of overpriced brew would cool his head. Not while Cassie was with Trevor.

From his position in the crowded bar area, Brian could see every move and gesture Trevor made. Not so with Cassie—she sat facing away. Probably for the best. With his nonstop staring, she'd have spotted him for sure.

He couldn't help himself. The sleeveless black dress hugged her body. When she swiveled to lift her bag from the chair, he caught a glimpse of her front. A long chain with some sort of oversized charm drew his attention to the low-cut neckline. She wore more makeup than normal—she didn't need it, but he'd bet that up close, the shimmery stuff brought out the blue in her beautiful eyes. Her hair had its usual adorably mussed style, the front pieces held back by shiny barrettes. She looked amazing.

Clearly Trevor agreed. The prick kept touching her—on the arm, covering her hand. When he reached over and made as if he were brushing something from the strap of Cassie's dress, Brian had to force his feet to stay where planted. If Cassie had protested in any way, he would've knocked everyone aside to get to her. She hadn't. By the smile on Trevor's face, the way she didn't flinch while his fingers made a slow descent down her arm, she didn't mind the contact. Or was it all an act—could she be doing this for him, because of Trevor's threats about his job? That didn't explain her shutting him out. None of it added up.

Trevor snagged a passing waitress. Whatever he said made Cassie stiffen. Twenty-five feet away and Brian knew something was wrong, but the idiot across from her didn't appear to have a clue.

Brian shifted on his barstool, angled to track the waitress as she headed for the kitchen. She reemerged a couple minutes later, and she wasn't alone. The hair on the back of his neck bristled. Fucking hell—the Italian from Cassie's driveway. No wonder she'd gone board-straight in her chair. Or maybe the guy smiling as he stopped to chat with patrons was the reason she'd dressed up tonight. Christ, what the fuck?

The man oozed pride and authority. The owner, maybe. Manager, at minimum. Both Trevor and Cassie stood to greet him. Trevor got a solid-looking handshake. The Italian then gave his full attention to Cassie. He cupped her elbow, kissed her cheek and spoke near her ear. Familiarity, oh hell yeah. The waitress hovering nearby collected their drinks and transferred them to a fancier table that stood alone, near the open-concept portion of the kitchen. Trevor's face reeked of victory. Not Cassie's. Her shoulders slumped the second his hand touched her back, propelling her forward.

She and Trevor had barely taken their seats when Cassie leaned in, smiled and excused herself. Brian darted a look at the Italian, then to Cassie, hot on his heels as he turned down a small hallway that probably led to restrooms or offices. He stopped for her. Listened to whatever words poured from her mouth, staring at her intently. Cassie's tiny hands covered her face. Still, the guy just stood there.

Enough of whatever bullshit was going on here. She'd requested space and Brian had respected her wish, but he refused to sit on his ass while two men who didn't deserve her caused obvious anguish. Fuck that.

He put the empty bottle on the bar and abandoned his seat. Using his bulk to push through the clogged bar area, he strode directly toward that hall. Cassie's back was to him and the Italian didn't toss him so much as a glance. He was about ten feet away when their conversation came into earshot. Not quite an argument, but intense.

"You have to tell him," the Italian said.

"I can't, Paulo, there are other people involved."

"I know, I'm one of them." The Italian—Paulo, his name was—put his hands on Cassie's upper arms, prompting her to look up at him. "If you don't, I will tell him."

"You can't. Please—don't."

Brian stepped behind Cassie, jumping onto both their radars. "Take your hands off the lady. And I'm not saying please."

"This is a private conversation." Paulo met Brian's eyes with polite reserve. "Thank you for your concern, but you can go about your business."

"Fine by me." He didn't think. Didn't plan. Just drew his arm back, then gifted the guy with knuckles to the jaw. "Cassie *is* my business."

"Oh my god, Brian…" She shoved at his chest, then spun away. "Paulo, I'm so sorry. Oh no, you're bleeding."

"Just a split lip. It's fine." Paulo wiped it with his fingers, then waved away the people who'd flocked to the end of the hall to gawk. "Everything's fine. Please, go back to your tables and enjoy your evening."

One by one, they filed away—except for Trevor, who leaned on the wall, hands stuffed in his pockets. "Brian, Brian. Stalking my date, punching her client... How'd you know we'd be here, anyway?" At this, Trevor's eyes drifted to Cassie.

"She didn't tell me. She's not even speaking to me." He needed to get Trevor out of the way so he could deal with whatever was going on between Cassie and Paulo. What a fucking disaster.

The snake smiled his slick best. "Good. For a second there, I thought I'd have to rip up those papers you're waiting to sign. I can't have a partner who lies to me." He extended a hand confidently. "Let's get back to our evening, Cassie. I have a lot planned for us."

Three sets of male eyes all focused on the same fidgety target.

"I-I..." Cassie's eyes darted between the men. So full of emotion, they matched the hands wringing in front of her petite frame.

Brian knew what Trevor wanted from Cassie, could make a good guess at what Paulo wanted. Hell, he wasn't innocent of wanting something from her, it was just more than these two bastards. Didn't really matter. In the end, it boiled down to what Cassie wanted. Maybe it wouldn't be him—this Paulo guy was obviously more important to her than Brian had thought. One thing he was sure about—having sex with Trevor didn't top her list. Hell, it shouldn't even be on the list.

That was his fault. "Does Cassie have the job to shoot the gym promo?"

"Yes." Trevor slid his empty hand back inside his pocket.

"Even if she walks out the door right now?" He had to be sure.

"Of course. I've committed, and I always make good on my word."

Yeah, there it was—the veiled reference he was looking for. "Like when you threatened to fire me if I didn't serve up Cassie for your sexual amusement?"

"Brian—" She shook her head. *It's only sex,* her eyes pleaded. Beside her, Paulo gently caught her arm.

Time to make things right. "No deal, Ritchie. I quit."

CASSIE

"Thanks for the ride," Cassie said when Paulo pulled into her driveway. "And for letting me hide out in your office. Oh, and I owe you a box of tissues."

After Brian had stormed out of Barolo, she'd said good night to Trevor, politely telling him they could discuss the details for the Iron Works project in his office, at his convenience. If he chose to yank the job, so be it, there'd be others. Finding more work wouldn't be so easy for Brian.

Paulo tipped his head toward the cell she clutched. "Have you heard from him?" At her head shake, he added, "Have you called him?"

"No."

He turned in his seat. "We are friends, correct?"

"Yes, of course." Though Paulo and Beth had started off as professional clients, then accidentally become her first private clients, they'd both grown into friends over the past couple of years. Good friends, people she could count on. Paulo had proven that several times over tonight. Including taking an unprovoked shot in the face. "Sorry about your jaw. I should've kept my mouth shut when you assumed Trevor was my boyfriend. If I hadn't chased you down that hall, if I'd left it alone and let you believe he was the special guy from the gym I'd told you about, all of tonight's trouble would've been avoided."

"You would've slept with Trevor to save Brian's job?"

Would she have? Thank god she hadn't had to find out. "Maybe…I don't know."

"Yet you won't call him."

"I can't."

"He loves you. Enough to fight for you and defend you, no matter the cost. As your friend, I think you're making a mistake, throwing that away."

"I don't have a choice—it's not only about me. Every person who has entrusted me with their privacy is involved." She hadn't shared all the gory details about Lance's threat to out her clients if she didn't pay him off, but Paulo and Beth knew the gist of what'd gone down.

"Just because one man burned dinner doesn't mean no man can be trusted in the kitchen."

"Leave it to a restauranteur to come up with that analogy." She opened the door and slid from the leather seat, into the warm night air. "Thank you."

Inside her house, she traded her dress and heels for boxers and a tank. She couldn't wear the robe hanging on her bathroom door. Just looking at it made her ache.

Paulo thought she didn't trust Brian to keep her secrets. That wasn't it, not anymore. He'd shown how much he'd do for her tonight, and in the process, shown her once again the value he placed on honesty and full disclosure. She just couldn't give him those.

Her stomach let out a frustrated growl. In all the commotion and subsequent crying jags, she hadn't eaten. She padded into the kitchen, Paulo's words replaying in her head. She pulled out a small frying pan. Cracked a single egg into the middle after it warmed, poked at the thinning edge with her spatula, gathering it into a uniformly thick mass. If Brian were here, he'd add spices, diced veggies or shredded cheese. He'd sit with her at her small table, their knees touching while they ate, talked and laughed. He'd wipe crumbs from her lips and look at her as if she were dessert.

She sighed and scooped her plain egg onto a plate. Dinner for one, from here out.

Chapter 12

BRIAN

HIS SHIFT at Blur last night had dragged. He'd half expected Ritchie to show up and antagonize him, but the prick hadn't made an appearance. Neither had Cassie. No movie-scene moments where the woman he loved pushed her way through the crowd to his waiting arms. Just six hours surrounded by drunk, dancing bodies while hoping his cell would vibrate. Hadn't happened.

This morning, a record-setting thirty-nine people had shown up for boot camp. Word was spreading, and that was great, especially now, but the one person he'd wanted to see hadn't shown. He'd taken the group through fifteen minutes worth of exercises before Sam pulled him aside to accuse him of pining, not pushing. Sam had been right. Few of the participants were out of breath. They'd paid their ten bucks for an hour with a drill sergeant, not a lovesick downer.

After the last sweaty boot-camper had left, he'd given Sam

the lowdown from Barolo. Asked him to keep an eye on Cassie at the gym, since he no longer worked there. An unemployed stalker via third-party means—didn't get much less classy. He didn't regret telling his lowlife boss to shove it, but another strike on his reference list wasn't going to make job hunting any easier. Shit. He'd think about that tomorrow.

Right now, he needed to *stop* thinking. He pushed off the couch. The heavy bag hung in the corner. He stalked to it, pulled on his gloves and drilled his fists into the vinyl. The chains suspending it from a hook in the ceiling creaked in protest, jangling more violently with each punch. Mrs. Hoffman in the apartment above stomped on her floor. Muffled yelling drifted through the registers in his ceiling. Probably hollering at him about this being a day of rest, or some shit like that.

He caught the bag in a hug to silence it. No point pissing off the neighbors when the bag wasn't doing the trick. Hitting it got him sweaty, pushed his heart rate up, but it wasn't enough. He needed a target who fought back. Somebody who wasn't afraid to sport a few bruises and who would relish knocking some sense into him. Only one person fit that description.

He tossed the gloves, mopped his face with his t-shirt and tapped out a text.

Feel like a beating?

The phone vibrated in his palm immediately.

It's on. Get the fuck over here so I can kick your ass.

For the first time in days, he laughed out loud. Family. Always willing to administer a whooping.

BRIAN

Brian peeled into the lot in front of the warehouse. "Hey, pretty boy," he called to his brother as he leaned out of the Jeep. "Got any meat here?" It was a running joke. Two years Ian had lived here and he'd never bothered to take down the old meat packer's sign. At least once a week, somebody banged on his door looking to buy a side of beef or a pig for spit-roasting.

"You're in luck, you ugly bastard." Ian flicked a cigarette butt to the pavement while sauntering to the Jeep. "Fresh meat just rolled in."

Oh yeah. It was on, all right. Brian hopped out and slapped Ian on the back. "I'd tell you to quit smoking, but it makes you that much easier to pummel."

Ian snorted as they walked to the blacked-out doors. "You wish."

Brian had hung out here plenty of times, and every time he did, his brain kicked into gear, redesigning the place. It'd make a great gym. Ian had come into ownership when an *acquaintance* needed to unload the property—and skip the country—in a hurry, but he had no long-term plans for the building. No short-term ones, either. Ian went with the flow, pushing the line of socially acceptable behavior sometimes, but always staying above board. The man had some crazy balancing skills.

"New TV. Nice." A sixty-inch flat screen stood opposite

the leather couches in what amounted to Ian's living room. The warehouse was mostly one space. Ian hadn't bothered to use the old offices along the front wall. All his stuff sat in the open, on display for anybody to see. Exactly like the man. They'd been raised to be honest and upfront. Ian took those philosophies to the extreme.

"Forget your gloves?" Ian asked when they reached the mats.

"Nah. Didn't want them." He cracked his knuckles, then peeled his t-shirt over his head and made a point of flexing as he chucked it aside. "Worried I'm going to mess up your face without them?"

"You'd have to hit me for that to happen." Ian's shirt joined Brian's on the floor, revealing his tattoo-covered torso. "And we both know I'm faster."

"That *is* what the ladies say," Brian said, raising his fists.

"Oh, ho…you're going to pay for that one."

They sparred about ten minutes, until both were slick with sweat and a bit of blood, then dropped onto the mats. They'd beaten each other black and blue once, neither willing to quit. It'd taken stitches at the emergency room and weeks afterward for their cuts and bruises to heal. Since that, they'd agreed to more sensible bouts of abuse. No winner, no loser, just a good mutual beating.

Brian ran his fingers over a tender spot where Ian had landed a solid right hook. "You might've cracked my rib."

"Fair trade for the shiner I'm going to have."

A glance at his brother revealed the beginnings of what would be a multi-colored semi-circle under his left eye. "Goes with your whole bad-boy look."

"It's not a look, it's a lifestyle." Ian grinned, rolled away and jogged to the fridge, where he launched a bottle of water at Brian. "But I think you're right. I bet the photographer I'm working with tomorrow will be all over the black eye."

"Shit, man, you should've told me you had work lined up. I would've worn gloves."

"And give you a reason to call me a pussy until the end of time—I don't think so." Ian drained his bottle and cracked the cap on a second. He joined Brian on the mat. "What's up with the brawling today? Woman troubles, work bullshit?"

"I can't come over for the sheer joy of pounding on you?"

"Anytime. That all it was today?" Ian raised one dark eyebrow.

They didn't look alike, lived very different lives, but still had a freakishly strong brother bond. Maybe it was all the blood and sweat they'd swapped over the years.

"It's both. A woman and work."

Ian arched his wrist and shot the empty bottle into a nearby can. "Work stuff first, get the boring shit out of the way."

"It's an all-in-one thing."

"Sounds like a fucked-up mess. Let's hear it."

"I've been seeing a woman from the gym. Yeah, I know," he said at Ian's grimace. "There's more. I got caught with her —as in, really caught—then a bunch of other shit went down, and last night, I quit my job."

"Whoa."

"That's the best you can come up with?" He hadn't expected Ian to spout some deep, meaningful philosophy, but more than one word would be good.

"You chose a woman over your career. I'm processing, give me a minute." Ian shuffled to lean against the wall. Folded his hands behind his head while he contemplated what, to a career player like him, must be the strangest decision a man could make. "She must be fucking amazing."

"She is. Mom and Dad like her too."

Ian's eyes bugged at that. "Damn. You gave up your job *and* you put this woman on Mom's radar. Is she knocked up—when's the wedding?"

"She's not pregnant." The image of Cassie caressing a big belly full of his baby appeared in his mind, so clear it could've been a memory. More torture for his shredded heart. "And since she's apparently done with me, even though she didn't say why, I don't think you need to run out and rent a tux."

The curiosity drained from Ian's eyes, replaced by cool indifference. "Fuck her, then. She doesn't deserve you. Forget her and come with me tomorrow. The photographer is your type—lean, great ass, dresses like a there's a worldwide shortage of fabric. She likes a good time, you know? I bet she'd happily help you forget your Mom-approved ex-girlfriend."

"Think I'll pass."

The perfect teeth that had graced magazines and catalogs gleamed at him from Ian's cocky grin. "I haven't been with this one, if you're worried she'll compare us and you won't measure up."

Trust his brother to force him to laugh, even when he felt like a bag of shit. "Not worried about that, *little* brother."

"Fucker." Ian's smile belied the insult. "Give me a good reason for refusing a hook-up with a hot 'n' willing photog."

"Hits a bit too close to home. You pretty much described my girl."

"The gym woman is a photographer?"

"Yeah. A good one. Grab your laptop and I'll show you her site."

"Pimping your ex's work—you're in worse shape than I thought."

"Shut up and get your computer." Didn't matter that

things had gone cold between them, if he could help Cassie he would. His brother had come a long way since breaking into the business, modeling for skin mags. If Ian liked her style of photography, maybe he could get her an in somewhere, or give Brian a contact to pass along. Ulterior motives, yeah, he had them.

"Here," Ian dumped the laptop on Brian's lap, "cue it up while I grab some ice. A black eye'll work for the shoot—having it swollen shut, not so much."

"Thanks for the fight, man. It helped," Brian said in lieu of an apology.

Ian dropped beside him on the mat, a bag of crushed ice pressed to one side of his face. "Anytime." His free hand motioned for the laptop. "Let's see what she's got." The gallery page on Cassie's site had dozens of thumbnail images to click on. Ian gave it a cursory glance, barked out a laugh. "Small fucking world. You're right, she's good. Better than any of these shots'll show." He opened a new browser window and keyed in an address. "Huh," he said when it displayed a blank page with an error message. "Maybe she's not shooting skin anymore."

"What?"

"Your ex-girl. She took my portfolio shots, the ones I used to get my foot in the door at Hot Heads. She had another site, but it's not coming up."

"You must have her confused with somebody else."

"Nope, don't think so. Cassie Johnson. I remember thinking how funny it was to have a Johnson taking pictures of my johnson. Plus, she's cute, right? Didn't make it so hard to get hard with her staring at my body."

Cassie'd taken the naked—as in, really fucking naked—pictures of Ian that'd landed him the gig with a gentlemen's magazine…for gentlemen. No way. That was two years ago, maybe Ian had similar names confused. Carrie or Cathy or something. He'd certainly dealt with a shitload of people since then.

Brian pushed up from the mats and retrieved his cell from Ian's coffee table. He brought up the picture he'd taken of Cassie and him lying on her couch. He'd snuck this one. For a person whose life revolved around pictures, she was camera-shy to a fault. The only ones she'd authorized him to take were...damn.

"Is this her?" Brian handed him the cell, adding, "Don't scroll through."

"Yup. Hair's shorter than I remember, and she's got a big red growth coming out of one side that wasn't there before, but that's her."

This time, he couldn't even force a laugh at Ian's ribbing. Pretty damn hard to laugh when it felt as if his chest had been cracked open, his beating heart yanked from the gaping cavity and splattered on the concrete floor. He'd been upfront about everything. *Everything.* So completely fucking honest, he'd forfeited his job and a slice of ownership. For her. Their physical connection had been intense and he'd have bet his left nut that she cared for him—she'd been willing to have sex with Trevor to save his ass, for fuck's sake. But when he thought back on their conversations, she'd been elusive from their first meeting to the day she didn't bother to say goodbye. While he'd fallen in love, she'd merely been falling into the sack.

He shook off the fury the best he could. "I have to go. Have to put a resume together."

"Any leads?"

His dark mood had gone unnoticed—good. He didn't want to learn anything else about Cassie from his brother. What he'd heard would keep him fueled with adrenaline until he got some serious space from it all.

"None. I'll probably have to move, put a bunch of distance between me and my history before I find a gym that'll hire me."

"That'll kill the folks. Hell, it'll kill me." Ian slapped the cell onto Brian's palm. "I got it. Fuck getting hired. Be an independent contractor, like me."

The burn in his chest subsided enough for him to snort. "Don't think I'm cut out for standing in front of a camera, with or without my clothes."

"No, dipshit." Ian put a fist to the bruise forming on Brian's ribs, grinning at the pained whoosh of air his gesture created. "We both know I got the looks in the family."

"And the ego. Christ."

"True." Ian laughed. "And you got the people skills. You're this giant, hulking thing who should scare the crap out of anybody with half a brain, yet they flock to you. How much did that gym charge for your personal training sessions?"

"One-fifty for an assessment, including a one-hour training session. Eighty-five for the following sessions."

"And how much of that did you pocket?"

"Around thirty-five bucks."

"That's bullshit. Drop the middleman, pocket the whole shebang."

"Not that easy. Most clubs don't allow outside trainers."

"Then I say, fuck them too." Ian tossed the ice pack and stood, arms spread wide, a borderline-lunatic smile on his face. "Start your own."

CASSIE

Jelly legs carried Cassie from the parking lot behind Brian's apartment building to the front vestibule. A wave of lightheadedness washed over her as she pressed the button for his unit. Hopefully he'd let her in to talk.

"It's open," rumbled through the speaker.

She grabbed the door before the buzzing ended. Even with the tension inching its way up from her stomach, the sound of his deep voice made her tingle in all the good spots. Get in, say what needed to be said, get out. She had to ignore the chemistry that was sure to erupt when she got close to him. Then again, she might not need to worry about it. The phrase "too little, too late" existed for good reason.

His apartment door opened before she'd raised her hand to knock. He filled the doorway, vertically and horizontally. God, he was big. A few weeks without her daily dose of ginger and she'd forgotten exactly *how* big.

"Cassie." The greeting—such as it was—held surprise, not warmth.

Looking at him, she had plenty of heat for both of them. He was shirtless, his chest rising and falling from obvious exertion, his pecs and abs slick with sweat. Shorts clung to his legs —and that's not all they clung to. Her eyes went to the ridge of his cock under the light-gray jersey. She cleared her throat and took in all of his exposed skin. A mouthwatering picture, until her eyes reached his face. Clenched jaw, narrowed eyes. Zero smile.

"I'm interrupting." Please, please, let it be a workout she had interrupted, not something else.

"It's fine, just giving it to the bag."

"Lucky bag." The words slipped out without thinking. But

he smiled, and oh god, it made her day. She missed that. She missed all of it.

"What're you doing here?" His tone hadn't hit the friendly zone, but it was getting warmer.

"Sam told me what he learned about Leanne—I knew you couldn't have hurt her the way she claimed." That bitch had caused her own injuries, overtraining, and blamed it on Brian to save her sponsorship contract. "How long before the conviction is repealed?"

"It won't be."

"But it has to be, you didn't do anything wrong. She lied."

"It's in the past. I'm leaving it there, moving forward." He leaned on the doorframe, eyes intent on hers. "Maybe you should think about doing the same."

If only she could tell him how she'd tried. That she'd put Lance's betrayal behind her—that she'd tried to choose love over money. But the sexy, naked ghosts of that business shared Brian's DNA. Ian Black had made a name for himself in mainstream modeling, but when she'd photographed him, he'd posed as Ian MacLean. There was no way around it. Out Ian to his brother, breaking a legal confidentiality agreement and devastating a wonderful family, or lie—even if by omission—to Brian. Walking away had been the only choice.

"I need to tell you something. It's important." His eyebrows rose at that. A little more of the Brian she adored, obsessed over and loved, slipped into place. She glanced at the other doors in the corridor. The walls in this building were probably none too thick, the doors even thinner. "And personal…"

"Come in." He stepped aside for her and closed the door behind them. Waited, while the room filled with awkward silence.

That efficient, fact-filled speech she'd prepared and practiced in her head—gone, now that he stood two feet in front of her, possibly for the last time. "I...it's about..."

He took a half step toward her, shook his head and backed up. Weeks of silence between them—at her request—yet he was clearly fighting the urge to take care of her. "You want a drink, or to sit down?" He glanced around the bachelor apartment. "Sorry about the mess, I'm getting ready to move."

Move? Sam hadn't shared that tidbit. "To a bigger apartment? You're not leaving the city, are you?"

BRIAN

"The new place definitely has more space." He curbed his smile the best he could. He'd given Sam permission to tell Cassie what they'd learned about Leanne, nothing more. Cassie frowning at the idea he might be moving away was the best thing he'd seen in weeks. "Still here, just a different part of town."

"Oh good." She fiddled with her purse strap. Shuffled where she stood and looked everywhere, except at him.

"You wanted to tell me something?" The nervous nod and accompanying lack of words told him this might take a while —unless he helped her along. In his experience, the best way to get Cassie to open up involved an activity with less talking. He just had to get them there. "Can you talk while I shower? I have a lot on the go today." He hooked his fingers over the top of his shorts. "It won't bother you to see me naked, will it?"

"Of course not." She waved at him nonchalantly, but when he shucked his shorts and boxers, her cheeks went deep pink, her eyes wide as saucers. This plan definitely had potential.

His cock had reached full attention by the time he reached the bathroom. And no, she hadn't missed that fact. Oh, she pretended to root through her bag, not stare at him through the clear plastic shower curtain, she just didn't do it convincingly. Her eyes tracked his hands as he lathered soap over his chest and arms. When he took his hygiene routine below the belt, a squeak slipped through her parted lips, audible over the pounding water.

"What's the important, personal stuff you need to tell me?"

"There's something you need to know about, um…" Consciously or not, she stepped closer. Close enough to brush the vinyl barrier. With the sparks flying between them, the thing might disintegrate.

He slowed the strokes over his cock. "Tell me." Her eyes fluttered upward and met his. "You can tell me anything. Anything."

The struggle showed in her eyes, in the set of her mouth. He was tempted to blurt it himself and relieve her of the burden—that he knew about the sexy photos she took, that it didn't fucking matter. But goddamn it, he wanted her to do it. To trust him with her soul the way she'd done with her body, even when he hadn't trusted himself.

"Maybe I should wait in the other room," she stepped back, "give you a few minutes to finish—"

"Or maybe you shouldn't." In a move that may well get him kneed in the balls, he snapped the curtain aside, curled his arm around her waist and hauled her into the shower, flip-flops and all.

"Brian…" Her whisper hinted at protest, yet she raised her hands and let him pull the stretchy sundress over her head, staring up at him while he unhooked her bra.

He crouched before her, his skin electrifying when her delicate hands landed on his shoulders. "So beautiful," he said, sliding her thong down and off. The spray pelted his back. Water rolled down his face, fat drops falling steadily from his nose. Not unlike the night on her doorstep. The night that had changed everything.

Today would change things too. Once she'd relaxed enough to open up, they'd be on solid ground again, better than before. He curled his fingers over her hips and pushed her back to the tiled wall. He nuzzled her clit, inhaled her scent, reveled in the whimper from above. Fuck, he wanted a taste. First, he needed to savor her lips and tongue, swallow the sexy sounds she'd make for him. He needed to get lost in her, starting at the top.

He stood, cupped her chin and tipped it up.

"No," she said, turning her face when he brought his lips down to hers.

"You don't want to kiss me?" No answer, no gesture—no eye contact. He caught her face again, this time less gently, and forced her to look up at him. "I could make you. Maybe that's what you want."

"You can try." This wasn't the playful Cassie who'd initiated hide-and-seek during a thunderstorm or mock-struggled to escape him while wearing a sinfully sexy smile. She'd come to tell him something big, wanted sex, but didn't want him to kiss her.

"What the hell, Cassie?"

"You're angry."

"Fucking right I'm angry."

"You should be."

Guilt, then? Christ, his fucking head was spinning. Not his cock, it knew exactly what needed to be done. He shoved his leg between her thighs, pinning her to the wall. He braced an arm above her and dipped low again. She tried turning away, this time unsuccessfully. His grip on her jaw tightened enough to force her lips apart. He got close. So goddamn close he almost dove in and claimed her mouth. Fuck, her warm breath on his lips. The whimper that filled his head. He had to pull back.

"Aren't you going to make me?" she whispered.

He grunted. Released her chin. Dropped his hand to her breast, squeezing while his mouth found the sensitive spot on her neck. He clamped down on tender flesh, making her cry out. He tugged at one perfect nipple, then the other, pinching and pulling hard enough to cause a deep-red flush. Christ, the sounds she made. The neighbors probably thought he was torturing her. He tugged harder, thrust his leg tight to her pussy and cursed between gritted teeth when she rocked her clit against his skin. Too close, both of them. He separated them by a step, bent and caught one hot nipple between his lips.

"Please, bite me. Hard."

"I'm not taking requests, I'm just taking." He circled her wrist and placed her hand on his shaft. "I'll start with your pretty mouth—wrapped around my cock."

A little smile lifted the corners of her mouth. "Is this where you order me to my knees and call me a bitch?"

There she was, his playful girl. He curled his fingers around her nape and guided her downward. "I'd never call you a bitch."

Slowly, she lowered to her knees before him. Caught his hand and brought it to his cock, replacing hers. At his raised eyebrow, she tucked her arms behind her back, arched her breasts forward and tipped her chin up, putting her mouth on level with his cock. "Take."

The beast stirred. He took her mouth the way he wanted, without hesitation. He pushed inside, hissing at her resistance, groaning once he'd filled her mouth and throat with every inch of his length. He held himself there until she adjusted.

Those eyes staring up at him. It was all there—love, lust and everything in between. He thumbed the misty drops from her cheek. "Fuck, baby. Your mouth feels so good." He slid free of the warm, wet suction, only to thrust to the hilt again. "Take it all, that's my girl."

And she did, sucking him hard, scraping his shaft with her teeth, nipping the head in resistance when he withdrew. Any more and he'd lose it.

"Enough. Up." He helped her to her feet, lifted her onto the bathmat. "On my bed, now." He didn't give her a towel. Didn't give her a choice either, going with a hard smack on her ass to move her along instead.

She crawled atop his unmade bed. On her knees, ass up, the way he liked. "Take anything you want."

His body folded over hers and he brushed the shell of her ear with his lips. "Careful. Only say that if you really mean it."

"Take," she whispered. "And don't hold back."

It'd taken three weeks, but she was here. In his bed, under his body, handing him an all-access pass. He had every intention of using it, in more ways than she knew.

As for not holding back… He slid one hand between her legs. Stroked her lightly. Already so wet. And responsive as hell. Like always. "You're mine now."

"As long as I'm here, I'm yours." Her breath hitched with a suppressed sob.

The sound twisted an invisible knife through his gut. So did her words. He straightened on his knees, cupped her hips and rolled her to her back, caught her delicate hands in his calloused ones and laced their fingers together. Stretched her arms above her head.

She stared up at him, pupils dilated, lips parted. The second his teeth scraped her neck, she arched. As if he could deny her. He lowered until they connected all over—legs twined, chest crowding her breasts, cock nestled along the sweet line of her pussy. He dragged his cock over her clit while inhaling her scent. Fuck, he'd missed that. Ditto the taste of her skin. Back and forth, he slid along her heat, grinding small circles over her clit at the top of each pass. He upped the pressure when her hips tilted toward him and her breath grew choppy. If she didn't come soon—if he didn't get inside her—he was going to burst.

"Missed you," he nibbled along her jawline, hovered over her mouth, "so fucking much." His arms framed her head, prevented her attempt at turning away. "Nowhere for you to go, baby." He chased her eyes, forced them to lock with his. "Taking what I want, and what I want is your kiss."

"Brian, please..." No need for her to voice the *don't* after those words, it was there in her wide, fearful eyes. Something had scared her so badly she'd bolted from him—was still trying to hide from him, even as she lay naked and willing on his bed.

Her body would never be enough. He wanted all of her.

"You'll kiss me because that's what I want. You're mine until you leave, remember?" He tracked a lone tear down her cheek as she nodded. "Maybe I won't let you go."

At that, she wriggled beneath him. Tried tugging her arms free—or pretended to, since her fingers stayed curled around his, telling him she didn't want to go anywhere.

He planned to make her admit that in every way possible. "Put your hands on me," he said, releasing her. "I want to feel your touch when I kiss you." This time she didn't argue. A million sparks shot through him when she smoothed her thumbs over his eyebrows, raked her fingers through his hair and down his neck, along his shoulders. He dipped lower, grazed her lips. Soft as he remembered. He went in for another taste. Groaned when she opened for him, letting him take what he'd demanded and doing some taking of her own. Including his soul, for the thousandth time.

"Brian," she whispered into his mouth between kisses, then locked her arms and legs around him, pulling him closer.

Message received. "Right here. Not going anywhere." He moved against her, giving her the friction she needed. "Come for me, baby."

Her body was a contradiction of movements. Clawing and biting his skin. Writhing upward one second, jerking away the next. Breathing so damn sexy into his ear he could've lost it from that sound alone.

When she said, "Please...I need you...right now," against his mouth, he slid inside her welcoming body and flew straight to heaven.

Single words. That's all his brain formed. Hot. Wet. Soft. Tight. Love. Cassie. He pushed deeper. Retreated, pulling out until his tip barely parted her lips. Thrust in hard and fast. And when she begged using only his name—goddamn. More, he needed to give her more.

He shifted position slightly. Like this, he could continue kissing her, squeeze one perfect nipple, press his quad against her clit and fuck her so, so deep.

"Oh god," she whispered at his first stroke. "Oh god, that's —*oh god*." Her legs curled around him. One hand clutched at his biceps, the other grabbed the thigh rubbing her clit, dragging it tighter. A deep-red flush spread over her chest, neck and cheeks. Her eyes fluttered closed and a low moan slipped through her lips. "W-what are you doing to me?"

"Loving you, baby." His damn balls were practically in his stomach. Fire churned at the base of his cock, threatening to unload each time he dared another thrust. Had to hold on—a couple more. He stroked again, using every drop of control to hit that spot for her. The one that made her eyes roll back. Made her pant like a wild animal. So fucking sexy, she was going to kill him.

A cry ripped from her, so sharp and intense it was almost silent. She bucked and scratched at him. And his name on her lips—fuck. He'd never heard anything as sweet. Her pussy hugged him and snapped the last of his control.

Chapter 13

BRIAN

"CASSIE, FUCK..." The room tipped sideways. Or it was just him, losing blood flow to every part of his body except his cock, which had to be three times its normal size. He dug his fingers into her hips. Held her there while he came like he'd never fucking come in his life. Collapsed half on top of her in a sweaty, breathless heap. "I meant what I said." He caught her chin, tipped her face to his for a long, deep kiss. "About loving you. And not letting you go."

She didn't speak. Didn't move. Just lay beneath him with closed eyes while her breathing settled and her normal color returned. After coming as hard and intensely as she had, she was probably borderline exhausted. Possibly hadn't heard a word he'd said. As much as he didn't want to move, he wanted to take care of her more. Now. Always.

This was the first time he'd given her that kind of orgasm, and the bed was wet from more than their damp post-shower skin. He loved restraining her, dominating her while she hungrily submitted—but this was the sexiest, most vulnerable he'd seen her. Despite scratching and biting the hell out of him, she'd been helpless beneath him. Completely at the mercy of the pleasure he'd given. And in accepting that ecstasy, she'd claimed him as thoroughly as he'd done to her.

He placed a soft kiss on her forehead. Gently strummed her nipple with his thumb. His cock, still semi-hard, stirred inside her, ready for more. Unbelievable after coming the way he had. He rose over her again and stroked upward, one time, to hear her soft little moan, before sliding slowly from her body. "Oh fuck."

Cassie's sex-drugged eyes blinked open. "What's wrong, are you going to be late for something?"

No, but she might, a couple of weeks from now. Unless she'd gone on the Pill. They'd discussed it a few weeks back and that'd been the plan. She must have, or she'd have stopped him, reminded him to suit up, as she had other times.

He shook his head. "Everything else on my schedule can wait." He leaned over and kissed her cheek. "Pretend you're chained to my bed like we talked about. I'll be right back with a towel and a drink."

CASSIE

She nodded. Managed a smile, even. But everything was such a mess, one hundred times worse than before.

They should've had hard sex, angry sex. One last bang, then she could've said what she needed and walked out the door, for good. But no…he'd made love to her instead. Oh, there'd been hard and it'd had plenty of bang—the fireworks-in-her-head-and-stars-shooting-through-her-body kind—but it'd been the opposite of angry. He'd told her he loved her. Again. Twice.

In an apartment this small, it didn't take long to hit the kitchen and bathroom, and Brian was already halfway back to the bed. Gloriously naked—the man had no sense of modesty, thank god—but he didn't look his usual, relaxed self. Tension bunched in his neck and shoulders. Shadows had found a home under his eyes. All of it her fault.

She willed some solidity to her bones and shuffled to a semi-seated position. Ridiculous as it was, she tugged the sheet that'd been twisted beneath them up to cover herself.

"Chilly?"

"A little," she lied.

A quick side trip to his sofa and he was back at his bed, one of his t-shirts in hand. "This'll work better. The sheets are kind of damp."

She ran a palm over the smooth cotton. Oh god. Damp was a polite understatement. "Sorry, that was, um, a first for me." And here she'd thought all the hype about G-spot orgasms was exactly that. Consider her among the thoroughly educated.

"The first of many, I'll make sure of it." Ego lived in the smile on his face, to be sure, but more than that, he looked—satisfied. As if he couldn't wait to make *her* feel that way again. He eased the shirt over her head, gently peeled the sheet away and guided her arms through the gaping sleeves. "Just your size."

Not even close on the shirt. The man whose scent was all over the shirt, on the other hand, was exactly that. And she had to let him go. Truly, this time.

"I—I'll be right back." Head down, she grabbed the towel he'd placed by her knee and scurried to his washroom. She wrenched his shirt from her body. Buried her face in the soft, warm fabric and choked back sobs that desperately wanted to escape. A new wave threatened each time she tried to set the t-shirt aside. Somehow, she had to pull herself together.

The door opened after a light knock she hadn't acknowledged. "Hey. You okay? Did I—" His Adam's apple rose and fell as he swallowed. He surveyed her face, her body. "I know I went pretty damn deep. Did I hurt you? Tell me the truth."

"No, god no." Nothing changed in his expression. Even knowing the truth about Leanne, he still didn't trust himself. That was the trouble with trust—once it'd been broken, deep inside, getting it back was almost impossible. She got that. Boy, did she ever. "You didn't hurt me. You never have, I swear." She wanted to throw her arms around him so badly. That'd only make leaving harder.

The cloud lifted, then he narrowed his eyes at her again. "You're still shaking—why'd you take off my shirt?"

Because she was terrified of losing her will if she stayed wrapped in the security of his smell. "I didn't want to get it wet. You know," she tipped her head, "from me."

"I don't care about that." Now he smiled and pulled her into his arms. "Besides, I'm equally to blame." His nose burrowed into her hair, found the spot behind her ear that always made her shiver. "You felt so good around me, so wet and warm…if I could've fucked you for hours, I would have. I could try that again, right now."

She should say no. "Brian…"

He slid his hand down her back, over the curve of her ass to her leg, which he hitched up and planted on the tub behind him. Clearly, he'd missed the *no* in the desperate way she'd said his name. The pad of his thumb settled above her clit. Two firm circles and her arms were around his back, clinging. He bent at the knees. Caught her mouth under his and coaxed her lips apart with his tongue. The head of his cock teased between her legs. He cupped her behind and thrust, filling her.

"Brian—stop."

His muscles tensed as he froze. "Too soon? Are you sore?"

"Condom," she whispered.

"What?"

"We need a condom." While her cheeks flamed, his had lost all trace of color.

"You're not on the Pill now?"

Realization dawned as her head shook in exaggerated slow motion. The heat of the moment, the wet sheets, the things he'd said. "Before…you didn't…?"

"No."

The emptiness as he withdrew from her body triggered the tears she'd held back minutes earlier.

"I thought—fuck, I didn't think. Don't cry. I'll take care of it. Of you."

"You can't."

"The hell I can't." His arms tightened around her, his lips moving against the top of her head. "We'll work through it. All of it. Whatever happened to keep you away, anything life throws at us, now and years from now."

Another sob heaved in her chest. "It's not that easy."

"It doesn't have to be easy to be great."

She should've pulled free. Put her clothes on and left. Instead, she pressed her face tighter to the warm, solid wall of his chest. "It can't work…you don't understand."

"So make me, Cassie. This time, *you* make *me*." He grasped her arms and stepped back, looming over her, filling the small space with his presence and deep voice. "You know how I feel. You know who I am, *what* I am, the worst things I've done. You're still here. What the fuck is it you think I can't handle about you? Or is it that you just don't trust me?"

"Some things aren't mine to offer in trust. I learned that the hard way."

"No more riddles and evasion. Just tell me. Goddamn it, Cassie." Raw emotions—anger, exasperation—played across his face, in the tight set of his muscles and his grip on her shoulders.

"I can't."

"Bullshit."

"Brian…" How could she make him understand without —making him understand. "My life, my secrets, involve other people. A lot of other people in intimate, compromising situations."

"So, what—you were a call girl, or you worked in a rub-n-tug or something?"

"Oh my god, no. That's disgusting." She shivered again, head to toe.

He blew out a frustrated breath and swiped the t-shirt from her hands. Popped it over her head for the second time. "Because it wouldn't matter."

"It'd be okay with you if I pay the bills by jerking guys off, or—more?"

"Fuck no. I'd work around the clock to keep you from doing that now." This time, when he held her shoulders, his touch was gentle. To match his eyes. "But if you'd done it in the past, even recently, it wouldn't keep me away or change how I feel. Nothing you could say will."

"I don't deserve you."

"You're right, you deserve a hell of a lot better. I'm just hoping you'll settle for an unemployed brute with a criminal record who'd do anything for you."

God, her heart. "I want to, so much."

"Good." The charming smile she'd fallen for months ago slid into place.

"But I can't make the same promise. Remember what you said to me, that you don't want a relationship that can't handle full disclosure? That's me. What I used to do…it's confidential."

"Not a hooker. Must be a spy then. Got it. No problem, Agent Johnson—if that is your real name—it's in the vault."

"You know I'm not a spy."

He winked. "Sure you're not."

Here she was, trying to explain, quite seriously, why she couldn't be with him, and he was being sweet and joking. "People aren't always what they seem." She bent to gather her discarded bag. "I have something to show you. The reason I came over." She fished out an envelope and handed it to him. "Look inside."

He pulled out the business check. "This is for the Iron Works job? Nice."

"That's the deposit, the project is still in progress."

"Very nice." He shot her a hard look. "Trevor backed off after that night at Barolo, right?"

"Completely. Thank you."

"Don't. My fault you were in that position in the first place."

"Wait," she said when he stuffed the check back into the envelope. "It's not the numbers I wanted you to see, it's the signature."

His eyes bounced from her face to the paper. "Leonard Ritchie."

"Trevor's dad. The real owner of Iron Works."

"What the fuck?"

"Trevor's supposed to be the manager and figurehead, but he has no real power. It took a little digging. I'm fortunate to have some well-connected friends in the local business world." Namely Paulo and Beth, who'd brought her the information on a platter, along with delicious takeout from the restaurant, to make sure she was eating while crying her eyes out. "Any contracts you signed that had Trevor's name on the bottom can go straight to the recycling box. They mean nothing."

"Christ. I had no idea. We're paid by direct deposit, I've never seen Leonard's name or met the man."

Now it was clicking. At least she could do this for him. "I have the senior Mr. Ritchie's number. I don't think he'll be too happy to hear how his son treats his employees. Or members. I bet you'll get your job back as soon as he finds out what happened, especially if you tell him what you've learned about Leanne's lies."

"That's the important thing you came over to talk about— how to get my job back?"

She could barely speak around the lump in her throat. "Yes."

"Not what's spooking you and how we can fix it."

"No."

Everything about him hardened. He yanked the towel from its bar and secured it around his waist. "Guess I'll let you get dressed so you can take off, then." And he left, jerking the bathroom door closed behind him.

No crying until she got to her car. Out of his apartment, at least. She tipped her head up while dressing, as if that would make the tears funnel back inside her head instead of spilling down her face, turning her nose red and mottling her cheeks. The mirror didn't lie—she was a mess, inside and out. She deserved to be at this point. She'd come here to fix things for Brian, not hurt him more. He'd thought he wasn't good enough for her...he was probably in the other room realizing how backward he'd gotten that one.

She scribbled Leonard Ritchie's contact info on a scrap of paper and tucked it behind the edge of the mirror. Gave her puffy eyes a final dab. She stepped into the body of his apart-ment, head down but peeking up through eyelashes and untamed damp hair. If she'd expected him to make this easy for her by giving her his back, no such luck. He stood beside the door, arms folded over his t-shirt-clad chest, eyes riveted to her every step.

"You're mine until you walk out this door, remember?"

She froze in front of him. He hadn't put an arm out to stop her, nor did he need to. They both knew that. A small blessing. If he touched her, softly or otherwise, she'd crumble.

"Answer two questions before you go."

"If I c—" She squeezed her eyes shut along with her lips, then forced herself to meet his probing stare. "Okay."

"What did your asshole ex do to burn you so badly?"

Answering this skated very close to things she hadn't told him, couldn't. The open door waited. Nothing prevented her from walking away right now. Nothing tangible, anyway.

"That's not an easy question to answer."

"I already told you what I think about easy."

Leather squeaked from her death grip on the purse strap. "I found out he was cheating, so I ended it. Then he used things I'd told him and blackmailed me out of my house and studio. If I hadn't signed it over, people who trusted me would've been hurt." God help her, bring on the next ques-tion. At least he could only ask one.

"I understand."

About taking responsibility for your actions even though it meant sacrificing your future—he'd certainly proven that. Multiple times. Exactly *what* and *who* she'd paid to protect, though, he couldn't possibly imagine. She shuffled on the spot while they stared at each other. Each second that ticked by seemed to soften his tense body language. Hers only ratcheted tighter.

KARLA DOYLE

"I should go," she whispered, putting one foot in front of the other.

"Do you love me?"

The four words froze her, mid-step. "What?"

"That's my second question. Should be an easy one—yes or no."

BRIAN

"Thanks for doing this, I owe you."

Ian grinned from his sprawled position on the couch. "Adding it to the ledger. Don't think I won't collect."

Total bullshit and they both knew it. Brian and his brother had managed to sidestep the sibling-drama thing since they were kids. They had each other's backs, period. Neither worried about keeping the scale even. Good thing, because Ian's tray would be on the ground right now. Today's favor didn't have monetary value like the other recent deeds, but it was sure as hell as important.

A little Ford pulled in, catching Brian's attention. "She's here. Get off your lazy ass."

"That's the thanks I get after my selflessness...I'm crushed." Nothing but lighthearted trash-talk—Ian's feet had hit the floor by Brian's second word.

Side by side, they watched Cassie through a strip Brian had cleared on the warehouse's front door. It'd been a week since she'd run from his apartment. Forever and too fucking long. He'd have resorted to stalking her if he hadn't been so damn busy working. Now that she was here, fifty feet away, he couldn't drag his eyes from her.

She gave the building a thorough once-over. Checked the

address against a piece of paper, then shoved it in her bag. She obviously had no clue who'd been behind the call to get her over here. Good news so far.

She set a shoulder bag on the asphalt, leaned into the backseat of her car to retrieve her portfolio case. What a great ass. And legs. Her skirt and blouse were all business, but on Cassie, they still looked sexy. When she closed the car, collected her bags and turned toward the building, it took everything in him not to throw open the door, charge out there and sweep her into his arms.

"Man, you've got it in spades."

Another time, he would've given Ian a shot to his grinning mug, or at least a sarcastic comeback. He shrugged, letting his gaze drift back to the adorable woman heading across the pavement. "Wouldn't you, if she were yours?"

Ian clapped him on the shoulder. "I hope this works."

"Yeah, me too."

Ian ducked behind a leg press machine about twenty feet back and rattled tools as if the thing weren't already fully assembled. Brian joined in the farce on a nearby piece of equipment. Good thing he wasn't actually putting it together, because his hands were actually shaking.

"Come on in," Ian called at Cassie's knock on the glass.

She hadn't recognized Ian's voice when he'd called to set up this meeting—and why would she, it'd been two years since she took his picture—so they'd used it again to get her into the building. If she'd heard Brian's voice, he bet she'd already be back at the car. No more running. This had to work.

"Hello?" Tentatively, she stepped through the door. "I'm Cassie Johnson, the photographer. We have an appointment to talk about…" Her eyes widened as he straightened, directly in her line of sight. "Brian," she whispered. "What is this?"

Yeah, she wanted to know why he'd lured her here. He'd

tell her everything soon enough. Meanwhile, he answered her question literally. "Right now it's a warehouse with some gym equipment. What it *will* be, after a shitload of renos, is Focus Fitness, my personal training studio."

"You didn't go back to Iron Works?"

"No. But I appreciate you tuning the old man into Trevor's bullshit."

The shrug she gave was loaded with tension. "The least I could do after…everything."

"It was huge. It meant a lot." The senior Ritchie had called two days after Cassie had shown Brian the check. She'd put her neck and the Iron Works gig on the block by telling Trevor's father what'd gone down between the three of them. The result, for Brian, had been an offer to be the *official* general manager of Iron Works—with Trevor as his underling. He'd almost said yes for the enjoyment that would have provided.

He set aside the wrench he'd squeezed so hard it'd left an imprint on his palm, then stepped around the vertical press machine, closing the distance separating them to a couple of feet. One small move and he'd be touching her. Even without direct contact, their connection crackled. The softness in her eyes stole his ability to speak. Yeah, this was going to work. Had to.

He edged a half step closer. "So, what do you think?"

"About what?"

Her scent filled his head. Citrus and roses and *Cassie*. "About this." He motioned, his fingers making a small oval between them. "The future." He let that sit a few seconds. "I've got enough room here for lots of equipment and I'll still have a large, open space. I'll be able to run the boot camp classes year-round."

"The gym, right. It's great, people will be beating the door down to get to you."

Damn, he wanted to touch her. Not yet. "Including you?" he asked, smiling and coaxing a small one from her in return.

"If you hire me to do promo shots, yes. Otherwise, I think your services will be outside my budget."

He relieved her of the bag and case, setting them on the floor. The simple brushing of fingers and he was done. All-in and going for it. He caught her hands and brought them—and her—to his chest. "My services will always be complimentary for you."

"Brian, don't."

"You said yes." Right before tearing from his apartment, not to be heard from since.

"Love doesn't solve problems."

"It's one hell of a motivator, though."

"Brian…" Everything shook. Her head in a side-to-side motion, her body in a fit of trembling.

"Hear me out." He leaned in, mouth grazing her ear as he spoke. "Or I could *make* you listen. Look at all these shiny pieces of equipment I could tie you to while I…talk." Playing on their physical chemistry hadn't necessarily worked out for him the other times he'd done it, but here and now, it kept her from bolting. Her shallow breathing and pink cheeks told him he had her attention, at least for the next few minutes.

"I won't be able to work with you if you insist on doing this."

"You mean this?" He caught her earlobe between his teeth for a firm nip. "What about this?" The sweet spot at the base of her neck received similar treatment. "I'd show you all the other things I insist on doing if my brother wasn't here."

Every muscle in her body stiffened. "I-I have to go."

Like hell. He tightened his grip on her wrists, knowing she

had to be freaking out and hating himself for causing it. Had to be done. "This is Ian's building. He's my not-so-silent partner, so he'll be around sometimes. And we'll use him in the promo pictures, since he'll work for free and cameras seem to like him, even though I think he's an ugly little runt."

"Hey, I heard that." Ian's good-natured laugh followed. Then he was on his feet, picking his way around equipment to join them.

Pure panic filled the eyes flitting between the men. "Brian, please—let me go."

"Not letting you run again. We agreed to deal with the bumps, remember? You asked me to never let you go and I promised you I wouldn't."

Her face had a deep flush, tears welled in the corners of her eyes. But he didn't release her. If this little intervention he'd staged didn't pan out as he hoped, she would truly never speak to him again, of that much he was sure. The other possibility totally justified the risk.

Only when Ian was a stride away did he free her hands. Amazingly, she didn't use them to smack him in the face or twist his balls into knots.

"Cassie, you remember Ian?"

She stared up at him as things clicked into place. "He's the one who called to set this up…"

Brian wouldn't apologize, that'd be a lie. "Did what I had to do to get you here."

"Hey, Cassie." Ian offered a smile. "It's been awhile. And I'm a schmuck for not keeping in touch. I always meant to email you and thank you for the fantastic shots you took for my portfolio. Got me my first big magazine spread."

"And he does mean *spread*," Brian threw in.

"Asshole," Ian said, driving a fist into Brian's unmoving shoulder.

"That too," Brian ducked a second jab, "though I don't think it was Cassie who took *those* pictures. If so," he grinned at her, "I hope you charged him double."

CASSIE

She stood, though barely, bottom lip in the vicinity of her knees, while Brian ribbed his brother about various nude shots and Ian halfheartedly threw punches in return. This couldn't be happening.

"You *knew*?" The giant space spun around her. Exactly what—how much—did he know?

"Whoa, easy. I have you." Brian's arms curled around her as the floor buckled. "Still not letting you go."

Somewhere between the pulse drumming in her temples and the steady thump of Brian's heart beneath her ear, a door clicked closed.

"Ian left, we're alone now. Hang on, going up."

She didn't resist as he scooped her into his arms. Or when he kept her there, on his lap, while seated on a long leather couch. The fight to keep her secret was over. All that remained was tallying the damage.

"How—when?"

"From Ian, after everything that went down at Barolo. He recognized your name when I showed him your website. He tried to bring up your *other* website, but it was gone."

"I'd already pulled it down by then. I quit doing those shoots the day I realized I was helplessly in love with you. I thought I could bury it and move on, with you. Then I saw Ian's picture at your parents' and knew it'd always be there, haunting me, even if I never took another erotic photo in my life."

The arms around her tightened and he pressed his lips to

her head. "Baby, I don't care what—or who, or how—you take pictures of. Don't change a thing for me, I love every part of you."

Baby—an endearment normally reserved for their most intimate moments. Only a fool would push a man like this away. Still, she had to ask. "At your apartment…why didn't you tell me you knew?"

"At the time, I thought if you loved me, you'd trust me enough to tell me yourself."

She shifted to a straddle, facing him. His close-clipped beard tickled her fingers as she cupped his jaw. "I *do* love you." Those words had never felt more right. And god, the instant smile on his face—it lit the whole, huge building. Probably would've lit the entire city. It definitely lit her world. "I love you, but there will always be things I can't share with you. Not because I don't trust you—"

"Because they're not yours to share. I get that now, and I respect it. Always will." His strong hands kneaded her butt through the hiked-up skirt, pulled the fitted blouse from the waistband and slid under the material, skimming up her back to her nape. He guided her forward, his eyes sparkling with a sizzling combination of love and raw lust. "Taking what I want."

"A kiss?" she whispered against his mouth.

"Your heart."

"Too late…you've already got it."

The squeak of leather masked her shriek as he reversed their positions. He stroked her face, tucked that one stubborn wave of hair behind her ear. Snug between her thighs, he rocked, pressing a hard ridge right where she needed it.

"What's that wicked little smile about?" he asked.

"Thinking of all the money I'm going to save on batteries in the future."

"Glad I can help with your budget." *His* lips were downright sinful. "I know another way you can save money…quit wearing these." A quick, singlehanded jerk relieved her of her red thong.

"Hey," she said when he tossed the torn silk to the floor. "Those were my lucky panties."

He raised one ginger eyebrow. "You came to a business appointment with a stranger hoping to get lucky?"

"Yes, lucky enough to land another big promo job."

"Then the panties worked. You're hired."

"Don't you think you should wait for my quote? I don't come cheap."

"As long as you come hard and often, I'm happy to foot the bill." He hovered over her, trailing butterfly-soft kisses and deliciously sharp nips along her neck, over her breasts as he freed them, then down, to the insides of her thighs. "I'll be running a tab," his eyes twinkled up at her, "starting now."

BRIAN

The grand opening. Four months in the making and a shitload of hard labor and debt later, it was finally happening.

"It looks incredible, let's go inside."

He unzipped his Focus Fitness monogramed hoodie, pulled Cassie's shivering body in front of him and wrapped her in fleece and his arms. "One more minute. Then I'll take you into my office and warm you up before the crowd gets here. Assuming anybody shows up."

"Of course they'll show. People been hitting the website, emailing and calling for over a month, asking when they can get in. You're going to have so many clients, you'll have to hire other trainers to keep up with the demand."

Anybody could say stuff like that. Because it came from her, his chest puffed out and his nerves eased off. Wild, the effect she had on him. She'd been there for him every step of the way. Pitching in, offering support, coming up with incredible ideas, telling him straight up when he was being an ass about stuff. She'd iced his bumps and bruises, massaged his aching muscles until he dropped into a coma-like sleep some nights. Others, she'd tested the limits of his cardiovascular fitness by fucking him into a pheromone-induced frenzy. Every day was different. Every day was the same—amazing.

"There's your parents." She giggled. "Your dad's wearing a kilt...in December. He must be freezing his you-know-whats off."

"Do yourself a favor, cutie, don't ask him if he's warm enough in the kilt." Though he had to admit, seeing Cassie turn deep-red might be worth it. She was adorable when she blushed.

"Oh look, Sam's here too." She tipped her head up and graced him with her beautiful smile. "Guess the quickie's out of the question."

As if they'd have had a quickie. Those didn't exist since he'd found Cassie. He could spend an entire day worshipping her, owning her, and still crave more.

Two more cars pulled in across the lot. His brother stepped out of a Camaro—his winter beater, unbelievably—and the Mancusos from their Cadillac.

"We should go, everybody's waiting for you to hang the *Open* sign."

"I'm one lucky son of a bitch."

She jabbed him in the ribs with one wicked-pointy elbow. "Hey, don't insult my favorite haggis maker."

And future mother-in-law, as soon as he thought Cassie was ready. Might take years, but they'd get there someday. He was sure of it. He kissed her nose, then her lips. One swipe of her sweet, talented tongue inside his mouth and his cock went to standby mode.

"This'll sound nuts, but I can't wait for this day to be over so we can hang the *Closed* sign and celebrate in private."

She turned in his arms, smiled up at him. "Me too."

"Your place or mine?" The pullout sofa bed in his office-slash-apartment wasn't the most comfortable for sleeping, but by the time they'd finished the *celebrations* he had in mind, he doubted they'd care where they crashed.

"How about both—at once." She disentangled from his arms and fished a single link of chain from her pocket. "Move in with me. I love you, I want to start and finish every day with you. I want to pull into the driveway and have my whole day made because you're already there, sharing every part of my life."

She'd obviously had the key ring custom-made, because it'd been soldered closed, making its contents permanent. A key for the front door, one for the back. He fingered a small, third key hanging alongside the others. "What's this for?"

"Say yes and you'll find out."

"Yes, baby. Always and forever, yes."

Epilogue

BRIAN

SIX MONTHS of living together hadn't dulled his need for Cassie. Not even a little. The new gym kept him insanely busy, but even when he was training clients, talking to suppliers or inputting data into one of the many spreadsheets operating his own business required, she was on his mind. From the moment he woke with his arms wrapped around her until the last second of consciousness before he fell asleep holding her tight. He craved her. Seven days a week. Just a bit more on Sundays—key day.

In the front pocket of his khakis, Brian located the link of chain with its three keys. Cassie's gift to him the day Focus Fitness opened. Also the day she'd asked him to move in with her, officially and permanently. One of the best days of his life.

He isolated the smallest key and rubbed it between his thumb and index fingers. The key opened a wooden box on their dresser. Another gift she'd given him that day. They didn't need props or accessories in the bedroom, hell no. Cassie was the only fantasy or sex toy he'd ever need and he was pretty damn sure she felt the same about him. The weekly contents of the box were just a bonus.

The first time he'd opened the box, he found two long, red silk scarves inside, along with a note. *Use these any way you can imagine.* That's exactly what he'd done, many times and many ways since. That first night, he'd used the scarves to blindfold her and bind her hands behind her back, after which he'd done all manner of things to her body. Yeah, that memory was a keeper.

Each week, Cassie put something new in the box. She might drop hints throughout the week, hints that made him fucking crazy with curiosity and lust, but he'd never strayed from her rule—no peeking. He could only use his key on Sunday evening, the one night of the week they'd set aside to share completely. No gym or photography-related commitments. Phones shut off and blinds pulled. Time for just the two of them…and whatever she'd put in the box.

Sometimes it was a sex toy. Sometimes an everyday article she wanted him to use during sex, such as the silk scarves. Sometimes when he opened the box, it contained a sexy photo of Cassie or a note detailing a fantasy she wanted him to bring to life. Those made him insta-hard. Brought his inner beast roaring to the surface. Not so long ago, he'd fought to suppress that side of himself. From their first night together, Cassie hadn't just accepted his rougher side, she'd enjoyed it. Craved it.

He pulled his cell from his pocket and tapped in a text while moving toward the office.

Just locked up. Little bit of paperwork to do

before I leave. Should be home in about 45 minutes. Can't wait to be with you.

Her reply popped up almost immediately.

If you knew what I put in the box, you'd skip the paperwork and come home now.

Nothing but truth there. Not only were Cassie's sexual preferences a perfect match for his, he already knew what she'd chosen this week. Nipple clamps connected by a silver chain. They'd seen them at a sex toy exhibition in Toronto a couple months ago. The pink in her cheeks when she'd picked them up had been all he needed to say, "We'll take it" to the sales rep. Cassie had shaken her head, tugged on his arm to lead him away from the booth.

She loved when he pinched her nipples hard. Really fucking hard. The idea of clamps turned her on—a lot—but she was afraid they might hurt *too much*. He'd never let that happen. Never. He'd make sure she got just enough pain to satisfy her appetite.

He hadn't tried to convince her though. Pressuring her into something she wasn't one hundred percent sure about was another thing he'd never do.

Also on that list—breaking her rule and opening the box in advance. Until this week. A necessary exception, because he had something very specific he wanted to do to her. Something more intimate than anything they'd done before.

Fuck it, the paperwork could wait until tomorrow. He changed course and headed for the exit. Killed the lights, locked the doors, then crossed the parking lot to his Jeep. He had another text typed by the time he settled in behind the steering wheel.

Doesn't matter what's in the box. I'll skip anything just to be with you. Home in 15.

CASSIE

If Cassie's heart beat any harder, Brian would be able to hear it all the way out in the driveway. She had sixty seconds, ninety max, to change her mind about the nipple clamps in the box on their dresser. The replacement item was ready to go. She could swap the glass butt plug for the clamps before he made it to the front door and he'd be none the wiser. Then the kaleidoscope of butterflies in her stomach could take a break for the night.

He hopped out of the dark-green Jeep—which had its doors off, of course—and met her gaze through the living room window. His sinfully sexy mouth curved into a smile. Oh, the things that mouth could do. Would do, once he got inside the house. Mouth, hands, cock, etcetera, no matter what he did, he always made it feel amazing. Better than amazing.

The clamps would stay in the box. She wanted this experience. Wanted it with the man who valued her mind, worshipped her body, and owned her heart.

She left the window to meet him at the front door. Just like the first night, she greeted him in her short, silky robe. She'd worn it around him so many times, he shouldn't even take notice, yet his blue-eyed gaze traveled over her body as if seeing her for the first time. Wait until he got a glimpse of what she had beneath the satin.

He closed and locked the door without taking his eyes off her. "You look incredible. I should've driven faster." His lunch bag hit the floor with a soft *thud*. He reached for her, snagged her by the waist and pulled her against his chest. "Maybe I'll rework the schedule so I'm home by noon on Sundays."

"That'd give us a lot more hours together," she said, sliding her palms up his big, hard body to the short, soft beard she loved touching. "What would we do with that extra time?"

"I have a few ideas."

"Oh? Refinish the deck? Paint the bathroom?"

His blue eyes twinkled as he smiled. "My do-to list starts in the bedroom."

"I think you meant *to-do* list."

He shook his head. "A to-do list is work. Errands and chores, obligatory shit." Without warning, he scooped her off the ground and into his arms, then headed for the bedroom. "My do-to list is entirely about pleasure."

"And there are only a few things on it? Uh oh," she said, baiting the big ginger bear.

"A few per day." Inside their room, he placed her on the bed, caging her there with his arms and heated gaze. "Maybe more than you can handle."

"Never."

His lips curved into a sexy smile. He rose, crossed the room to the dresser, to the box.

Time to see if she truly could handle *more*. She held her breath as he picked up the box. The metaphorical butterflies in her chest resumed their mad fluttering. She shifted to her knees, loosened the robe to reveal her new demi-bra. One that barely covered her nipples. Perfect for tonight. Inside the sheer, lacy cups, her nipples tingled as they hardened. Heat rippled through her, anticipation pushing her temperature higher with each step he took toward the bed.

The clamps were going to hurt. That was the point. But it

259

wouldn't be bad pain, because Brian would be delivering it, controlling it. He'd make her come because it hurt so good.

He set the box in front of her and withdrew the custom-made key chain she'd given him from his pocket. Metal softly met metal as he inserted the smallest key in the lock. "About that 'never' you mentioned..."

She swallowed hard. Reminded herself to breathe. Something she'd only had the courage to fantasize about was about to become reality. Because of this incredible, sexy man she trusted like nobody else in the world. Her dream man.

He didn't open the box. Instead, he turned it until the lock faced her. They didn't have a scripted routine for these evenings, but this isn't how they did things. He always opened the box. Always.

He knelt by the bed, lifted her hand and placed it on the key. "Never's a long time. So is forever, but even that won't be enough time with you."

"Brian," she whispered, unable to shut down the scenario running through her head. Another thing she'd only fantasized about. Something they hadn't discussed, not even casually. It couldn't be that. "What is this?"

He nodded at the box. "Open it and find out."

With shaking hands, she turned the key, lifted the box's lid. "Oh my god..."

The nipple clamps were still inside, but he'd pooled the connecting chain into a small pile, which served as cushioning for a ring. *A ring.* One that took her breath away.

A large, sparkling diamond nestled in the middle of a Celtic knot, the loops of which wrapped around a diamond-studded rose-gold band. Delicate yet strong, it was absolutely stunning.

"It's beautiful, but too expensive a gift."

"If I did this on a weekly basis, yeah. But since I only

intend to buy one engagement ring in the rest of my life, I wanted to do it right."

Her gaze snapped from the ring to his waiting eyes. Engagement ring. He'd said engagement ring.

He clasped her hands inside his large, warm ones. "I've wanted you since the day I laid eyes on you. Liked you the first time we talked. Loved you since that rainy night when you lured me to your house with a conveniently forgotten cell phone."

"Hey, I *did* forget it," she said, giving his shoulder a light-hearted, and utterly pointless, shove. "In my rush to leave the gym before I made more of a fool of myself drooling over you, the phone fell out of my bag."

"Sure it did, cutie." He winked and lifted the chain from the box, letting the ring slide off, onto his palm. Their eyes met as he offered the ring between his thumb and index finger. "I'm going to spend the rest of forever doing everything in my power to make you happy. If you'll have me, I'd like to do that as your husband. Will you marry me?"

Marriage. The real deal. She'd be legally bound to him, sharing everything. Her secrets would be his secrets. His scars would be her scars. The future, though, would be theirs. They'd build it together. She couldn't think of anything she wanted more. That didn't mean she had to make it easy on him. He'd be disappointed if she did.

"Hmm..." she said, trailing her fingertips over the gorgeous ring. "Depends. Will you wear a kilt to the wedding ceremony?"

"Depends. Will you let me push it up so I can fuck my beautiful, sexy wife as soon as she's mine forever?"

"No," she said, as straight-faced as possible, her smile and giggle winning out at his speechless, wide-eyed response. "I won't *let* you fuck me, I'll demand that you do."

"Guess I should have called you my beautiful, sexy, bossy wife."

She slid her palms along his broad shoulders. "Call me whatever you want, as long as the description starts with 'my' and ends with 'wife'."

"Is that a yes?" He turned the ring in his fingers, casting sparkles around the room

"Yes," she said, offering her trembling left hand. "A million times yes."

"I like those odds." He stilled her shakiness with his strong, stable touch, then slid the ornate band onto its new and permanent home, circling her ring finger. "Fits perfectly."

"Like you do."

"Like we do," he said, easing her onto her back as he joined her on the bed. He stretched her newly adorned hand above her head, smiling down at her as his thumb rubbed back and forth over the ring.

"Like we do," she said, copying his perfect words. "Though it wouldn't hurt to check the fit."

"I can do that." He dipped down, brushed his lips over hers. Gently at first, then deeper. He slid his free hand inside her panties, teasing her pussy and clit with his fingers as he stroked in and out of her mouth with his tongue.

"Future husband…" She nodded upward, used her eyes to direct his attention to the nipple clamps, where they'd been pushed off to one side of the bed, above her head. "I wouldn't mind if it *actually* hurt a little when you do that checking."

Raw desire flickered in his eyes. She'd roused the beast. *Her* beast, officially, for the rest of forever.

I HOPE YOU ENJOYED BRIAN & Cassie's forbidden love story! If so, I hope you'll leave a review or star-rating on Goodreads, Amazon, or wherever you enjoy discussing books.

~ *Karla*

YOUR NEXT VERY PERSONAL training session is with Brian's best friend, Sam, in **Worth the Wait**. Start reading it now!

> When personal trainer Sam bumps into his favorite former client, their chemistry reignites instantly. Leigh is everything he pictured in his sometime-down-the-road woman. Sexy, funny, independent, mature—in more ways than one. He never cared about their age gap, he just wasn't ready to get serious before. He's ready now. But when his prior playboy ways come back to bite him in the ass, it'll take more than sizzling sex and charm to convince Leigh to stick around.
>
> Leigh's life is humming along according to plan. Her custom bakery is thriving. Her daughter is a well-adjusted ten-year-old. Romance is the one area that's lacking. Completely. Until the universe fulfills her

request for some hot lovin' and puts Sam in her path—
for a second time. Sam gives her exactly what she was
missing, and more. Maybe more than her well-structured life plan can handle…

WORTH THE WAIT

Chapter 1

LEIGH

Leigh jogged across Dundas Street, waving a thank-you at the
rare gentleman who'd stopped to respect the pedestrian cross-
ing. Another minute and she'd have given up and turned back
to her shop. She had three-dozen cupcakes to transform into
superheroes, a double-layer, red-velvet cake to bake, and an
appointment with a bridezilla before this day ended—and it
was already two-thirty. But first, she needed a coffee.

Correction, she needed somebody else to make and serve
her a coffee. A big fancy one with a triple shot of eighteen-
percent cream and a generous dose of sugar. Every minute of
her day was allotted for something specific. This minute, along
with the next five, were scheduled for coffee. The schedule
kept her sane. On busy days like today, so did a big fancy
coffee.

She pulled the door and stepped into Bean There, blinking
as her eyes adjusted from the bright, June day to the coffee
shop's interior lighting. A couple more blinks and the darkness
morphed into shadowy outlines of tables and chairs, dotted
with midafternoon patrons—one of whom was looking her
way. Intently.

Leigh checked over her shoulder, ready to apologize for

blocking somebody's path, but saw only the door. Maybe she'd been wrong, maybe the lighting had played tricks with her vision and he hadn't been staring in her direction.

She glanced at the guy again while walking toward the counter. Nope, she hadn't been wrong.

He was definitely watching *her*. Maybe she had flour in her hair or a smear of icing across her t-shirt. Whatever the reason, she'd take it, because the guy staring from under the low brim of his ballcap had the best shoulders and arms she'd seen on a man outside the gym. The body of a hot *younger* man. And, oh god, he was smiling.

Something about him pinged on her radar. More than raw attraction, there was a sense of familiarity. Hard to know for sure while her vision was still muted. The fact that she couldn't see any features above his sexy, smiling mouth didn't help either.

He'd probably been in the bakery with some equally young fiancée, checking out wedding cakes, and had smiled at her out of recognition. Or, since she'd been cursed with one of those faces that never lie—and his good looks and the blip of attention he'd given her had initiated a pleasant tingle to the south—he was simply amused by the cougar drooling over him.

Regardless, no more ogling. But, oh boy, his sexy grin was a keeper for later.

"Large vanilla latté with whipped cream and cinnamon, please. To go." She poked at a handful of coins while the coffeehouse barista prepared her order. A total ruse, she'd brought exact change plus a fifty-cent tip, as always.

The money gave her something to focus on. Her peripheral vision still worked though, and it was in overdrive, thanks to ballcap guy's muscle-filled, army-green t-shirt. He was yummier than the dessert coffee she'd ordered.

And he was leaving. He stood, slapped his male companion on the shoulder, and disappeared from her subtle sightline.

She exhaled slowly, smiling politely when her cup of comfort landed on the counter. Back to reality.

"Hey, Leigh." A deep, friendly voice slid into her ear from behind. "Haven't seen you in a while."

She knew that voice from the gym—or house of pain, as she'd once renamed it, thanks to her former personal trainer's rigorous sessions.

"Hey, Sam," she said, turning—and nearly dropping the five-dollar latté when the source of the deep voice came into view.

Hat. Army-green t-shirt packed solid with muscles. Handsome, smiling face, which she could now see more of than just his mouth. Sam was *the guy*.

She'd only seen him in gym attire, not in street clothes. And never wearing a hat. She wouldn't have thought he could get hotter than he'd been at the gym. He could. He absolutely could.

"Got it?" He still held her hand where he'd caught it and the fumbled takeout cup, saving her drink and preventing a giant, sticky mess.

Which had her mind conjuring other sticky messes she and Sam could create. Sexy ones. Not a good train of thought with the object of her lusty infatuation looking into her eyes.

"Yes, I've got it now, thanks," she said, finding words that wouldn't get her in trouble. "I didn't recognize you without your gym clothes." Heat flooded her cheeks as Sam's smile stretched into a wider grin. "As in, wearing clothes other than your gym clothes. Obviously, since I've never seen you naked." So much for finding words that wouldn't get her in trouble. "Well, I didn't make this awkward at all, did I?"

"Not one bit."

That should have been the end of it. They should be exchanging polite goodbyes and going their separate ways. Only he didn't say goodbye. Nor did he let go of her hand.

"Are you rushing off to somewhere, or do you have a few minutes to sit and catch up?"

Zero minutes, that's what she had. Negative minutes, actually. Yet the words that came out of her mouth were, "Sure, yes."

"Great." He released her hand, then placed his at the small of her back, using the contact to guide her toward a booth at the back of the café.

Maybe she'd stepped through some crack in reality and this wasn't her neighborhood coffee shop, but an alternate version. One where a hot young gym trainer wanted to spend his unpaid, personal time with a woman at least a decade older.

"So, what's new, how're you doing?" he asked after sliding onto the opposite bench. "Still hitting the gym a lot? Because you look fantastic. As always." He couldn't be flirting, he was just being nice. Because he was a nice guy. A nice, super-hot, too-young-for-her guy.

She fiddled with the cardboard sleeve circling her cup. Dared a glance across the table and found him smiling at her. A genuine smile, or one damn good facsimile thereof. Either way, it warmed her more than the coffee she sipped.

"Nothing new with me, everything's good, and yes to working out regularly." She toyed with her cup, contemplated. If he laughed in her face, so be it. What was a little more embarrassment in the grand scheme of things? "I miss seeing you at the gym."

"New trainer not kicking your ass hard enough?"

"I don't have a new trainer."

His eyebrows rose, then his gaze drifted lower, over every inch of her body not obscured by the table. "I know I said it already, but you look great. You definitely don't need a trainer anymore."

"Thank you."

"That's one of the things I've always liked about you. You know how to take a compliment." He leaned forward and folded his arms on the table. "Confidence is a sexy thing." His gaze tracked her tongue as she licked a spot of whipped cream from her lips. "So is watching you drink that coffee." He'd just called her sexy, after complimenting her physique.

This was officially the best coffee break ever.

"I find confidence sexy, too," she said, meeting his eyes straight on. "I like it when a man knows what he wants and isn't afraid to go get it."

"I'm glad you feel that way, Leigh."

Apparently, she'd used up her allotment of boldness and flirty banter, because she didn't have a comeback. Nothing she could actually say, anyway. The only words in her head were, *Let's go to my place and get naked.* And those were staying put.

"How's the new job working out?" she asked, directing conversation into safer territory. "What's it been, five or six months?" Such a ruse. She knew exactly how long he'd been missing from her gym.

"Six, and they've flown by. It's great. Brian's got an amazing setup going. Clients are loving it." Sam shifted to dig his wallet from deep within the front pocket of his jeans— damn lucky wallet—then pulled a business card from the worn leather. "Stop by sometime and I'll give you a tour."

"Are you trying to lure me away from Iron Works to Focus Fitness? Is that ethical?"

He relieved her of the coffee cup, then pulled her hand

toward him, halfway across the table. "Whatever it takes to get you there," he said, slipping the business card into her palm.

"Anything to snag a client?" Hopefully he'd missed the breathy quality so evident to her ears. From a simple, innocent touch. She needed to get laid soon. Any sex would be better than no sex at this point.

"I don't want you as a client, Leigh."

Music and the buzz of voices wove together in the background, disappearing as her pulse pounded harder and faster in her ears. Sam's hazel eyes twinkled and his smile accented the perfect, square jaw she'd wanted to touch since their first personal training session. God, that jaw. That face. That body.

She probably had drool trailing from the corner of her mouth. But she couldn't feel her face—only her hand, where he continued to tease her skin with soft strokes. And her clit, where all the sparks he'd created were headed.

A loud, startling ringtone jerked her from her Sam-induced trance.

"Shit, sorry," he said, withdrawing his hand to pull his cell from a back pocket. One glance at the screen and he answered with, "Hey, man."

This was her chance to save what little composure she had left. She waved at him, shuffled along the bench to escape, but he reached across and caught her wrist. Shook his head. Nodded toward the spot she'd just vacated. As if on command, she slid back to her original place in the booth.

"Yeah, I can cover that, no problem. I'll be there in fifteen. Hope she's okay." With that, Sam pushed the phone aside and focused on her. "I wouldn't have answered that, but Brian's girlfriend hasn't been feeling well and I knew he might be calling me to back him up at Focus."

Leigh had never been formally introduced to Brian's girl-friend, Cassie, but she'd said hello to her at Iron Works plenty of times. That was before Brian had resigned to open his own fitness studio. And taken Sam along with him.

"It's nothing serious, I hope?" she asked.

"Me too. If anyone deserves a happily ever after, it's those two."

"Do you believe in those? In happily ever afters, I mean?"

Sam leaned back, fingers laced behind his head, the casual position making his biceps pop in a dangerously distracting way. "If you'd asked me that a year ago, I would've said hell no. After seeing Brian and Cassie together, the way they click and the sacrifices they were willing to make for each other when they *weren't* together…yeah, I'm a believer."

Wow. And simultaneously, ugh. "You're going to make some young woman very happy one day." She scooped her cup off the table and shimmied out of the booth with relative fluidity, thank goodness. "I've got to get back to work. It was great to see you, Sam. Good luck with everything."

SAM

Instinct beat down the reaction to follow her out. A woman in that big a rush to get away needed space, not a tagalong.

Sam forced his butt to stick where it was planted and watched Leigh's ass sway as she cut around the tables, en route to the door.

She looked fantastic. The strictly male part of him appreciated the view. The professional part took pride in it.

She'd been a member at Iron Works for over a year, doing classes and cardio five days a week before approaching him at the desk about personal training.

His schedule had been packed, but he'd made room for her. As much time as she'd wanted. Hadn't taken long for him to see the changes in her physique. Increased muscle tone all over, making her ass even better than it'd already been. With her dedication and work ethic, she hadn't needed the quantity of training she'd bought. And had continued to buy.

He probably should have cut her loose, but he'd enjoyed the time with her too damn much. Not just for the opportunity to admire her hot body and pretty face up close. He'd enjoyed talking with her too.

Leigh had brains, a sense of humor and maturity. The whole package. She also had a kid. One she talked about frequently. And yeah, at the time, it'd spooked him.

Then he'd packed it in at Iron Works and gone to work for Brian at Focus Fitness. While he hadn't sat around pining over Leigh, she'd always been there, in the back of his mind. A what-if? Questions should have answers, one way or the other. Seeing her today brought that nagging what-if back, placed it front and center in his brain.

He stepped out of the coffee shop and headed toward his truck. Walked right past it and crossed the street, mid-block. He had to get to work, but he wanted a look at Leigh's bakeshop first.

An eye-catching sign hung over the door. *Short'n'Sweet* was written in black lettering on a bubblegum-pink background, with the words *custom bakery* in smaller letters beneath. Cute name for a business, especially since it described the owner perfectly.

No sign of her inside as he walked past the shop's large front window. Probably for the best. He didn't have time to go in if she'd waved at him. And if she hadn't, if she'd looked at him as if he were a creepy stalker, that would've sucked too. Majorly.

He made a mental note of the business hours and circled back to his two-door Sierra. Drove to the gym on autopilot, thoughts of Leigh filling his head along the way. Her easygoing laugh. The way her dirty-blonde hair shone, begging him to find out if it was as silky as it looked. Pretty face that gave away much more than her words.

He'd seen the way she looked at him all those months ago at the gym. The attraction had been there, yet she'd never come on to him. Not directly and not in any playful, joking way that might've been intended as a hint. Even after he'd flat-out asked if she was single. Either she hadn't taken *his* hint or she'd chosen to ignore it.

Today had been different. Different was good.

"Thanks for doing this," Brian said as Sam stepped through the door of the warehouse-turned-gym. "Cassie insisted I go to work this morning. Didn't want me to cancel client appointments when she just had a stomach ache." Clouds descended on the big man's face. "When I called to check on her, she said the abdominal pain had gotten worse. So bad she can't stand straight. I never should've left her alone."

"Stop beating yourself up and go home." Sam gestured toward the door. "I'll handle everything on this end."

"I don't know how long I'll be gone. Her regular doctor can't get her in, so I have to take her to the hospital. No telling how long that'll take. I might not get back here tonight."

"I've got you covered, now get going."

Brian nodded, grabbed his keys and wallet from a drawer beneath the counter, then headed out like a man on a mission.

Covering Brian's evening clients would mean postponing the visit to Short'n'Sweet, since Leigh's bakery closed at six. He'd waited this long to make a move, one more day was no big deal. Until he pictured her face, the way she'd checked him out at the coffee shop, before she'd recognized him. The way her face had lit up when she did. The desire in her eyes each time they touched.

He made his way to the changeroom. Swapped his clothes for a club t-shirt and sport pants, shoving his thickening cock to one side in the process. Sport pants hid chicken legs and weak glutes, not hard-ons. No more thinking about Leigh while he was on the clock. Piece of cake.

Cake. Bakery. Leigh.

This was going to be a long, hard night. Emphasis on hard.

SAM

With less than half an hour to spare, Sam found a parking spot up the street from Leigh's shop. Covering Brian's schedule had stretched from Wednesday afternoon into evening, then all day Thursday and most of Friday. Not that Sam blamed the guy for wanting to be by Cassie's side, but man, covering Brian's client appointments as well as his own had made for a couple of long-ass days. When his friend had shown up at the gym unexpectedly a while ago, Sam hadn't declined Brian's offer to take off.

He pocketed his keys and repositioned his hat while walking up the street. Waiting to see Leigh had given him time to think. He'd hooked up with single moms before, but he'd never wanted to add Leigh to that list.

Oh, he wanted to have sex with her. Had since day one. Spending several hours together every week, month after month, had allowed him to get to know her. The more he'd learned, the more he'd liked her mind and sense of humor as much as her shapely body.

Hadn't taken him long to realize she was relationship material, a sometime-down-the-road woman. Not somebody he'd been ready for back then. Now, though… Maybe it was time to check out that road.

He pulled the door and stepped into the bakery. Warm, sugary-scented air surrounded him, making his stomach groan. No sign of Leigh or any other adults, only a kid sitting on a stool behind a diner-style counter, with a sketchpad balanced on her lap. Whoever she was, the little girl didn't acknowledge his presence.

Until his stomach growled again, longer and louder than the first time.

"Better give that thing a cookie," she said, pointing toward a covered tray on the counter without giving him a glance.

"No thanks, I'm good."

The girl paused whatever she was working on and looked up, squarely meeting his gaze. "Don't worry, they're free." Totally deadpan. Saucy kid.

"All right." He lifted the clear glass dome and plucked a cookie from the tray. "Thank you." He bit off a third of the cookie to be polite, then inhaled the remainder because it was the best damn cookie he'd ever tasted.

The little girl continued watching him as he swallowed the last bite. "Guess you'd better have another one."

"I think you're right." The second cookie went down as fast as the first. He wasn't usually one for sweets, but if the kid turned her head, he could devour the rest of the batch in about sixty seconds.

Based on the girl's smirk, she read minds in addition to drawing pictures. "I can get your order," she said, setting her sketchpad aside and sliding off the stool. "What name is it under?"

"I haven't placed an order yet."

"Then I'll get my mom to help you."

"Actually, I'm here to see Leigh."

"Same thing," she said while walking to a door at the rear of the room. She pushed the swinging door open a crack and called, "Mommy…customer."

At Leigh.

"You're Lennox?" he asked when the girl hopped back onto the stool.

"Yup."

Shit. All the times Leigh had referred to her kid, she'd either said "Lennox" or "my ten-year-old". She'd never said daughter, and he'd always assumed son.

"Can I help y——" The voice sweeter than any cookies stopped short, as did the voice's owner. "Sam. Hi. What are you doing here?"

"Hey. I came to buy something." Smooth opener, not so much. Her kid—her daughter—being here had thrown him off his game.

"Okay." Leigh's gaze shifted to the girl, whose full attention had already returned to her drawing. "Honey, would you go in the back and keep an eye on the timer for me?"

"Sure, Mommy."

Leigh patted the girl's head as she passed. Alone with him in the front of the store, Leigh wiped her hands on an apron that was obviously utilitarian, not decorative, and came around to his side of the counter.

"You have a daughter," he said.

"I do."

"I always figured you had a son, because of the name."

She shook her head, her lips curving into a shy smile. "From the beginning, we planned to use my surname as the baby's first name, regardless of gender. It's not a typical girl's name, but if you knew Lennox, you'd see that it suits her."

"I'm sure." Nice response, idiot. Man, he was rolling on the suave today.

The *we planned* in Leigh's statement had thrown him for another loop. She'd never been married, he knew that much. He'd assumed her pregnancy had been an accident, or the product of a now-defunct former relationship. Her explanation made it sound the opposite of accidental.

He'd done way too much assuming where Leigh was concerned.

"So," she said, fidgeting with her apron. "Tell me what you're interested in and I'll show you what I can do."

He choked on a laugh, at which she shook her head. "Sorry. What can I say? I'm a guy, you're hot, and that was one perfectly dirty offer."

Another head shake came his way, then she turned and leaned over the counter to retrieve a large binder. "I'm afraid you'll have to settle for checking out my cupcakes and cookies."

Jesus, that ass. He tilted his head, angling for a better view. "I had your cookies when I came in and they were amazing. Gotta say, so are your cupcakes."

Her head jerked in his direction, catching him in a full-blown, wide-eyed ogling of her backside. "Were you just—" Pink flooded her face and she shook her head.

He shrugged and grinned. "Yeah, Leigh, I was."

Another binder landed on the counter as she straightened and faced him, one eyebrow raised, arms crossed over a pair of nice, full breasts. Damn, that spunk. So cute. And hot. With her kid in the next room, meaning he needed to behave. Wasn't going to be easy.

LEIGH

"If you weren't *you*, Sam, I'd think you were hitting on me."

"You'd think right." He winked, of course. Typical Sam—
sexy, playful, charming.

What woman was immune to that? Certainly not her.
"Uh-huh. What are you really here for?"

"You."

And she'd thought today couldn't get wilder. The bridezilla
from Wednesday hadn't had a single complaint about her
engagement-party cake when she picked it up. A last-minute
order she shouldn't have agreed to, but couldn't afford to turn
down, had fallen into her lap. Then Tim had called, asking to
take Lennox to the cottage to celebrate the start of summer
vacation, meaning Leigh could work on that rush order until
the wee hours, guilt-free. Now Sam was standing in her store,
claiming to be here *for her*. Whatever that meant.

But God, look at him. Broken-in jeans rode low on his
trim hips. A black, V-neck t-shirt showed off his hard,
muscular upper body. The same olive-green cap he'd worn in
the coffee shop completed the sexy-young-stud look. His smile
and comments made her stomach do backflips on top of the
somersaults that'd started when she pushed through the
kitchen door.

The coffee shop had been a coincidence. This meeting
was intentional—and entirely Sam's doing.

"I would like to buy something too."

A business transaction. She could work with that. "Okay."
She flipped one binder open. Attempted to reclaim her
normal, businesslike posture, even though his innocent flirting
had made her hotter than the ovens in the kitchen. "What's
the occasion? Wedding or engagement?"

"Neither."

"Haven't found your happily-ever-after girl?"

He chuckled. "Not since Wednesday, no. Still looking."

Totally teasing her, but it was her fault, she'd initiated the topic.

"Birthday? Graduation? Getting the guys together to watch the fights?"

"Nothing like that." He moved closer, covered her hand on the book. "Something small and simple for a friend. Maybe a box of those cookies your daughter introduced me to?"

"Oh, well..." She kept her eyes on his face, but it didn't help her concentrate on baked goods. Hard to do with his fingers stroking her hand, as he had in the booth at the coffee shop. "I don't actually sell those cookies. I don't have anything pre-made and ready to buy. Less risk of waste."

"I can't imagine they'd go to waste."

"Me either, since I'd probably eat all the leftovers rather than throw them away. Then they'd be going to *my* waist."

"That wouldn't be all bad. You'd need to hire me again, meaning I'd have an excuse to spend time with you regularly."

She ought to pull her hand away and laugh at his innocent flirtation. She didn't. "How soon do you need the cookies for your friend? I'm going to be baking tonight anyway, I could make you some, if you don't mind waiting a couple of hours. Not actually waiting around, of course. That's not what I meant. You could come back later to pick them up. Or in the morning, since it's Friday and you probably have plans." Great, she'd become a rambling mess. From a simple touch. She really needed to work on that *getting laid soon* plan.

"Or I could wait, hang out with you. We can talk while you bake. I'll help, if you tell me what to do." His eyes drifted to the kitchen door, then back to her face. "Unless that's a bad idea with your daughter here?"

"She won't be here. She's spending the weekend with her dad. He'll be here to pick her up any minute."

Sam trailed his fingers up her arm, sending sparks racing along her skin. "Is that a yes to hanging out?"

"It's Friday night. Don't you have a date?"

"I don't know, Leigh, do I?"

Keep reading WORTH THE WAIT!
Visit www.karladoyle.com
or buy it from your favorite book retailer.

Also by Karla Doyle

Worth the Wait
Very Personal Training # 2

When personal trainer Sam bumps into his favorite former client, their chemistry reignites instantly. Leigh is everything he pictured in his sometime-down-the-road woman. Sexy, funny, independent, mature—in more ways than one. He never cared about their age gap, he just wasn't ready to get serious before. He's ready now. But when his prior playboy ways come back to bite him in the ass, it'll take more than sizzling sex and charm to convince Leigh to stick around.

Leigh's life is humming along according to plan. Her custom bakery is thriving. Her daughter is a well-adjusted ten-year-old. Romance is the one area that's lacking. Completely. Until the universe fulfills her request for some hot lovin' and puts Sam in her path—for a second time. Sam gives her exactly what she was missing, and more. Maybe more than her well-structured life plan can handle…

Gift Wrapped

After catching her boyfriend cheating two weeks before Christmas, Brinn is seriously lacking in holiday spirit. So when she looks into the eyes of a last-minute shopper after closing on Christmas Eve, she's sarcastic rather than sympathetic. But Brinn is ever the good girl and her conscience wins out. She offers the handsome stranger ten minutes to select a gift and ends up with a present of her own— a date. On Christmas Eve.

Davis hates Christmas. Especially this year, since a neighborhood heist liberated him of his hard-earned belongings and the few gifts he'd purchased. But the robbery led him to a cute store manager with a sense of humor, smokin' body and no plans for the evening. Mistletoe might be in order after all.

Their Christmas Eve date is like gift-wrapped, sexy satisfaction. But the best gifts keep on giving, and one naughty night may not be enough—for either of them.

Cup of Sugar (Close to Home #1)

Nia has one rule—don't date neighbors. Simple, except the guy next door is single, handsome, and not inclined to close his blinds while naked. When her car dies, Conn takes "being neighborly" to a new level by offering a ride to her long-distance destination. Nia has resisted his looks and charm for months. Surely she can handle a few hours in his truck…

For months, Conn has blatantly put himself on display, hoping his pretty blonde neighbor would tire of secretly watching and come knock on his door for a cup of sugar—or more. No such luck—until an unusual opportunity arises. After a six-hour drive turns into a sweet-and-sexy weekend, Conn wants more than neighborly status with Nia. To get it, he must convince her to break the rule protecting her heart—by putting his on the line.

Icing on the Cake (Close to Home #2)

Nia and Conn's wedding will be fairytale perfect…if their siblings can get along.

Free-spirited, anti-establishment Sara has always been on the outside of her family's fairytale mold. Now she's being forced smack into the middle of it at her sister Nia's wedding. Alongside the cocky and annoyingly sexy best man—Conn's cop brother.

Curtis doesn't buy in to organized romance and fairytales. But for his brother, he'll throw on a tux and fake it for a few hours. His flak vest would have been a better choice around the maid of honor. He should have brought his handcuffs too, because somebody needs to restrain the dark-haired spitfire—and he's just the man for the job.

One night to indulge the spark between them, then goodbye—that was the agreement. Curtis isn't looking for a relationship and he sure doesn't want a troublemaker for a girlfriend. The last thing Sara needs in her daily life is a cop looking over her shoulder, no matter how hot he is.

But giving in to their chemistry is much more fun than giving it up…

Sweet as Candy (Close to Home #3)

To survive and thrive in her line of work, Candace has become a master at reading people. With most of her customers, it's easy. Until the off-duty cop with golden-boy good looks starts coming around. He pays for her services but never collects, even though it's obvious he wants her. Candace can't afford to get to know or like him. Whatever his angle, he's still a cop, and she's breaking the law to provide for the only person who matters—her five-year-old daughter.

Between his looks and his police uniform, Jake never lacks for female attention. But when a favor for his partner Curtis lands Jake in a massage parlor, one sexy "masseuse" fries all his circuits. He should enjoy her services and move on, but it wouldn't be real. It wouldn't be enough. When he and Candy get together—and they will—it won't be a paid transaction.

12 Days (Hope Harbor #1)

Kelly Horne and Adeline Mission have been best friends since the third grade. Yes, he thinks she's pretty. And hot. Smart. Funny. But they're buds. Roommates. End of story.

Until he opens a package delivered to his house without checking the name on the label, and finds Addie has ordered a vibrating cock ring for some guy who doesn't deserve her, because no guy does.

There's a gift receipt in the box, meaning she intends to give the sex toy to somebody for Christmas…in 12 days.

12 days to undo a lifetime of "just friends". 12 days to change the name she writes on that gift tag. 12 days to win the girl he just realized has always been the one for him.

Crossing the Line

Lifelong best friends Derrick and Jeremy met Hanna at a bar ten years ago. Both wanted her—one married her. Now the other man has been invited to join in for one hot weekend.

Everything would've been fine if they'd had their fun that weekend, then gone back to normal. But they didn't. And when past demons resurface, things will never be the same—for any of them.

More Than Words

A brutal mugging two years ago left Calli terrified to go out after dark, and incapable of real dating. Hanging out with a resentful Chihuahua every night hasn't filled the void, and all the sex toys from the store she owns could never replace a flesh-and-blood man. An online Scrabble site promising anonymous, flirty fun sounds like just the ticket. A like-minded geek, that's what she needs. Unbeknownst to her, the man on the other end of the game is anything but geeky.

Tired of the party scene, Travis seeks a venue where he can meet a woman who is drawn to his mind, not his profession. Having women chase after his bad-boy musician persona has grown stale. After heating up the tiles online with Calli, he knows he must meet her in person. Touch her in person. And when he does, their chemistry is undeniable. She stimulates him, mind and body. But when he discovers her tragic past he realizes it will take more than words to win her heart…and her trust.

Game Plan

Recently divorced after seventeen years with a snooty, uptight, controlling man, forty-year-old Andie is definitely ready for some casual, sexy fun when a hot younger man "accidentally" hits her with a baseball. Mason's interest is clear and he looks like a lot more fun than her overworked vibrator collection, so she goes for it, despite the obvious age gap. The young veterinarian is as easy to be with as he is on the eyes, making him an ideal summer diversion and the perfect man to help her make up for lost time and missed orgasms.

Mason had to meet the sexy woman at the ball diamond. The chemistry between them is instant and completely addictive. Andie is more than beautiful, she's uninhibited and independent—totally unlike the needy twenty-somethings he's been dating since his ex-fiancée deceived him five years ago. And yeah, Andie is ten years older than him, big deal. The more they're together, the more his heart wants her as badly as his cock. Too bad Andie isn't playing for keeps.

Stealing Home

When Paige's latest attempt at happily-ever-after with a nice guy tanks, she decides to quit fighting her destiny. She craves bad boys. Men who deliver short-term, panty-melting excitement, not reliability and settling down. If she's going to embrace her true nature, who better to start with than the dark-haired, tattooed ballplayer whose cocky attitude gives her more thrills than any steady boyfriend ever has…

Alex had major league plans for his life until it threw him an unexpected and unwelcome curve ball. Switching gears to pursue his other passion was a rough road, but things are good—aside from his MIA muse. When a chance meeting with a blonde firecracker stirs his creative juices—and more—Alex is game to see where their chemistry leads. Trouble is, his potential Miss Right thinks she's only capable of playing the field.

Check Karla's website for the most up-to-date listing of all her books!

Thank You for reading!

About the Author

Karla is a small-town girl with some big-city experience, happiest living somewhere in between. She studied fashion design in college and spent over two decades in that industry before following the writing muse. Karla resides in Southwestern Ontario with her two amazing kids and smokin' hot husband. When she's not writing the sexy stories that swirl around in her head, you can find her cuddled up with a steamy romance novel and her beloved pets.

Subscribe to Karla's Newsletter

www.karladoyle.com
karla@karladoyle.com

ISBN 9780994098443 (Print Edition ISBN 9780994098450)

Original digital publication May 2013

Editor: GraceBradleyEditing.com

Cover design: BookishDesigns / Cover image by oneinchpunch

Electronic book publication June 2016 / Print book publication July 2016

For questions and comments about this book, please contact the author at karla@karladoyle.com.

ISBN: 978-0-9940984-4-3